# An Inconvenient Marriage

## ALL FOR LOVE
## BOOK 1

# WREN ST. CLAIRE

Dragonblade Publishing, Inc. is an imprint of Kathryn Le Veque Novels, Inc.
P.O. Box 23
Moreno Valley, CA 92556
ceo@dragonbladepublishing.com

Produced in the United States of America

First Edition July 2025
Trade Paperback Edition

## ARE YOU SIGNED UP FOR DRAGONBLADE'S BLOG?

You'll get the latest news and information on exclusive giveaways, exclusive excerpts, coming releases, sales, free books, cover reveals and more.

Check out our complete list of authors, too!

No spam, no junk. That's a promise!

### Sign Up Here

www.dragonbladepublishing.com

*Dearest Reader;*

*Thank you for your support of a small press. At Dragonblade Publishing, we strive to bring you the highest quality Historical Romance from some of the best authors in the business. Without your support, there is no 'us', so we sincerely hope you adore these stories and find some new favorite authors along the way.*

*Happy Reading!*

*CEO, Dragonblade Publishing*

# Prologue

*London, 7th of March 1800*

YOUNG MASTER ROBERT, Marquess of Thornbury, fidgeted on the leather squabs impatiently as the carriage drew up outside a four-story house in Pall Mall. Barely waiting for the carriage to stop, he jumped down into the road and said to the driver, "Wait here. I will bring the duke," and hurried up the steps of the discreet establishment.

With his heart beating fast, he knocked and was answered, a few agonizing moments later, by a superior looking doorman, who looked down at Robert and widened his eyes in surprise.

"Young sir, I fear you must have the wrong establishment."

Robert drew himself up to his full height, which reached to the middle of the big man's chest, and said with every bit of dignity he could summon, "I am the Marquess of Thornbury, here to see the Duke of Troubridge. I understand he is within. Please conduct me to him immediately. It is a matter of the utmost urgency."

The doorman blinked and bowed. "Follow me, my lord."

Robert straightened his cravat and followed. The man led him up a flight of stairs to a salon on the first floor, where two rooms branched off. From one, the hubbub of conversation emanated, and Robert caught a glimpse of gentlemen seated around tables drinking and playing cards. The second room also contained gentlemen playing cards, but unlike the other room, was deathly silent. The men sat staring at their cards with grim concentration.

The doorman wove through the tables to one at the back, where a large, handsome man with dark hair and dark eyes sprawled in a chair, rouleaux at his elbow and cards before him. A glass half full of amber liquid, glinted in the light from the candles overhead. The doorman waved Robert forward and stood back.

"Robert!" said the Duke of Troubridge, blinking at him owlishly. "What are you doing here?"

His twelve-year-old son bowed to him with stiff propriety. "Mama's time is upon her; you must come with me now!"

The duke changed color and dropped his cards. "Good God, it's too early surely." Rising, he waved at the other players. "Sorry gentlemen, you must excuse me!"

Relief caused Robert's shoulders to drop and his fists to unclench—it had been easier than he'd anticipated. He turned and led the way out of the house and back to the waiting carriage. Clambering in after him, the duke slumped on the seat as the carriage lurched into motion. His hands were visibly shaking as he ran his fingers through his hair, which had come loose from its ribbon.

"How is she faring?" he asked, leaning forward toward his son.

Robert pursed his lips and said repressively, "As well as can be expected, sir."

"It's too early," fretted the duke.

"In fact, it isn't, sir. She began her lying in last week," said Robert calmly. It was typical that his father paid so little attention he didn't know when his wife's time was come. Since the duke spent many of his days either drunk, in a gambling hell, or both, this was not surprising. He sat back, blinking. "Is that so? Why didn't someone tell me?"

Robert just looked at him in silence. The duke gave a weak smile and put out a hand to grip his son's arm. "Good thing she's got you, eh? A sight more reliable than me." He rubbed his face tiredly. "I'm a sorry excuse for a man. You, my boy, are a true gentleman, I'm proud of you."

Robert lowered his eyes to hide the unmanly moisture in them. "Thank you, sir. I shall endeavor to live up to your expectations."

"Oh, you far exceed them, my boy. Far exceed them. You'll make a fine duke one day, much better than me."

"Don't speak of that sir," said Robert softly. "We none of us want to lose you." Whatever his faults, he loved his sire and while he could no longer hero worship him as he had done when he was younger, he was no more proof against the man's natural charm than anyone else. Everyone loved the duke.

"I don't plan to shuffle off the mortal coil yet," said the duke heartily. "Where are the boys?"

He spoke of Robert's younger brothers, Hereward and Kenrick, aged eight and four respectively. "Asleep, I believe. It is after three in the morning, sir. I was sitting with Mama when her waters broke, and I sent for the doctor and the midwife. When her pains came closer together, Mama sent me to find you."

"Was it going well when you left? Nothing untoward?" asked the duke anxiously.

"The midwife assured me that everything was progressing as it should, sir."

The duke nodded. "I shall not be easy until she is safely delivered, and the babe also."

The carriage drew up just then outside their house in Berkeley Square and the duke was out of the carriage and up the steps like a cannonball shot. Robert followed a little more slowly, not because he wasn't anxious to know how his mother fared, but because someone had to ensure the carriage was dismissed correctly and the driver well compensated for being hauled out of his bed in the middle of the night.

He followed his sire up the steps and into the house where their butler Creighton bowed to him. "The duke has gone straight up, Master Robert."

Robert nodded, stripping off his hat and coat. "Thank you. Any news?"

"Any minute now I was told, half an hour ago. The staff are all praying for the duchess, my lord."

Robert smiled a half smile. "Indeed—"

A sound above stairs made him drop his gloves and sent him flying up the stairs two at a time, with Creighton at his heels. He arrived on the first floor to be greeted by the duke with a squirming, crying bundle in his arms.

"It's a girl!" he exclaimed, tears on his cheeks. "A baby girl. She's so beautiful, look." He held the bundle out and Robert got his first look at his baby sister. Her little face was scrunched up and red and her little mouth was open, squalling fit to burst, little fists waving about. Her fingers were perfect. In fact, everything about her was perfect. Robert's heart, which had been worried in spite of his outward seeming calm, gave a little leap of joy. He allowed himself to smile and looked up at his jubilant sire. "How is Mama?"

"Well—tired but well. I'm so proud of her." The duke wiped tears off his face with his cuff, clutching the baby close. Robert passed into the bedchamber where his mother lay banked against pillows, her blonde hair confined in a plait.

"Robert." She reached out a hand toward him, and he came to her bedside, taking her hand in a sustaining clasp. The duke followed, still clutching the squalling infant.

"How are you, Mama?" Robert scanned her face to satisfy himself that all was well. One heard so many horror stories of women's labor. But to his relief she seemed, as his father had said, tired but well. She smiled at him.

"Well, Robert. What do you think of her?" Her eyes strayed to the duke, with a warm light in them, a look she reserved only for him. Robert felt like an intruder between them. "A girl at last, Costin. I think I shall call her Ava."

"My dearest Jocelyn," said the duke fondly, leaning forward

to deposit their daughter back into her arms. "I couldn't be happier. Ava it is." He kissed her cheek and then her lips. Feeling decidedly *de trop*, Robert backed out and left his parents to it, going up to the next floor to inform his brothers they had a baby sister at last. He wondered how the boys would take the news, but he for one, was pleased. She was a dear little thing, and it would be his privilege to guard and protect her.

*London, 7th of February 1818*

MADELEINE KINSELLA ADJUSTED her mask and entered the ballroom, her sky-blue domino billowing over the full skirts of her old-fashioned ball gown in rose pink brocade. Her powdered wig and the patch beside her mouth completed an ensemble that would have been the envy of Marie Antionette, before she lost her head. It was the first time she had ventured out of her house in Clarges Street since the Duke of Troubridge delivered the news that their "arrangement" was ending. He had been generous, she had to give him that. He had extended the rent on the house until the middle of the year, including the servants' wages, and made a present of the carriage and two horses that drew it. And of course she got to keep all the clothes, jewels, and knick-knacks he had given her over the years. You couldn't accuse him of being stingy.

On the contrary, he had been exceedingly generous and kind. Which resulted in her suffering a greater degree of heartbreak over the severing of their relationship than was wise for a lady in her profession. She had wept and been inconsolable for two months. But it was time she moved on. She needed to find another protector, as unpalatable as the notion was. But first, before she did, she needed a palate cleanser, a man to rid her of her deep-seated hankering for the duke.

Thus, here she was at this masked ball in search of such a man. She moved farther into the room, skirting the dance floor where couples twirled to the tune of a waltz, dominos flying. The candles glinted off the chandelier's cut-glass teardrops, and the room was filled with the murmur of conversation over the music.

She found a position with a good view of the room, near an alcove that offered privacy if required, and waited, plying her fan lazily against the growing heat in the room and the overpowering smell of pomade, perfume, and human sweat. Behind her mask, she tracked various gentlemen around the room, looking for a suitable quarry.

She was surprised by a soft voice in her ear, "all alone, Princess?" Startled, she turned to gaze upward into blue eyes dancing with wicked delight behind a black mask, a sensuous mouth curved in a charming smile and a thatch of blonde hair cut in a fashionable Brutus. The man was tall, well-made, broad through the shoulders, and lacking any signs of a paunch. Beneath his black domino he wore unrelieved black evening dress, a stark contrast to the whiteness of his neckcloth. A diamond glinted among the snowy folds and a gold signet ring upon his finger, with the coronet of a peer, told her that she was looking at a perfect specimen.

She smiled. "Not anymore, it would seem."

# Chapter One



*London, 7th of March 1818*

"I TELL YOU, I have no choice," said Robert Layne, 7th Duke of Troubridge morosely. "It's an heiress or be hounded to death by debtors." He raised his whisky, catching a flash of his neatly groomed, curly brown hair and brooding, grey-blue eyes reflected in the glass, and downed it in one swallow. His tall frame was sprawled in a comfortable chair in Boodle's with his cronies. The four men sat in a half circle drawn cozily up to the fire, enjoying a post-dinner drink. But even the warm and familiar surroundings of his favorite club couldn't dispel the twinge of unease in his gut at the prospect of seeking a wife for purely mercenary reasons. It went severely against the grain and left him feeling empty and depressed, an unaccustomed emotion for one of his temperament. It was making him irritable.

"An heiress ain't so bad, Rob," said Jerome DeVere, the Marquess of Ravenshaw, one elegantly booted foot crossed over his knee. "Provided she's pretty of course!" Ravenshaw added with a rakish smile.

*That is easy for him to say. He doesn't have to marry the damned chit, whoever she proves to be.*

As always, the marquess's attire was immaculate. His black hair was sleek as a groomed horse, and his devastatingly handsome face was perfectly shaved.

"Pretty isn't going to be a criterion," Robert said gloomily. He was looking for something beyond skin-deep beauty and would be lucky to find someone who didn't repulse him utterly, as he was particular in his tastes. *Am I too particular?* A pang in his chest reminded him of what he did want, a wife he could love with his whole heart. *The perfect woman I have never met. And never will now . . .*

"Marrying for love's not all it's cracked up to be," remarked Emrys Fitzgerald, Viscount Ashford, with a rueful grimace, finishing his glass of red wine and refilling it. He was the only one of the four of them who was married. Robert was surprised by the comment; to his knowledge Ashford's marriage was a happy one. He and his wife Caroline had three children, the eldest of which was eight or thereabouts. Robert made a mental note to follow up on this hint of marital discord. Ashford's match had been the gold standard in his mind for a love match—outside of his parents of course. It was disturbing to think things might not be as smooth sailing as they had always appeared to be.

By contrast with Ravenshaw, Ashford was disheveled, his brown hair was too long to be fashionable, his jaw sported a faint stubble. His clothes were loose fitting with a stain on his waistcoat, and his boots were in sore need of a shine. In short, he looked like something the cat had dragged in, which was nothing unusual. He'd never been a good-looking man, and he was now slipping into comfortable middle age, with a slight paunch developing round his middle.

"Well, they won't haul you off to the fleet. You're a bloody duke!" said Deodonatus Kininmounth, the Earl of Pendrell. Inspecting his own glass and finding it empty, he reached for the decanter on the table and absently refilled Robert's glass while he was at it. Pendrell was the biggest of the four men, with shoulders like an ox and a muscular physique that topped out at over six foot three. He was built on similar lines to Robert's brother Hereward, although Pendrell was taller. Combined with his height and bulk, his hawkish features made him somewhat intimidating. And to add to his striking appearance, his head was covered in a shock of bright red hair, and his skin was freckled from long hours in the sun on some dig or other. The man was obsessed with antiquities and not known for his social address. He became quite tongue-tied in the presence of females.

Robert waved a hand dismissively. "No, but I'm damned sick of not being able to pay my debts and trying to balance the books. My esteemed papa was not a good steward, I am sorry to say, and I'm paying the price for it now. Whichever way I try it, there are more outgoings than incomings." He sighed. "The estate has been abused for too long. It requires significant investment to begin showing a profit again, and I can't raise the ready because everything is bloody entailed." He ran a hand through his hair, disturbing his valet's neat handiwork, and unconsciously created an artistically disheveled look worthy of Byron.

"I've tried to get my mother and brothers to practice some economy to no avail, and with three sisters to provide for as well as the boys . . ." He scrubbed a hand over his face and sighed. *God I'm tired.* "I'm resigned to my fate, but I don't have to like it!"

Robert had always envisioned that when he did marry he would do so for love, the kind of passionate, life-long love and devotion his parents had enjoyed. He had searched for ten years for the deep-soul connection among the debutantes of the *ton* that he was convinced was possible, but it was to no avail. He now realized with a sinking heart that he would have to choose a lady based first and foremost on the size of her fortune. The chance of him finding the love of his life among the ranks of this year's crop of heiresses was reduced to a very small, if not non-existent, percentage indeed.

"To make it worse, Mama and Ava will arrive soon for Ava's come out, and the expense doesn't bear thinking of," he added with a frustrated sigh.

"My parents dropped a bundle for my sister's debut," nodded Ravenshaw. "But she nabbed De Crecy, so it was worth it. Ever thought Lady Ava might solve the problem for you?"

"Damn it, no! I'll not sacrifice Ava. It's my lot to solve. Ava shall marry where she chooses."

He had not confessed his intentions to his family. He did not plan to tell them that he was bent on making a marriage of convenience. Instead, he would do his best to convince them he had chosen a bride he loved, even though it wasn't true. Or was unlikely to be true, he amended, the small amount of hope in his heart persistent to the last.

"What are the choices this year?" asked Ashford.

"I don't know. I'm going to Almack's tomorrow night to find out." He swallowed another mouthful of whisky. "I've enlisted Maria Sefton to help me. She and Mama have been thick as thieves for the past twenty-odd years, so I'm hoping I can trust she'll keep a discreet tongue in her head. The last thing I want is the *ton* catching wind of the fact I'm hanging out for a rich wife!"

The notion still turned his stomach and gave him that strange ache behind his sternum, but he really couldn't see any way out of it.

"Wish me luck, gentlemen." His three closest friends raised their glasses to the successful hunt for a suitably endowed bride.

"What ho, chaps!" said a cheery voice, breaking in on Robert's morose thoughts. He raised his eyes from the fire to focus on the beaming expression of Reynard Fairbanks, 6th Earl of Lannister. Tall and loose-limbed, with blonde hair and blue eyes, Lannister had the sort of devilish good looks that seemed to drive women wild. "Care for a game of cards?" he offered. "Greathouse and I were looking for a table. Want to join us?"

Lannister indicated his companion, Fabian Lidcombe, Baron Greathouse. Greathouse was of a different stamp altogether, still dashingly handsome, but being of only medium height, with brown hair and dark, dreamy eyes, the two together made a clear contrast.

Pendrell rose to his great height, his shock of red hair falling into his eyes. "Not for me, thank you. I've a paper to finish editing for the Quarterly Journal. All the best tomorrow, Rob.

Good night, gentlemen." He gave a short bow and strode away.

Ashford, who was a close friend of Greathouse, rose and tugged his ill-fitting coat into order. "Not tonight, Fabian, I'd best be getting home. Caro had a headache and stayed in tonight."

"I'm sorry to hear that, Emrys," said Greathouse with a moue of sympathy. "Do give her my regards. I hope she feels better in the morning."

Ashford nodded. "Thank you, I will. Rob, you want to play?"

Robert put down his glass and rose. "No, I'll go with you."

"Which leaves Ravenshaw. Come on, man—say you will play!" coaxed Lannister.

"I wouldn't, Ravenshaw. He wants to fleece you!" warned Robert. Lannister's pockets were notoriously to let. The man lived hand to mouth on the turn of a card, a vice his youngest brother Kenrick seemed to share, one Rick had inherited from their sire. *Another drain on the Layne finances.*

"Let him try," said the marquess rising and shucking his elegant cuffs. If he weren't such an athlete, he'd be taken for a dandy, the care he expended on his wardrobe.

The two groups of men parted, and Robert and Ashford made their way out into the street, collecting their coats and hats on the way. "Sorry to hear Caro's not feeling well," said Robert as they strode out. It was a fine night with a half-moon giving some light to supplement the streetlamps. "Nothing serious I trust?"

"No, just one of those female things, I think. Care to share a hack?" he asked.

"Why not?"

Ashford flagged down a hackney coach, and when he had given the directions—Berkeley Square then Cavendish—and they were settled against the leather squabs, Robert cleared his throat and asked delicately, "Everything all right between you and Caro?"

Ashford raised his brows. "Yes, why?"

"Just your comment earlier . . ."

Ashford lounged on his side of the coach as the carriage

swung round a corner and said carelessly, "Oh, that? When you've been married as long as I have, you learn that there are good days and not so good days. Doesn't mean there's anything seriously wrong."

Robert nodded thoughtfully. "You're my pattern for the perfect marriage, old chap. I've always wanted what you have."

His friend smiled. "I was lucky, I'll admit. Prettiest girl of the season and she said yes to me!"

Robert chuckled. "I recall! You snatched her right out from under Everly's nose. All the clubs had short odds on him winning her hand. Just goes to show the power of sincerity and a good heart. There's not a better man in London than you, my friend. I'm glad Caro had the sense to see it."

Ashford shook his head at the compliment; he was inordinately modest. "You've had the pick of the crop of every season for the past ten years, Rob. Yet you've not found what you're looking for. Are you setting the bar too high?"

"Why, because I want my own Caro?" He frowned. "I just want a woman I can give myself to wholeheartedly, who will love me, not my title and position. I didn't expect it to be so dashed difficult."

Ashford coughed and Robert looked at him suspiciously. "What?"

Ashford hesitated.

"Out with it, man. You're my friend. If you can't be honest with me, who can?"

"Very well. If you want a woman who will love you for who you are, perhaps you should show her more of your private self. There's a deal of difference between the Duke of Troubridge and Robert Layne."

"Being a duke is part of who I am. I can't change that."

"No, but Robert is a darn sight more approachable than the duke."

Robert chewed that over. "I'm not sure I fully understand, but I'll think about it. Here's my stop. All the best to Caro," he said, getting out of the cab and paying the jarvey for his share of the ride.

He ran up the steps of his four-story London townhouse in Berkeley Square with a thoughtful frown on his brow. *Perhaps there is something to Emrys's words. But it is probably moot anyway, because I am about to embark on the search for a bride who is willing to trade her wealth for my title.*

For a moment he wished he could eschew the title and all its trappings and find the woman he wanted as a commoner. But that was a fairy tale, and this was real life. He needed a wealthy wife and quickly if he was to be able to continue to provide for his family and all the retainers who relied upon him. They were his priority, not his selfish desires. He needed to keep reminding himself of that.

# Chapter Two

M ISS SARAH WATSON bundled up the letters from home, received by this morning's post, with a sniff and a wipe of her cheeks—she missed them all so! Mama's letter was full of the doings of the four younger children and three letters from her sisters, Deb's of the latest Assembly she had attended with Ruth. Ruth's letter told her all about her latest rescue, a starling fallen out if its nest. Mary's letter begged her for all the details of her handsome beaux. And dear Papa's letter told her of the doings of the parishioners and his most recent reading of Tacitus, which he highly recommended to her. The letters were a timely reminder of her duty to them all.

Glancing at the clock, she reached for the bell to ring for her maid. If she didn't bustle, she would be late. Tonight was to be the first visit to Almack's for this season, and her first social appearance since becoming an heiress. Her chaperone Daphne, Lady Holbrook, would be up any moment to look her over, and she didn't even have her hair done yet!

She had spent far too long reading *Glenarvon* this afternoon. With only a few pages to go, she had hoped to finish it, but she had run out of time. Then she had got distracted by Deb's mention of Mr. Cheevly's attentions to herself at the Assembly. Mr. Cheevly was the younger son of the Squire and not the most stellar match for Deborah, who of all the Watson girls was by far the prettiest.

With a shiver of discomfort as she gathered up her family's correspondence, she recalled her own experiences with Mr. Cheevly, including an ill-advised kiss behind the arras in the vestry. No, he would not do for Deb. She must write to warn Deb against him. All the more reason for her to make an impression tonight.

Her maid, Esme, opened the door. "You rang, miss?"

"Yes, will you dress my hair? I'm horribly late—Daphne will be wild as fire with me!"

"Of course, miss. Which dress was you going to wear?"

"The pink silk with the net overskirt, please, Esme," she said, seating herself at the dressing table and removing the pins from her simple chignon and combing out her mahogany-colored hair. It was thick and wavy and took a lot of pins to hold it in place. Esme laid out her corset, petticoats, dress, stockings, reticule, gloves, slippers, and shawl before coming over and taking the comb from her hand and beginning to weave her magic on Sarah's head. She had just added the last comb when the door opened and Daphne sailed in.

"Sarah, you're not dressed yet!" Daphne was a widow, short, plump, and forty, with blonde hair just beginning to silver a little.

"Sorry, Daphne, I got distracted," she said, putting in her pearl ear bobs and passing the simple silver cross on a light chain to Esme to drape round her neck. "I shall be ready in a trice, I promise you!"

"Yes, well, you know the doors shut at ten!" scolded Daphne mildly. She inspected the pink silk gown. "I was in two minds about whether you should wear that one or the white muslin with silver trimming, but on the whole, I think the pink will do nicely. The color becomes you."

Sarah rose and let Esme strip off her day gown. She'd had a leisurely bath this morning, and could still just smell the traces of lavender from the water on her skin. Really, London life was terribly indolent. She felt so guilty having all this indulgence when her family was living in genteel poverty.

Changing her stockings, corset, and petticoats for ones more suitable to wear under a ball gown, Esme then helped her on with the gown itself, twitching the folds of silk into place and lacing it up the back. Sarah viewed her décolletage with misgiving. As a vicar's daughter used to more modest neck lines, the latest fashion for positively indecent bodices made her blush. Sliding her feet into her matching pink silk slippers, she presented herself for Daphne's inspection.

"Very nice, my dear. I venture with the little extra touch of class, this year you will turn heads. The gown is delicately understated and just screams quality. I expect all the girls will be asking who your modiste is." She frowned. "A pity you don't have the jewels to match it."

Sarah shook her head. "I wouldn't feel comfortable in expensive jewels, Daphne."

Daphne sighed. "I suppose not. Still, that cross placed just there is in exactly the right spot to draw a gentleman's eye, so I daresay the effect is the same."

Sarah blushed and looked back at herself in the mirror. Sure enough, the cross was nestled just above her bust. Was there time to shorten the chain? Not really. Then she thought about what her mission was: to snare a titled gentleman. *If it takes some slightly embarrassing tactics, is that so terrible? I am doing this for my sisters.* She straightened her shoulders and turned away from the glass.

"I will see you downstairs in five minutes, Sarah," said Daphne, leaving the room.

"Will that be all, miss?" asked Esme who had gathered up her clothes and tidied everything away.

"Yes, thank you, Esme. And you needn't wait up, I can manage when I get home." She smiled. She wasn't accustomed to having a maid at home, but Daphne insisted she have one during her season, so Esme, who was the senior housemaid, had been pressed into service during her first season and had been serving in that capacity in Daphne's house for her ever since. As she needed to be up at the crack for her other duties, Sarah thought it cruel and unnecessary to ask her to stay up just so she could help Sarah undress.

With a small bob and a sunny "Thank you, miss. All the best!" Esme left her alone.

Sarah sprayed herself lightly with rose water, took one last look at herself in the mirror, and on impulse grabbed her spectacles and *Glenarvon* and stuffed them in her reticule. She should get a few minutes to read that last few pages at some point. Her experience of Almack's was that it was mostly excruciatingly boring, punctuated with short stints of embarrassment.

# Chapter Three

ROBERT SURVEYED THIS year's crop of debutantes at Almack's assembly rooms, with a somewhat jaundiced eye. He was resigned to his fate, but he couldn't summon enthusiasm for it, no matter how hard he tried. Having made his requirements plain to Lady Sefton, much to the injury of his pride, and requested her discretion, he waited expectantly.

She smiled up at him. Maria was short, and he was just over six feet in height. "You are in luck Robert; we have five heiresses this year, and I believe they are all present tonight. None of them smell of the shop, you understand. They wouldn't gain entrée if they did. Let us take a stroll round the room and I will point them out to you. That way you can have your pick."

He nodded and offered her his arm. "Thank you, Maria. I appreciate you helping me in this fashion."

The hubbub of noise covered their conversation as they began a slow perambulation around the room.

"As if I wouldn't. I've known you since you were in short coats, Robert. Now, see the young lady to our right with the brown curls and the white gown with too many flounces on the hem?"

Robert discreetly glanced in the direction indicated by Maria's fluttering fan.

"Miss Emily Grenfell, twenty, her maternal grandfather owned tin mines in Cornwall and left his whole fortune to his daughter, Ernestine. She was snapped up by Gerald Grenfell, Viscount Lockwood. Despite all their efforts, Emily is their only child and stands to inherit more than forty thousand pounds. Her dowry in the meantime is said to be generous."

Robert nodded, observing the lady's long nose and rosebud mouth. She was not unattractive; her skin had a milky smoothness, and her figure was slender. "And the lady herself?" he asked.

Maria glanced up at him. "Her disposition?"

He nodded.

"She seems a pretty behaved young woman. I know no ill of her, at any event. Somewhat reserved in company I believe. Her mother is a little, how shall I put it? Dominating? I suspect Emily would show to better advantage away from her mama's eagle eye."

"Noted," he said. Miss Grenfell had definite potential.

They strolled on, and Maria swirled her fan artistically. "The young lady with the guinea-gold curls and the jonquil-colored gown, standing beside the plump woman in the puce turban."

He glanced in her direction and beheld a peaches and cream beauty of delicate frame and short stature. He was not a man given to poetical flights of fancy, but this girl was worthy of a sonnet. His expression must have given him away because Maria chuckled. "Yes, they all do that when they see her. Her name is Cecelia Woodrow, and she has thirty thousand pounds and an estate in Bedford. She is eighteen, this is her first season, and she won't last long. You have an advantage being a duke, but I'd move fast. She's an orphan, and her guardian is her uncle Sebastian Monk. He'll drive a hard bargain."

"I see," he smiled ruefully. "And her disposition?"

"She is young, possibly a little spoiled."

He pursed his lips. The lady's looks were enticing, but he wasn't sure that he could cope with a child of eighteen, the same age as his sister Ava. "Next?" he said.

Maria raised her eyebrows and moved on. "If you prefer someone a little older, there is Isabella Mortimer, Countess of Esbury, twenty-five. Her husband was thirty years her senior when they married six years ago, and she has been a widow for two years. This is her first appearance in London since his death. He left his whole fortune to her. She has no financial reason to remarry and no one to force her into it. It will be entirely down to your address to convince her." Maria cast him a twinkling look. "Not something beyond your capabilities, I should think."

"Does she have children?" he asked, his heart quickening a beat as he surveyed the tall dark-haired woman in a cream and gold gown, conversing easily with a group of three, made up of two men and one other woman. She was striking rather than classically beautiful but carried herself with an elegance and confidence that was very attractive.

"No. It wasn't for want of trying I understand, but whether the fault was his or hers is anyone's guess. He married her for an heir, and it didn't happen."

It was his duty to obtain an heir, but he did have two younger brothers, so the line wouldn't die out necessarily, unless all three of them failed to reproduce. But still, children were something he actively wanted, not only because he needed a son to succeed him, but he also looked forward to daughters as well. Children were a definite part of his vision of a happily ever after. But how did they fit into a marriage of convenience scenario? Would they be a solace for the lack of affection between him and his (as yet unknown) wife, would they underline the emotional gulf, or— best of all possible worlds—bridge that gulf, bringing happiness closer? *I can only hope for the latter.*

"In the blue satin with red hair and, most unfortunately, freckles—Elinor Carlisle, nineteen. Her father was the Laird of McKlintock. Her uncle holds the title now. Scottish, obviously. The uncle is sponsoring her season in the hopes of snaring a title for her. Lady Merton is bringing her out as a favor to the family, some sort of connection between the families."

"Does the hair ring true?" he asked with a slight smile.

"I believe the lady has a reputation for her temper, yes. She is certainly no simpering miss."

Did he want to risk having a termagant for a wife? His siblings caused enough chaos as it was. He shuddered internally at the thought. They moved on and the music commenced for the first of the country dances. Couples began pairing up and moving onto the dance floor in the middle of the room. He glanced around and noted that both the blonde and the widow had partners for the dance. Both ladies were patently in high demand. But there was one more lady for him to sight. "And the last one?" he asked.

"Yes, I'm just looking for her," said Maria peering around. "Ah! Behind the potted palm in the corner. "Miss Sarah Watson, age twenty-two. You may actually have met at some point. This will be her fourth season, she missed last year due to being in mourning. Her father is the vicar of Littledon, an obscure little village in Hampshire. She is the eldest of five daughters and three sons."

"How can a vicar's daughter be an heiress? And if she is, how has she remained unwed for three seasons?" He couldn't see much of the lady; she was literally hiding behind a monstrous plant in the corner. Her gown as far he could tell was rose pink, but everything else was a mystery.

"Her great aunt, Lady Agnes Fairchild, sponsored her seasons and died last year leaving her whole fortune to Sarah, on the condition she was married by the end of this year to a titled gentleman."

"How extraordinary," he murmured, feeling sorry for the woman, sight unseen.

"Lady Agnes was an eccentric."

"Evidently. Tell me more about Miss Watson."

"As you might have surmised, she didn't take. She is what is colloquially called a wallflower. She is not ill favored, but I believe, due to her upbringing as the eldest of such a large brood and raised in a country vicarage, she is disastrously direct in her speech. And to be blunt with you, she is rumored to have bluestocking tendencies."

He nodded thoughtfully. "And her fortune?"

"A principle in excess of fifty thousand pounds plus an income of six thousand a year."

Robert's eyebrows went up in surprise. "And if she doesn't fulfil the terms of her aunt's will?"

"The lot will go to a home for orphans."

"Lucky orphans," he murmured.

"Needless to say, once the word gets out about her fortune, she will be besieged."

"Who is her chaperone?"

"Lady Daphne Holbrook. Percival Holbrook's widow. She is a cousin of Miss Watson's father and a niece of Agnes Fairchild. She has supervised all Miss Watson's seasons."

He took a breath and let it out slowly, passing the five ladies under review quickly.

"So which lady would you like to meet first?"

He was most drawn to the widow. Physically, if he had a preference, it was for dark beauties. Being older, she might be the least complicated of the options available, and she would understand a marriage of convenience, as she had already had one. *Then again, why would she choose a second husband if she doesn't need one? What can I offer beyond a title and a pile of debt?*

But he was intrigued by the lady hiding behind the potted plant. He would at least like to see her face.

"Miss Watson," he said with a smile.

Maria arched her brows and gave a little shrug. "Very well, come this way. You're wise to get in before the rush."

She led him over to the corner where his quarry lurked, and as they rounded the screen of plants, he caught his first view of the lady. She was of medium height, with a figure that was neither voluptuous nor thin. The gown she wore was of net over a pink underskirt. It was well cut and of obvious quality. She wore long white gloves and carried the ubiquitous fan and reticule. The gown's décolletage was modest by fashionable standards, and a simple silver chain with a cross suspended from it and a pair of pearl earrings were her only ornaments. Her hair was a deep mahogany, a rich brown with red highlights, and had been piled on top of her head, confined with an arête and let to curl round her face in the latest fashion.

She might be quite pretty, but it was hard to tell because she had her head bent over a book and a pair of spectacles on her nose. Maria coughed and the young lady started, dropped the book, snatched the spectacles off her nose and blushed furiously, the expression of a startled hare on her face.

"Lady Sefton!" her voice was soft and slightly husky and sent a shiver through him that went straight to his groin. *Promising?*

Something vaguely familiar about her teased his memory, but he couldn't recall actually meeting her. Yet he may very well have done so, as Maria had indicated. But he met hundreds of people a year in his role as a peer and dozens of young ladies. They tended to all blend together after a while.

"Miss Watson, I would like to introduce you to someone who is eager to meet you," said Maria smoothly, ignoring the book which had fallen at the lady's feet and was sitting up on its end. He longed to know what it was.

The lady clasped her hands nervously, the spectacles still clutched in her fingers, and dipped a curtsy, her eyes widening at the sight of him. Her high color fled and for a moment he thought she would faint. *What is there about my appearance to cause such a violent reaction?*

"Miss Sarah Watson, may I present the Duke of Troubridge?"

The lady gulped and dropped a deeper curtsy, her eyes on the floor. "Your Grace."

He offered her a bow in return. "Miss Watson, I am delighted to make your acquaintance."

This was greeted by silence and the continued view of the top of the lady's head. Maria faded away with a mouthed, "Come and find me." He nodded and turned back to Miss Watson. He bent and picked up the dropped book and glanced at the spine. Volume three of *Glenarvon*, Lady Caro Lambs' roman-à-clef. He grinned. *So the lady is a bluestocking?*

"I believe this is yours?" he said gently, holding it out.

"Yes! Um, thank you." She took it back and stuffed it and the spectacles in her reticule.

The country dance was finishing up, and he said, "Would you care to dance, Miss Watson?"

"Are you asking me to dance?" came the peculiar reply. *Really, is the woman mentally deficient? Surely not. Just shy perhaps? Or overcome by my title? It does do odd things to people.*

"Well, yes, it is generally customary," he said with a slight smile. She glared at him for a moment. At least he thought it was a glare, but then her lids dropped, and he wondered if he had imagined it. She smoothed her hands down over her dress. A nervous gesture?

*The lady is an original, I'll give her that.*

*YOU DIDN'T THINK it was customary two years ago!* fumed Sarah. But she didn't say it out loud, because she longed to dance with him. Had longed to do so since the first time she'd clapped eyes on him in her first season. The Marquess of Thornbury he was then, and the handsomest man in the room. He was tall but not too tall and was blessed with a fine pair of shoulders and trim waistline. His handsome features were enhanced with slightly wavy brown hair and devastatingly blue eyes. And a smile that would melt the coldest of hearts. She had lost hers to him on sight.

She might have gotten over her girlish infatuation, for that was all it was, smitten by a handsome face and elegance of manner, if she hadn't encountered him on two more occasions where he'd come gallantly to her rescue.

The first time was toward the end of her first season. She was in Hatchards bookshop and trying to reach a book on the top shelf just out of reach. Being so much taller, it was the easiest thing in the world for him to reach it down for her.

"Here, let me," he'd said, pulling the book off the shelf and offering it to her with a smile and an elegant bow.

Like an idiot, she had blushed and stammered something unintelligible, and he had turned and continued on his way down to the ground floor. By the time she had recovered her countenance, he had left the shop.

The second time was in her second season. She was just leaving Hyde Park where she had been taking her daily walk with Esme her maid, when she had been caught in a sudden squall of rain. In moments she was drenched, as the wind turned her umbrella inside out and whipped it out of her hands. The umbrella, turning end over end, had scooted down the sidewalk away from her, as she had given chase. Another gust of wind picked it up and, much to her mortification, hit the gentleman in front of her squarely in the back.

He'd turned, and through the drenching rain she recognized him, *Thornbury! Oh, if it had been anyone else. How humiliating!* His great coat flapped in the wind and his hat flew off before he could catch it. Despite that, he had grabbed her broken umbrella as the wind threatened to whip it away again, just as she reached him full of apologies.

"I'm so sorry! The wind took it out of my hand!" she'd said, breathless. She had blinked up at him through the rain.

"Perfectly all right, ma'am," he had said politely, straightening it out and shutting it to prevent it flying off again. "Let me hail you a cab!" he'd said over the rush of the wind and rain. In the next moment a cab appeared at the curb, and he handed her up into it with Esme.

"Your direction, ma'am?" he'd asked.

She had given it, and he had paid the jarvey and waved the equipage off, standing in the rain until he was sure they were safely on their way, his coat running with rivulets of water, bareheaded in the downpour, his brown hair plastered to his head.

On neither occasion had he introduced himself or enquired after her name.

And when he had been finally introduced to her formally in this very room in her last season by Countess Lieven, he neither evinced any sign of recognizing her, nor asked her to dance.

*And now here he is, promoted to the dukedom and asking me to dance? Why? Why has he sought me out now?* There was only one answer, and it smote her in the chest with an ache that turned her stomach. *Because he knows about my fortune and suddenly that makes me, a mere vicar's daughter, worthy of his notice.* She had never felt so conflicted in her life. Part of her wanted to slap his face and storm off, part of her wanted to flee, and a treacherous third part ached to accept his offer. *Just once, to be held in his arms . . .*

Her desire to fulfil her fantasy won out. After all, was it not her goal to snare a titled gentleman? All the same, she could not but be conscious of the disparity in their social standing. A vicar's daughter and a duke? Not likely. She did not harbor any real illusions that the duke had matrimony in mind where she was concerned. *But then what has prompted him to seek me out at all? It is a mystery, perhaps if I dance with him, I can find out why.*

So she dropped another curtsy and said with becoming humility, "Thank you, Your Grace," and held out a gloved hand.

ROBERT TUCKED HER hand into the crook of his arm and led her onto the dance floor. He had been almost certain she was going to refuse him there for a moment. He had caught a flash in her sherry-brown eyes before she lowered her lashes that slashed him with fury. *Is she angry with me? What have I done? Is she mad? Is that why she is a wallflower?*

Taking her hand preparatory to bringing her into his embrace, he said, "Forgive me, Miss Watson, but have I done something to upset you?"

She glanced up at him as a pink stain spread over her face and his memory kicked him.

"We've met before!" he blurted with less than his usual sang-froid.

"We have," she admitted.

"I apologize for not recalling the event," he said, flushing faintly. He prided himself on his good manners, and clearly, he had been remiss here. Try as he might, he couldn't recall the exact circumstances of their meeting, but that blush tickled his memory.

"Several times, actually," she said. Damn, why couldn't he remember her? She was pretty enough. But then a vicar's daughter would be beneath his notice in normal circumstances, wouldn't she?

"Then I do most deeply apologize," he said, bowing to her as she curtsied to him. He slipped an arm round her waist and drew her into his embrace. A waft of rose water and lavender enveloped his senses as he brought her closer to his body and an unexpected rush of heat threw him off balance. *That was a surprise!*

She had a deliciously trim figure that fit neatly in his arms. Her head reached his chin . . . *which is a nice height for kissing . . . Good God, where did that come from?*

Although, it had been months since he had been with a woman. Knowing he was going to have to seek a wife this season, he had broken off his arrangement with his long-time mistress before Christmas. He might not be able to make the kind of love match he had been hoping for, but he intended to make every effort toward that endeavor; keeping a mistress in those circumstances he felt would be unfair to both ladies. Consequently, his natural needs were beginning to make themselves felt. *It must be that circumstance that has prompted me to think such things so precipitously.*

He led off and she followed with ease, her eyes fixed resolutely on his cravat.

Objectively, her face was pleasing but not beautiful. Her best features were her eyes, wide set and fringed with dark lashes, followed by her lips, plump enough for kissing—*ah, those thoughts again!* Really, he should be showing better control than this. It was most unusual for him. *Perhaps it denotes my tumbled state of mind?* He had thought he had himself in hand better than this. Her chin would be thought a smidgen too resolute for a woman, and her nose had a slight bump. *There, that is better, more objective, less feeling!*

Her reticule slid from her wrist to her elbow, pushed out of shape by its rectangular burden, and swung about awkwardly with the movement of the dance. He recalled with quiet amusement her fright when caught with her nose in a book.

"How are you enjoying *Glenarvon?*" he asked.

She flushed and glanced up at him. "I was almost finished, just a few pages to go. The story isn't much, but the satire is delightful."

He nodded in agreement. "Indeed. Did you recognize the players?"

She chuckled. "Absolutely! It is what makes the whole thing so delicious."

"If you like satire, have you read Voltaire?" he asked, curious to discover how far her education stretched.

She looked up startled, her eyes wide, her lips slightly parted. *I do like that expression. What would her lips feel like? No, no . . .*

"Yes, but don't tell anyone!" Something tugged in his chest at the unconscious intimacy of that. As if they were compatriots who shared a secret. *Was it possible . . . ? Don't get your hopes up. You know nothing about her yet.* All the same, his lips twitched at her hunted expression.

"I won't. What else have you read?" He was wholly unable to resist encouraging her.

"Are you trying to trap me?"

It was his turn to be startled. "No. Why should I?" He had a reputation for starchiness he knew, but in this particular realm he held more progressive views than most.

"You know perfectly well it is not appropriate for young ladies to read things like Voltaire."

"It is true that society thinks so."

"You do not?"

"I am somewhat more liberal in my ideas," he said mildly. "My sisters have all received a very good education," he added by way of illustration.

"I had no idea," she said softly.

"No idea about what?"

"Nothing!" she said abruptly. "What do you like to read, Your Grace?"

"I am partial to history," he said apologetically.

Her eyes lit up. "Roman or Greek?"

"Both. I read classics at Cambridge."

"Oh, how I envy you!" This was the most unusual conversation he had ever had with a young lady, her kissability notwithstanding, and he would rather like to prolong it. Unfortunately, the dance was drawing to a close, and he had four other young women to speak with. He returned Miss Watson to her chaperone and made a mental note to call upon her tomorrow. Unless, of course, one of the other young ladies proved to be more compelling.

And by the end of the evening, having danced with all five, he was only able to eliminate immediately the blonde and the redhead. His first impression of the widow held firm. She was definitely at the top of his list, and he had made an appointment to call upon her tomorrow to take her driving in the park. The other one, what was her name? Grenfell, yes Miss Grenfell, had been underwhelming. He'd had a devil of a time getting her to talk beyond monosyllables and her general demeanor was disinterested. *Which was a bit of a facer.* He wasn't used to being treated as someone of no interest. He might have been intrigued if he weren't so interested in the widow.

As for the wallflower, he would hold her in reserve if the

widow failed. He had enjoyed their conversation, but her changeability of mood made him wary. The widow was older, she would know the rules of a contract such as this. Miss Watson, he had a feeling was more vulnerable. There was a sweetness to her, an innocence that gave him pause. There was also that disturbing spark of heat that threw him off balance; that wasn't something he was accustomed to.

SARAH RETURNED TO her chaperone's side after her waltz with the duke, only to be pounced on by Daphne, who had been drawn away when the duke appeared at Almack's, which was why Sarah had snatched the opportunity to read her book in the first place.

"Troubridge?" she said, fanning herself. "My dear, I never thought you could look so high. Who introduced you?"

"Lady Sefton," she said, trying to hide her smile. When he had slipped his arm about her waist and drawn her close against him, her heart had threatened to jump out of her breast. And the heat that rushed up her body at his proximity made her blush in remembrance.

"Ah!" said Daphne looking mighty pleased. "And a waltz, too! Well, that will get you noticed, I guarantee it. You will be besieged now, mark my words!"

As proof, just then, Mrs. Drummond-Burrell floated across the room trailed by two gentlemen eager for introductions and that was the start of the avalanche. Sarah had no further opportunity to read her book because her hand was requested for every dance, a hitherto unknown experience. While she was dancing, though, she could not but be aware of the duke's movements also, and it did not escape her notice he danced with four other ladies known to possess substantial fortunes, and her initial euphoria drained slowly out her toes.

She hoped in vain that he would solicit her hand for another dance, but he did not.

Daphne repined this, too, but said, "It would give a singular particularity if he were to do so, my dear, and he would not commit such a solecism, I'm sure. The duke is known to be very correct and punctilious in all matters of *ton*, you know. He is very proud, but then the Laynes can trace their lineage back to the Conqueror."

By the time Sarah retired to bed, she had a headache, and it was all the wretched duke's fault. Her dormant infatuation was awakened again, and all her foolish longings she had thought packed away for good were back to taunt her. Really, it was absurd to be so swayed by a handsome face. Papa would be ashamed of her. *Where is strength of character and heart? I barely know him; it is ridiculous to harbor such powerful feelings on the strength of one dance.*

And yet her foolish heart persisted in looking for the things to support her feelings. *What of his interest in antiquities and books? His teasing me about Voltaire? And his admission that he supports liberal ideas for women's education? When he said that, my heart fairly melted.*

*Perhaps, if he is truly interested in pursuing my acquaintance, he will call upon me or seek me out at the next entertainment.*

# Chapter Four

"YOU HERE AGAIN, old chap?" said Ashford walking up to Robert at Almack's a week later. "I thought you were pursuing the widow?"

"I was," said Robert disgustedly. "I popped the question yesterday, and she turned me down flat."

"That's a shame," Ashford sipped the terrible lemonade they served here, for lack of anything else to drink, he supposed.

"Yes, I've lost a week," fretted Robert. "I was hoping to find the Watson girl, but she's not here yet and it's just minutes to ten o'clock."

"Doesn't look like she'll show."

"No." Just then Caroline swept off the dance floor on Greathouse's arm and came up to them. Caro was a tiny woman, one of those ethereal sorts, with strawberry blonde hair and deep green eyes. She smiled up at him.

"Robert! Lovely to see you." She looked about and lowered her voice to a conspiratorial whisper. "How goes the hunt?"

"Not well, I'm afraid," he admitted ruefully. "I'm glad to see you looking well."

"Thank you. Emrys, will you fetch me a drink? I'm parched!" she said with a waft of her fan.

"Of course, my love," said her obliging spouse, breaking off his conversation with Greathouse.

"Did Lannister fleece you the other night?" asked Robert.

Greathouse laughed. "No, his luck was damnably out."

"Fabian!" scolded Caro with a light slap of her fan to his arm.

"Sorry, my dear," he said absently. "Ravenshaw won."

"Doesn't he always?" replied Robert. Ravenshaw was nothing if not competitive.

Ashford reappeared with a glass of lemonade for his wife, and Robert excused himself. He'd spotted the Grenfell girl, standing in the corner with her mother, staring at her feet. *If Miss Watson wasn't here . . .*

Approaching Miss Grenfell, he bowed. Her mother beamed and jabbed the girl with her fan, none too subtly. Robert winced internally. Could he bear such a woman as his mother-in-law? Lady Lockwood was a tin-miner's daughter, and it showed. Miss Grenfell straightened, glanced up at him, and dropped a curtsy. "Your Grace," she murmured.

"Would you care to dance, Miss Grenfell?" he asked with what he hoped was an encouraging smile.

"She would love to, Your Grace! Wouldn't you, Emily?" said her mother, almost pushing the girl in his direction. He offered her his arm and drew her away from her dreadful mama onto the dance floor.

"Are you enjoying the season, Miss Grenfell?" he asked, looking for a way to open the conversation.

"Yes, Your Grace." This was uttered with such a listless tone, it was clearly a pelter.

"You don't care for dancing?" he queried, wondering what in blazes she did care for.

"No, Your Grace." Silence.

"If you could do whatever you pleased, what would it be?"

"I hardly know, Your Grace." At this point he was longing for Miss Watson's lively conversation. Silence ensued after that as he was at a loss as to how to draw the lady out, and she made no attempt to engage him in conversation. She performed the steps of the dance competently enough, but with little enthusiasm. Her whole demeanor was of someone who wanted desperately to be somewhere else. Yet when he gave her to opportunity to express that desire, she declined to take it.

He returned her to her mother's side and beat a hasty retreat. Really, the whole evening had been a blasted waste of time. He sought out Ashford and Caro and bade them goodnight. Ashford offered him the opportunity to come home with them and share a drink, but he wasn't in the mood to be sociable.

His mood wasn't improved when he got home and discovered a pile of bills waiting for him. Including a debt of his brother's, Lord Kenrick, for five hundred pounds! He dashed off a livid note to his youngest brother demanding that he explain himself, then took himself off to bed to fume and fret. Between ridiculous debts, the widow's refusal, and the inability to find Miss Watson this evening he was in a rare taking.

The next night, at his third ball for the evening, close on one o'clock, he finally found Miss Watson. She was just coming off the dance floor on the arm of Lord Exforth, whereupon she was besieged by a bevy of admirers. Word had got out about her fortune, clearly. It was easy to see, even at this distance, that this unaccustomed popularity was flustering her.

He crossed the room with rapid strides, managing to avoid being waylaid by several matchmaking mamas, and reached her side. Catching her eyes with his, he smiled and offered a bow and an arm. "Excuse me, gentlemen, but I believe the next dance is mine."

Holding her gaze, he challenged her to deny him. For a split second he thought she might. Then she inclined her head in acknowledgement and, placing her hand on his arm, let him lead her away from the disappointed group of males. There were some advantages to being a duke, after all.

Tonight, she was wearing a white muslin gown over a sea-green satin slip with silver trimming. And her reticule did not appear to contain any books. "Do you care to dance, or would you like to take a stroll in the gardens? It is disgustingly hot in here," he said.

"Yes, some fresh air would be most welcome," she said with a rather fixed smile. "Your rescue was quite timely," she added with a sideways glance that made his heart trip in an odd fashion. He could have sworn that was another glare she threw at him. The lady seemed to change mood faster than the weather. *Or is it just a trick of the light in her sherry-colored eyes?*

"You looked besieged," he said, holding the curtain aside for her.

"I was." She frowned as they stepped through the open French windows onto the terrace. "Word of my fortune has spread, and now I am the cynosure of all eyes."

"The world is regrettably mercenary," he said with a twinge of guilt as he led her down the steps into the garden proper. There were a number of couples taking advantage of the cooler air, and he set a sedate pace for their stroll down a path between trees forming a canopy overhead. The moonlight filtered through the branches and gave the illusion of privacy, although they were not truly alone. The murmur of the other couples' voices could still be heard against the backdrop of the fainter sounds of music and conversation from the ballroom. "I looked for you in vain at Almack's last night," he said.

"Lady Holbrook had a headache, so we didn't go," she replied.

"I was disappointed," he said, deciding to go all in. "I wanted to see you, perhaps reprise our waltz?"

"Really? It has been a week, Your Grace." Her voice was gentle, but he fancied there was a slight edge to it. He flushed.

"Yes, I've been a little busy."

"I gather that your pursuit of the Countess of Esbury did not prosper," she said flatly. He stiffened as if poked with a hat pin. His instinct was to protest that he didn't take her meaning, but she didn't give him a chance. "You haven't seen the latest caricature?"

"No, I haven't," he said slowly.

"It's quite amusing." She didn't look amused. "But then you must be used to being the butt of satire, being a duke and all," she added with a drawl.

"You have a sharp wit, Miss Watson." He spoke shortly, more than a little annoyed.

"You see, I couldn't fathom why you suddenly took an interest in me after three seasons of ignoring me. Now I know why." She came to a stop and turned. "I have had enough fresh air now, Your Grace. Please return me to the ballroom."

He felt winded for a moment. The problem was he couldn't deny that she was right without making a liar of himself, and that went against all his principles. "You are perfectly correct in your assumptions, Miss Watson. My circumstances make it imperative that I find a wealthy wife. I can assure you it is something that I find of equal abhorrence to yourself."

It was her turn to stiffen. Then her mouth fell open. "I have been insulted in all sorts of ways in my three years on the marriage mart, Your Grace, but I think you have just topped the list! If I am so abhorrent to you—!"

"Good heavens, I did not mean you were abhorrent!" he said testily. "I meant that the circumstances were as abhorrent to me as I am sure they are to you. Contracting a marriage of convenience was the last thing I wished to do."

"Why? I would have thought that for one of your station it would be expected."

"That may be, but I can assure you it is not the expected thing in my family."

"It isn't?"

"No. We have a tradition of marrying for love. Something I had long cherished hopes of doing. Unfortunately, I have never met a lady of suitable birth in my ten years on the marriage mart who has inspired more than mere liking or a fleeting physical attraction." He flushed faintly to be so blunt, but since the gloves were off, he felt it best to be brutally honest.

"I see. Well, if the widow was your first choice, I make a pretty poor consolation prize," she said, her color heightened. The lady was clearly still annoyed with him.

"You do yourself a disservice to make such an unflattering comparison, Miss Watson. You are not a consolation prize."

"It is kind of you to say so, Your Grace, but I doubt that you are sincere."

"Damn it all to hell, Miss Watson!" he said, losing his temper. "You know me not at all if you think that I am in the habit of offering ladies Spanish coin!" Her eyes widened in shock, and he flushed with embarrassment. "I apologize for my intemperate speech, but you're the most exasperating female I've ever met!"

"In that case, Your Grace, it is fortunate that if you were able to bring yourself to offer for me, as distasteful as the notion is to you, you can be assured that I would not accept!" On which, she turned and walked away, leaving him standing alone under the trees.

"Damn and blast!" he muttered. *This is not going according to plan at all!*

He returned to the ballroom to find to his horror that the lady was dancing with Lannister. *Bloody hell, is there no one to protect her from the likes of him?* Lannister was not only a gazetted fortune hunter, he was a loose screw to boot. Not the sort of unsavory character that ought to be let anywhere near young ladies of virtue. He was banned from Almack's for that very reason.

Aware, with a twinge of conscience, that he was as guilty as Lannister of chasing a fortune, he still maintained that at least he was aboveboard about it. He had no intention of trying to make the girl fall in love with him. *Well, not unless she felt the same.* He would never stoop to a pretense of feelings he didn't have.

The girl's father wasn't here, and she had no adult brother to watch out for her, or even an uncle. Was her chaperone unaware of Lannister's reputation or just lax? She might be unaware, of course. Lannister was charming, the ladies loved him. His more extreme behaviors were probably only known to the gentlemen.

*Damn it, what could he do?* If he attempted to speak to her again tonight, she would likely react badly, and he could hardly warn her against Lannister without sounding like a hypocrite. She wouldn't know of Lannister's reputation, and he wasn't about to tell her.

Then he spotted Ashford, Caro, and Greathouse returning to the ballroom from the refreshments area. He headed in their direction and intercepted his friend. "Can I have a word with you quietly?" he said in the other man's ear.

"Of course, old chap," said Ashford. "Caro's going to dance with Fabian. I'm all yours."

They retired to an alcove out of the main flow of traffic, and Robert said, "Would you do me a favor?"

"Anything you like. What is it?"

"I just spotted Lannister dancing with Miss Watson."

"Good God!"

"Yes, precisely! She has no one to protect her from his sort. Her father isn't in London, and she has no male guardian here, only her chaperone, Lady Holbrook, to advise her. Would you keep an eye on her? She and I"—he flushed—"had a little misunderstanding earlier on, and she is a trifle annoyed with me at the moment. I don't think she would take kindly to me offering her unsolicited advice at this juncture."

"Pot calling the kettle black?"

"She would perceive it as such, I fear. There is a clear difference, but she wouldn't know that and nor should she."

"You can rely on me, old chap!" Ashford clapped him on the shoulder.

"You're the best of good fellows, Emrys. Thank you!" Robert shook his hand fervently, a sudden weight lifting. "I shan't be staying. I only came to speak with her, and it all went rather horribly wrong. I won't do myself any favors attempting to approach her again tonight. I mean to leave it until tomorrow."

"In hot pursuit?"

"I am."

"Best of luck, Robert," said Ashford in all sincerity.

"Thank you. I'm going to need it. I never thought myself lacking in address, but there is something about the lady that seems to get me wrong footed. Dashed if I know what it is. She's a vicar's daughter, for God's sake!"

Ashford gave him an odd look and shook his head.

"What?" asked Robert.

"Nothing, old man," Ashford smiled but wouldn't be drawn.

Robert glanced back at Miss Watson. She seemed highly amused by Lannister, and it made him uneasy. He would call upon her tomorrow. Paradoxically, now that she had thrown down the gauntlet, he was quite determined to pursue her. *For in truth, what other choice do I have?*

SARAH WATCHED THE duke leave with mixed feelings. On the one hand she was glad, or ought to be, that she had sent him off with a flea in his ear; on the other, the ache in her breast gave the lie to that. She couldn't help but think that if he'd wanted to, he might have tried to talk to her again. But then she had been quite rude to him. He was a duke after all. If Daphne knew she had spoken to him like that, she would have a fit of the vapors.

She had been so elated when she'd seen him coming toward her and so angry at the same time. When he had very high-handedly demanded the next dance, she ought to have given him a set down and chosen someone else, but the temptation to accept had been irresistible. However, when he had then tried to pick up where they had left off a week ago and pretend he hadn't been dancing attendance on the widow all that time, her fury had come blazing back.

"I've lost your attention, my dear," said her dancing partner, recalling her scattered wits. He gave her a droll smile. "A penny for them?"

She had met the Earl of Lannister for the first time three

nights ago at Lady Morton's party. He was handsome, witty, and charming and had claimed her for two dances. His attention had been a balm to her heart, bruised from the duke's neglect.

She flushed and said lightly, "Nothing of consequence, my lord. You were telling me the tale of the horse that won?"

"Yes, first bit of luck I've had in a while. But with a name like Tickle My Fancy, how could it lose? I got excellent odds, too." He slid an arm round her waist as they circled each other in the steps of the dance, bringing her close against his side with a smile. "I think my luck is decidedly in at the moment. Perhaps it is you bringing me good fortune, Miss Watson?"

"How absurd, my lord!" she said with a laugh. His flirtatious manner was a little flustering. She wasn't accustomed to flirting and didn't know how to do it successfully. *The duke didn't flirt with her.* The thought was a little depressing.

He let her go, sliding his arm away slowly, his hand running across her back, his gaze holding hers longer than it should. This assault on her senses was confusing, and she felt peculiarly light-headed. They stepped around each other and came back together, his fingers brushing her side again through the fabric of her gown, before seizing her hand and twirling her under his arm. His arm came round her waist again for the promenade, and he murmured in her ear, "You're a dashed attractive young woman, but you know that, don't you?"

Her cheeks flooded scarlet, and she shook her head. "I wish you wouldn't, my lord."

"Wouldn't what?" They turned to face each other, hands clasped.

"Wouldn't say such things. They put me to the blush. I'm not accustomed to them and do not for a moment think them true."

"Did no one teach you how to flirt, Miss Watson?"

She shook her head again.

"Then I shall have to teach you. It is a useful skill for a lady wishing to intrigue a gentleman."

"What makes you think I wish to intrigue a gentleman?"

"Ah, that is better. But of course, you do. You cannot tell me that none of your many beaux have taken your fancy?"

She opened her mouth to say that there was no one, and he cut her off with a shake of his head.

"Tut, Miss Watson, do not tell me lies, for I will not believe you. Someone has you in his snare, and I'll warrant it is not me. Despite my best efforts." His expression was so woebegone at this, she had to laugh.

He grinned, which made his startlingly bright blue eyes dance. "You will make a first-rate flirt with a little coaching," he said, adding conspiratorially, "I will help you land your chosen one, for if I cannot have you for myself, I will do my very best to see you happy."

This statement, as outrageous as it was, made her heart flutter in an odd way. She didn't really believe his nonsense, but the notion that someone would be her champion was attractive. *To have someone care for me enough to want to make me happy?* She was not so foolish as to think the earl was the one who would do so, but the idea was nonetheless attractive.

With a pang, she wished the duke showed such an inclination. So far, she had to admit that the only inclination he had shown was in service of his own needs. He was, she realized sadly, remarkably self-centered. Although she acquitted him of being so deliberately. It would be a side effect of his upbringing. He would never have been taught to consider others' needs above his own, except in a noblesse oblige kind of way. Though she was sure he would be horrified to be perceived as selfish and would vigorously deny it.

The dance was drawing to its close, and she looked up at the earl and said with a smile, "You, my lord, are full of nonsense. I will not be drawn into it."

"That's put me in my place," he said, not one whit bothered by her attempt at a set down. She laughed and decided that she liked him in spite of his attempts to flirt with her.

Returned to the circle of her admirers, all clamoring for her hand in the next dance, she was confronted by a plethora of choice. A gentle cough behind her made her look round, and she found Viscount Ashford bowing to her.

"May I have this dance, Miss Watson?" Something in his kind smile made her lay her hand on his arm.

"I would be delighted, sir," and she let Ashford lead her away to the groans of the other gentlemen. If she didn't know for a fact that all this attention was caused by her fortune, she would be in danger of getting a swelled head. As it was, she knew precisely why she was so popular, and it was a delight to swan off with the viscount who, being married, was unlikely to have such ulterior motives. Viscount Ashford, despite his disheveled appearance, was a surprisingly good dancer.

"Don't look now," he murmured, "but Exforth's about to tread on Lady Keighley's skirt."

"Oh dear! He is remarkably clumsy. He trod on my toes twice earlier," she confessed. "I do feel sorry for him."

"Yes, poor chap, he should stick to horses. Excellent rider to hounds, hopeless on the dance floor."

"Well, one can't be good at everything,"

"No indeed. Unless you're Ravenshaw, of course." At her look, he added, "Friend of mine, Marquess of Ravenshaw, have you met him?"

"Oh yes, I believe I have had an introduction. Splendidly handsome and very polished."

"Yes, that's him, devil of a fellow with the ladies, they all love him."

She smiled but didn't respond to that. Ashford went on, "Fact is, Miss Watson, I've noticed you don't have your father here, no one to keep an eye out for you."

She flushed, "Why should I need that?"

Ashford smiled kindly, "You're an heiress, my dear, and are going to be a target for all sorts of unscrupulous fellows. If you feel at any point unsure or uncomfortable, I hope you know you can come to me. Not a relative of course, but—well, you seem to need a friend?"

Her heart lifted, and she smiled into his merry, hazel eyes. There was nothing flirtatious in his manner, unlike Lannister. He made her feel comfortable and safe, as if he truly was her friend. She appreciated that; she had precious few friends in London.

"Thank you, my lord. You're most kind."

ROBERT, WAITING ON the steps for his carriage to be brought round, was conscious of a lowness of spirits that was uncharacteristic. The evening had gone disastrously wrong from his perspective, and he was frustrated with the situation and himself. What was it about Miss Watson that made him so wrong-footed?

His thoughts were interrupted by a plaintive mew and the pressure of something brushing up against his leg. Looking down, the lamplight revealed a black cat with emerald-green eyes rubbing round his leg, long tail curling round his stocking-clad calf.

"Hello, where did you spring from?" he asked, removing a glove with his teeth and bending down to pat the creature. It wasn't much bigger than a kitten, yet it had already been in the wars, judging from the ragged state of one ear, and it was thin, and its fur was damp. It butted his hand with its head and rubbed its cheek against his calf.

"You've been having a rough time of it, haven't you, little fellow? Or perhaps lady?"

The cat lifted its head, so he could rub it under the chin, closing those magnificent green eyes. His carriage rattled to a stop in front of him, and he sighed at the kitten, bent, picked it up, and got into the carriage with it. Setting it on the seat, he watched it kneading the upholstery with its little claws.

"What shall I call you, little lady or laddie?" She or he blinked at him and settled on the seat, Egyptian cat fashion. The carriage drew up at his door and he scooped the cat up, and letting himself into the house—it was late, past three o'clock—he shut the front door and set the cat down to explore the entrance hall while he divested himself of his hat and cloak. Then he scooped the cat up again and headed down the rear stairs to the kitchens.

It was years since he had been in the kitchens at Berkeley Square. Probably not since he was a boy, he thought. But he remembered enough to find his way around. The fire in the great hearth was banked but still gave off a strong glow and plenty of heat, making the room one of the coziest in the house. A lamp on the big refectory table gave some light, and he set down his guest while he took the lamp and investigated the pantry. Having found the milk, he spent a bit of time finding a bowl. Filling the bowl, he set it down for the cat.

"That meet with your approval?" he asked.

The cat sniffed and began to lap delicately. Robert went back to the pantry to find something more substantial and came back with a ham, some bread, and butter. He was setting these out on the table and reaching for the carving knife when a shocked voice made him look round.

"Your Grace, what are you doing here?'

He smiled. "Mrs. Holloway, I brought you a mouser," he waved at the cat. "Both of us could do with a snack." He waved the carving knife.

Mrs. Holloway, his housekeeper, dressed in a robe and slippers, came toward him protesting. "Let me do that, Your Grace. It's not seemly, you waiting on yourself and a cat."

He smiled whimsically. "I don't mind. Fetch me some ale while I carve this ham. Would you like some?"

"Your Grace!" she said, scandalized.

The knife hovered over the ham as he raised an eyebrow.

"Just a sliver if you insist, Your Grace," she said coyly, disappearing to find the ale. She came back with a jug and two tankards, a plum cake, and a wodge of cheese. She poured the ale, sliced and buttered the bread, cut the cheese into generous wedges, and cut two slices of the plum cake. She fetched plates and made him a ham sandwich and served the cat some ham and cheese on a plate.

"Where did you find her, Your Grace?"

"Is it a female?"

"Aye, judging by . . . the look of her," she said.

"I shall call her Emerald for those magnificent eyes, Em for short," he said, tucking into his sandwich. "She found me. I was waiting for the carriage, and she just appeared, rubbing round my legs. I don't think she's fully grown."

"Let's hope she hasn't got a litter on board yet." She sat down opposite him with a smaller plate of food. "You haven't been down here since you were a lad, Your Grace."

"I know, I was just thinking that I should do it more often. What is it about illicit midnight snacks that make them taste so good?" he said, popping a bit of crumbly cheese in his mouth. The sharp salty taste was delicious with a bit of the sweet plum cake.

"I'm sure I don't know, Your Grace, but Mr. Creighton will be shocked when I tell him, and if Mr. Le Bow should learn of it, I'll never hear the end of it."

"Le Bow?"

"The chef, Your Grace. He will be very French about it."

Robert shrugged and took a deep draught of the ale. "She should keep the rats down for you anyway." He polished off the rest of the cheese and plum cake and drained the tankard. "Thank you, Mrs. Holloway, I'll bid you goodnight, or should I say good morning? I'll expect a report on young madam there and how she is earning her keep." He rose and bowed to his housekeeper.

"You want me to rouse Mr. Bridges for you, Your Grace?"

"No, I'll manage. I'm feeling very independent tonight, Mrs. Holloway. Tell Bridges not to wake me before ten at the earliest."

"Right you are, Your Grace."

He gave Emerald another scratch round her ears and under her chin and made his way up to bed, feeling a little better about the evening than he had before, his resolve to pursue Miss Watson firmer than ever.

# Chapter Five

SARAH WAS SITTING in the parlor sifting through the cards, gifts, and bouquets of flowers delivered that morning from her bevy of admirers. She noted that there was nothing from the duke. Not surprising after her performance last night. He would never speak to her again, of course. Her temper had got the better of her.

*The gall of the man, to spend a week pursuing another woman (also possessed of a large fortune), and only when his suit clearly didn't prosper to attempt to lure me into making an idiot of myself over him. Again . . .*

Daphne looked up from a note and exclaimed, "This one is from Viscount Moorcroft. It is very pretty; he likens your eyes to pansies."

Sarah snorted.

"Don't snort, my dear, it's not ladylike," said Daphne absently, reaching for another note. "Oh, here is a lovely one. It's a bit of Keats and accompanies a lovely bouquet of rosebuds. Shall I read it to you?"

Sarah was about to decline the treat when the door opened and Latham, the butler, announced, "His Grace, the Duke of Troubridge."

Daphne dropped the note and rose, flustered, touching her

hair and smoothing her cambric gown. Sarah rose more slowly, her heart doing an odd thump in her breast. Had he come to scold her for her unseemly behavior last night? But then his speech had been quite shocking, so why should she apologize?

In the next moment, the duke entered the room, dressed stylishly in a maroon-colored coat that fit his admirable figure to perfection, pale eggshell-colored breeches, and top boots. His cravat was tied with style, and his shirt points were starched perfectly. His hair was arranged with casual elegance. In short, he was beautifully turned out. Which just emphasized how undeniably handsome he was. *Drat the man, why does he have to be so attractive? Papa would say I am being horribly shallow!* She dropped into a curtsy with Daphne.

"Your Grace!" Daphne rose and held out her hand, quite pink with pleasure. "You honor us. Latham, fetch refreshments, please."

"Please don't trouble yourself, Lady Holbrook. I called in the hopes that I could entice you ladies to visit the museum with me. There is an exhibition of Greek and Roman statuary that I thought might be of interest to Miss Watson." At his words, her heart turned over with a palpable thud and all her bad temper drained out her toes.

He took her hand as he spoke and kissed it with the lightest of touches. It was a formal, old-fashioned gesture, and it sent a quiver up her arm that landed in her belly. She could feel herself blushing.

Sarah swallowed. *It was really so unfair of him to be so charming.* Before she could find her tongue to reply, Daphne said, "How delightful! Of course we would love to go, wouldn't we Sarah?"

"I'm not dressed for an outing!" protested Sarah.

"I'm sure His Grace will be happy to wait while you change, dear. I'll order that tea, shall I, Your Grace?"

Daphne waved Sarah away and she left reluctantly. She ought to refuse after last night. She was mortified with embarrassment when she recalled all the horrible things she had said to the duke, and now he was being perfectly civil and offering her a treat. *How did he know I have been dying to see the exhibition?*

She flew upstairs and rang for her maid, Esme. She selected her new walking dress in green poplin with a high collar, a fawn-colored pelisse with green ribbons, fashionable high poke bonnet, kid boots, and gloves in matching green.

She was dressed in record time and returned to the parlor where she found Daphne offering His Grace a second biscuit. The duke looked up as she entered, and his eyes, a devastating blue, appeared to register approval. Setting down his cup, he rose immediately, and Daphne bustled out to fetch her pelisse and bonnet, which had miraculously appeared downstairs while Sarah was dressing.

Quickly arriving at Montague House, they purchased a program for the exhibition and made their way to the new exhibit's hall.

They had gone only a few steps into the hall when Daphne said, "I don't know how it is, but I am a little fatigued. I'll just take a seat on one of the couches in the middle of the hall and let the duke show you around, Sarah." She smiled at the duke, taking a seat and waving them off.

"How did you know I wished to see this exhibit, Your Grace?" Sarah asked, consulting the program as they approached a large sculpture featuring Zeus and a nymph.

"I guessed that you might when you expressed an enthusiasm for Greek and Roman history. And I confess I had a desire to see it myself."

"And I confess I am surprised to see you today after our . . . heated passage of arms last night," she said frankly.

"If you meant to deter me, your object failed. I'm made of sterner stuff than that," he said with a smile which made her grow unaccountably hot.

"Evidently," she said, attempting to make a recover.

"I must offer you an apology," he said with every evidence of sincerity. "My speech was intemperate in the extreme, my foul language was unforgivable."

She smiled; it gave her a little thrill to have him apologize to her. "I have three younger brothers, Your Grace. I have heard worse."

They continued their perambulation around the exhibit, consulting the program as they went, and fell into a heated discussion of the rival merits of Greek versus Roman sculpture. She argued that Greek statuary had more artistic merit because of its simple and graceful style, and he that as Roman statuary was more realistic, *it* held greater artistic merit.

"We shall have to agree to disagree, Your Grace," she said firmly. "You shall not budge me from my position."

"And I shall not budge from mine, so yes we will have to agree to disagree," he spoke with a smile, however, that made her heart dance. *If only he weren't so dashed handsome,* she thought. *What would Papa make of him?*

Her father was a man of the cloth and would not be swayed by considerations of status and titles, nor beauty of countenance. Papa would look for moral fiber and solid worth. He had been opposed from the beginning to Great-aunt Agnes's plans to marry her off to a titled gentleman. But Mama had persuaded him to consent to Sarah having a season. And as each year rolled around and Sarah was whisked off to London for yet another round of frivolity and still no husband, he grew if not reconciled, at least grudgingly accepting.

With a large family and small income, it became impossible to refuse Aunt Agnes's whims, as she held the purse strings so tightly that without her generosity, the Watsons would have suffered severe privations. As it was, Sarah would, if she fulfilled the terms of the will, be able to supply the funds for her sisters to have seasons with the opportunity to find suitable husbands, and her little brothers would be able to attend Eton and Oxford. Something they could never have afforded otherwise.

"I'm sorry, what was that?" she said, startled to realize he had spoken, and she hadn't heard a word he'd said.

"I asked your opinion of this piece," he said, stopping before a statue of a Roman general.

"Ah, Julius Caesar!" she smiled. *Is he trying to test me?*

"So, you recognize him?"

"Of course! Did you think I wouldn't?"

"I detect a competitive streak in you, Miss Watson."

"It comes of being the eldest of eight siblings, Your Grace. Everything is a competition."

He pursed his lips as if considering her statement. "I am the eldest of six and have never felt the need to compete with my siblings."

"Perhaps not, but I would bet my best bonnet *they* have felt the urge to compete with *you*, probably unsuccessfully. Do you always win?"

He frowned. "I've never thought about it. It's my duty to lead the way and protect them. I was trained to be the Duke of Troubridge from the day I was born."

"Which explains your unconscious arrogance." She smiled to soften the blow.

"I am not arrogant!" His expression and tone took on that testy edge again, and she cocked her head and continued to smile but said nothing for a moment.

"I am not arrogant!" he repeated. "In fact, if anything, I am too easy in my ways."

"I said it was an unconscious arrogance, Your Grace. Of course you don't realize it."

He stared at her for a moment and then resumed their perambulation. "I shall take your opinion on advisement, Miss Watson," he said a little stiffly.

"I've offended you again, haven't I?" she said ruefully.

"You seem to make a habit of it," he admitted. He looked down at her again and frowned. "You're an original, I'll give you that. I begin to see why you didn't take. Let me inform you, Miss Watson, that no man likes to have his shortcomings pointed out to him."

Her cheeks flooded with heat, and unable to keep her tongue between her teeth, she said tartly, "As someone of consequence, of course you're unused to anyone offering you critique, no matter how justified!"

He stared at her baffled for a moment, and she dropped her eyes, suddenly mortified. "I apologize, Your Grace. That was very rude of me."

"No, don't. I suspect you're right; I've just never seen myself that way. I still don't necessarily count it as a fault. I can hardly help something that is bred in the bone, so to speak. I'm a privileged person by birth. I had hoped I didn't take it for granted, but I see from your comment that I do need to be more mindful of my good fortune."

"Well, I wouldn't have said it if you hadn't been rude first," she said.

"Was I? I suppose I was. For which *I* apologize, Miss Watson. It must be your frankness that tempts me to be equally frank in return." He was still frowning at her as if she were a puzzle he couldn't fathom. "I've never met a woman who disconcerts me as much as you do. You are leading me to show a lack of manners, for which I am heartily sorry. Please forgive me."

The sincerity in his tone made her heart turn over. She didn't know if she was on her head or heels. He made her pulse race with his smiles and the merest touch of his hand. Then he said something abominably rude or arrogant, and she wondered how she could possibly think him attractive.

Really, after the way he had behaved over the last week, she ought to be over her infatuation with him. She needed to remember that he was only interested in her for her fortune, not anything else. He had made it abundantly clear that he was sacrificing himself on the altar of familial duty. Seeking a bride with money to support his family. If it were not for her fortune, he would never have looked twice at her.

After an inner struggle, she said politely, "You are very gracious. I shall mind my tongue in future."

"Pray don't. I find the fact that I never know what you're going to say next vastly entertaining."

She smiled tightly and nodded but didn't offer any further animadversions on his character for the rest of the tour.

BY THE TIME Robert had returned the ladies to their house and taken his leave, he had decidedly mixed feelings about the whole experience. He could not deny that the more he saw of the lady the more intrigued he became. There was definitely something between them, but he was damned if he knew what it was. He wondered seriously if he could live for the rest of his life with a woman who could so accurately and devastatingly point out his faults to him.

She was certainly nothing like the woman he had envisioned one day marrying. She was not easy or comfortable to be around, and they did not fall into a harmonious synchronicity, the kind he had always imagined his soul mate would provide. On the contrary, she made him prickly and defensive, argued with him, and held her ground when he challenged her. He wasn't used to that. He realized that people toadied to him all the time, but he hadn't realized until she pointed it out that he expected it and was mildly annoyed when they didn't.

Miss Watson aroused a bewildering array of emotions in his breast. He had to admit he was *not* indifferent to her, although he was unsure if irritation or liking was uppermost, since he seemed to feel both in equal proportions. She also sparked a physical reaction. Ever since he had taken her in his arms at Almack's that first night, he had wanted to do it again, but the opportunity had not arisen.

His next plan of attack must include a kiss, he decided, to test that spark. If he was going to marry the lady, he needed to be able to expect that their union would not be a chore to either of them.

All the signs were there for a felicitous physical union, but he persuaded himself that testing it was imperative. Just a kiss, nothing more.

He recalled the sensation of holding her in his arms. Her slender waist, her perfect height for kissing, as he had noted at the time. Yes, he definitely needed to get her alone and kiss her. That would be the deciding factor.

*But how to contrive such a thing without causing a scandal?* An idea occurred to him, and he sent off a note to Caroline to elicit her assistance.

# Chapter Six

"MY DEAR, LOOK at this!" said Daphne, sorting invitations beside her breakfast plate. "It's from Lady Ashford. Such fun! Her ladyship begs the company of Lady Holbrook and Miss Watson to watch the fireworks in Vauxhall Gardens on Friday next at eight o'clock. All guests are to wear masks and dominos . . ." Daphne looked up with her eyes sparkling. "My dear, in my day such entertainments were a little improper, but today they are much more respectable. I wonder who will be in Lady Ashford's party?"

Sarah looked up from her correspondence, "Weren't we going to Lady Partridge's ball on Friday?"

"I shall write at once and beg off—this is an opportunity not to be missed. The fireworks are splendid and the gardens very pretty. You may be sure, Lady Ashford's request to wear masks is to protect the identities of all concerned. Because, while they are much tamer than in my day, public masquerades are still not quite the thing, my dear."

"If they weren't the thing, how did you come to attend one, Daphne?" asked Sarah, highly amused.

Daphne blushed. "My sister and I sneaked out and went with our cousins Leopold and Gerald. It was most reprehensible, but such fun. Mama never found out, thank goodness, and the boys took good care of us, I promise you. But if we had been caught and unmasked, we would have been ruined. On no account should you remove your mask for the duration of the event, Sarah."

Sarah frowned. "Should I go? Would Papa approve?"

Daphne pursed her lips. "Probably not, but do not let that put a damper on your spirits, Sarah. You will do nothing untoward. Lady Ashford's guests will not cross the line, and you may be sure you will be perfectly safe, or I would not countenance it."

The presence of Viscount Ashford in the party reassured Sarah. He at least she felt safe with. It occurred to her to wonder if the duke would also be in the party. Ashford was a friend of his, she knew that. *But surely the duke is too stuffy to attend a public masquerade? Even in disguise?*

As it transpired, that Friday, the Ashfords collected them by carriage.

"The rest of the party will meet us there. We have booked a box on the second tier away from the hoi polloi," said Lady Ashford, looking perfectly splendid in a white and silver gown beneath a black velvet domino, which set her strawberry-blonde curls aflame.

Sarah was also dressed in white, but she had to admit that her ensemble was plain by comparison with Caroline's.

The blaze of light from the thousands of colored lamps strung among the trees, temples, and pavilions of the gardens took Sarah's breath away, and she was glad that she had come, despite her misgivings.

Daphne squeezed her arm and murmured in her ear, "I told you it was splendid!"

The Ashfords led the way to their box in the pavilion, where an orchestra was playing and couples were dancing beneath the trees. In the box they found two gentlemen awaiting them in masks and dominos.

"Lady Holbrook, Miss Watson, I would like to present the Marquess of Ravenshaw, and I believe you are already acquainted with the Duke of Troubridge," said Lady Ashford, her green eyes dancing behind her mask and a broad smile on her lips.

Seeing Ravenshaw beside the duke, he was slightly shorter and had much darker hair, a sleek ebony color. He smiled, bowed with inestimable grace and kissed first Daphne's then Sarah's hand. It was rapidly obvious that Ravenshaw had been invited to monopolize Daphne and leave Sarah to the duke.

*Could the duke have asked Lady Ashford to organize this party just for me? Surely not.*

Yet it appeared that was indeed the case. A little thrill ran through her at the notion. She needed to remember that he was in pursuit of her fortune. But for him to exert this much effort to please her, particularly after the insults they had exchanged in their last encounter? At the very least, it argued for persistence on his part.

Each couple had a table in the box, and Sarah was conscious of a shiver of excitement when he held her chair for her and smiled, his eyes glinting through his mask. Even knowing who he was, the mask gave him an air of mystery that was intriguing.

"Am I forgiven for my rudeness the other day, Miss Watson?" he asked, passing her a plate of ham and salad and pouring her a glass of champagne.

He spoke in a light tone, almost teasing for him. He was different tonight, and it encouraged her to tease back. He did seem bent on charming her. She wasn't sure that she was proof against a charming duke.

"Perhaps. What will you do to earn my good graces?" she asked, sipping the champagne.

"I will turn that back upon you and ask you how I may do so, for if past behavior is any indication, I have a poor success rate. I must confess you throw me off balance, Miss Watson. I am not accustomed to it."

"In days of yore, it was the custom for knights to perform acts of valor for their ladies," she said whimsically. *Is it wearing a mask that is making me act this way, or is it the champagne? Or both?*

"I see. Will you set me a quest, my lady?"

Hugely enjoying herself, Sarah said, "I think I shall. See that lantern over there, the blue one in that huge tree? Will you fetch it for me?"

He followed the line of her pointing finger and bowed, "As my lady wishes."

He left the box, and, in a moment, she saw him reaching up to detach the blue lantern from the branch on which it was suspended. It was done in a trice, and he was back with his trophy. Which he presented to her on bended knee. Hugely tickled, she laughed and accepted it, placing it on their table where its flickering light threw blue shadows over the tablecloth.

She then held out her hand. "Sir Knight, you are forgiven."

He took her hand and kissed it before rising to his feet and resuming his seat.

She placed her hand in her lap, trying to pretend that a little tingle hadn't travelled up her arm from the touch of his lips upon the back of it.

"Now I am restored to your good graces, my lady, I must endeavor to stay there. There will be a display of fireworks later. Have you seen such a spectacle before?"

"No, I have not. I am most excited to see it," she confessed, sampling a mouthful of the wafer-thin ham. It melted on her tongue, its salty flavor a nice contrast with the sweetness of the honey glaze. She sipped more champagne, a warm glow filtering through her body.

She glanced sideways at Daphne who was blushing at something Ravenshaw said to her and rapping his knuckles with her fan. The Ashfords had left the box to dance.

"Would you care to dance, Miss Watson?" he asked as if divining her thoughts.

"Very well, Your Grace" She removed her napkin from her lap and took his hand as he conducted her from the box down to the dance floor. Less formal than Almack's or a ball, couples joined and left the dance floor when they chose, and the orchestra continued to play. Currently, their choice seemed to be the waltz.

Sarah's heart skipped and thudded as he slid his arm round her waist and drew her close against him, closer than he had done at Almack's. Between the rush of warm heat from his proximity, the champagne, and the general giddiness of the moment, she felt lighter than air as he led off. Their cloaks swirled outward with the movement of the dance as they circled the floor, and she found his eyes holding hers in a compelling fashion that she could not look away from.

*Intoxicating.*

She nearly held her breath wanting to hang onto this moment of perfection forever. She could almost believe she had stumbled into a fairy tale. For the first time in their acquaintance, she felt an accord with him, as if the rhythm of the dance had got into her blood and her heart. She had been dazzled by his good looks from the first, but this, this was something altogether different and more powerful than the girlish infatuation she had previously nurtured. She felt herself in serious danger of plunging headlong off a precipice. And the worst part about it was that she desperately wanted to.

As the eldest of eight children, and Papa's favorite, she had always been a good girl, the responsible one, the one everyone relied on, the one who gave for the benefit of others. She was the one who put her own needs, wants, and desires behind those of her loved ones. It was second nature to her to do this, and she didn't resent it, but just in this moment, she felt the temptation to reach for something for herself. *Something that perhaps Papa would not approve of?*

The duke's arm tightened around her, bringing her closer against the hard heat of his body, and a pulse of a different kind thrummed through her. He bent his head and murmured in her ear, "There is something very freeing about wearing a mask, I find. Do you agree, Miss Watson?"

She nodded. "Yes," she said softly. A shiver provoked by the warmth of his breath against her ear skated down her spine. A heat was building low in her belly that she had never felt before, and it was making her breathless and reckless. She felt wicked for the first time in her life. And contrary to her expectation, it felt delicious.

His mouth lingered near her ear, and he murmured, "Your scent is intoxicating."

She shivered with delight, and a soft breath escaped her in a sigh. The champagne must be making her giddy. *So wicked. So delicious.*

"Would you care to take a walk with me amongst the trees before the fireworks?" he asked softly.

"Yes," she breathed, quite convinced she was going to combust with wickedness.

He swirled her away from the dancing couples and out among the trees. Bringing their dance to a graceful close, he tucked her hand in his arm and conducted her down a meandering walk among the trees, lit by lanterns of different colors. The stars twinkled above in an almost black, velvet sky and the night air kissed her cheek with a breath of freshness. A three-quarter moon gave some additional silvery light, and Sarah thought she had never experienced anything so romantic in her life.

"It's beautiful," she whispered. "Like a fairy land."

"Yes, it is," he murmured in agreement, and they strolled in silence, neither it seemed, willing to break their silent harmony.

Their path brought them to a small temple nestled among the trees; the scent of blossoms heavy in the air. He led her up the shallow steps into the dim interior of the little round temple. Within, they found an altar with a dozen candles lit, the flames dancing in the night air. More candles stood waiting to be lit, and he took up a taper and said, "We should light a candle and make a wish together, hm?"

"What a lovely notion," she said with a smile up at him.

He smiled back and said quietly "Put your hand over mine." She obeyed, and he lit the taper from one of the other candles and moved it toward one of the unlit ones. "Ready to make your wish?"

She nodded and closed her eyes as his hand guided them to light the candle.

*Please, God, let me love the man I marry, and let him love me!* she prayed silently.

ROBERT BLEW OUT the taper and set it aside, turning her in his arms. *Was it the masks?* When he had held her on the dance floor, he had felt such a strong desire to kiss her it had almost overwhelmed his reason. His desire for her was more powerful than he had anticipated. She looked up at him, her eyes glinting in the candlelight, her lips plump and tempting. He bent his head and said softly, "Let us seal that wish with a kiss."

He thought she might pull away, but she remained still, and he closed the distance to press his mouth lightly against hers. A feather-light kiss. It was hardly necessary, dancing with her had given him his answer in regard to physical compatibility. He wasn't certain she felt it, too, but knew unequivocally that he did. Her scent, her shape, the feel of her in his arms pressed against his body, had hardened him so much he feared she would detect it through the layers of their clothing.

He meant it to be a light caress and nothing more, something symbolic that would not alarm her. But one touch, one taste, was not enough, and he dove back for another and another, losing his sense in the delight of her soft, luscious lips. The tingling glory of it was a new and seductive drug that he quite suddenly couldn't get enough of. Could he persuade her to open for him? *Sarah, you're delicious . . .*

Shifting his hold to draw her closer, he discovered her slipping from his grasp and fleeing before his senses had fully comprehended what was going on.

"Sarah! Miss Watson!" His heart thudded, dismay displacing desire, and he gave chase, concerned that she might lose herself amongst the trees. And worried he had frightened her.

SARAH, OVERWHELMED BY the sensation of his mouth on hers, fled on instinct alone. Shocked by her own response, she ran blindly from the temple and into the tangle of trees coming out in a different path altogether and running slap into the broad chest of another man. Mortified, she bounced back and would have fled if he hadn't grabbed her hand.

She looked up, blinking to bring her gaze into focus, and recognized him for he wore no mask, just as the duke crashed through the trees and said, "Lannister! Let her go!"

The Earl of Lannister smiled down at her engagingly, seemingly ignoring the duke. "That depends on whether the lady wishes me to or not. Do you, sweetheart?"

"I said let her go!" growled the duke.

"Take a damper, Troubridge," he said, his eyes still on Sarah.

"Please let me go, sir," she said softly.

He loosened his grip. "Of course, my dear." Then he leaned forward and whispered in her ear, "Your secret is safe with me."

"I'm warning you, Lannister, move away from her, or I'll hurt you!" said the duke.

The earl stepped back lifting his hands. "No need for violence, Your Grace." He bowed to them both. "Good evening to you," he said and strolled off down another path.

The duke swore under his breath, watching the earl walk away. Turning to her, he said roughly, "What made you run? If he recognized you, it could be all over London by morning."

She swallowed, her heart thudding hard. "I'm sorry, I panicked."

"It was my fault. I frightened you, I'm sorry. Come, we should return to the others."

All his playfulness was gone, the mood broken. Her pleasure in the evening destroyed by a moment of panic. She had never felt such sensations take a hold of her before. It was absurd to have panicked so, he would think she had never been kissed, and that wasn't true. But no other kiss had stirred such a reaction in her, and all from the merest brush of his lips.

And then to run into the Earl of Lannister like that. Had he recognized her? His words implied that he had. He certainly knew she was with the duke. Would he spread the tale as the duke feared?

*Am I ruined, all for an innocent kiss?*

ROBERT'S SLEEP THAT night was disturbed by a dream. He was dancing with a woman in a mask in the moonlight, among the trees. He was kissing her, and the tingling desire was intoxicating. Suddenly, she was beneath him on an altar in the middle of a clearing, and he labored to bring them both to crisis. The desire curled through his body, persistent and strong, yet the peak was out of reach. The trees moved closer and closer the more urgent his growing desire became until it was a race to reach the finish before the trees devoured them . . .

He woke with a jerk and gasp, his cock hard and throbbing on his belly. *Sarah . . .*

*God, my physical needs are becoming demanding.*

He touched his rigid cock with a tentative hand. This wasn't going away on its own. He tried to think of Madeleine, his former mistress, but his mind kept slipping away to Sarah. It was undoubtedly her he'd been making love to in that clearing. Actually, he'd been rubbing himself on her in the most lewd fashion imaginable, he was shocked by his own dark need. Yet it wouldn't let go. As he stroked himself, he tried to block out images of Sarah and failed miserably.

With a groan he stroked harder, the wild action of his dream taking over his imagination and he came hard, hot seed spurting across his belly and the tingling pleasure of release pervading his whole body with an intensity that made him groan repeatedly.

Catching his breath as his heart rate dropped to a slow heavy beat and his body relaxed into a blissful lethargy, he blinked in shock.

*That was so intense!* Even now his body was still tingling with the aftermath. *Three months without a woman were starting to take their toll.*

One thing he was sure of, after tonight he couldn't deny that he wanted Miss Sarah Watson, and in a base, physical way that shocked him. She was an innocent, virtuous woman. She had run from him tonight because he'd frightened her with a simple kiss. *What am I going to do with this passionate desire? If I let that loose on her, I'll terrify her.*

He moved his feet restlessly and a disgruntled *mrrp* told him he had disturbed Emerald. The cat had quickly decided his bed was her favorite place to sleep, and no attempts to remove or keep her out had succeeded. Not that he tried all that hard. Her presence was a comfort, and he now allowed her free run of his bedroom, day or night, as she saw fit. In fact, she had full run of the house from basement to attics and had become a fast favorite with many of the staff. Including Le Bow, their very superior French Chef, who saved the best tidbits for her from his cooking and spoiled her rotten.

He rolled over and closed his eyes, letting sleep take him, insensibly comforted by the purring of a stray cat with a torn ear and the greenest of green eyes.

# Chapter Seven

THE NEXT DAY Robert waited for the rumors to circulate, so convinced was he that Lannister would not be able to keep his mouth shut. The question was, had Lannister recognized Miss Watson as he had himself? If not, the story was probably not worth much. Catching the duke in a mask with an unknown damsel at Vauxhall might cause a minor ripple, it was after all out of character, but if the identity of the damsel became known . . . Therein lay the main issue, for it would ruin Sarah's reputation instantly.

However, two days later there was not so much as a murmur as far as he could tell, and he had Ravenshaw, Ashford, and Caro all keeping an ear out. Nothing. And nothing in the gossip columns of the papers, either. No veiled hints of the activities of a certain duke with a Miss W or anything of that nature. So, he must conclude that Lannister was choosing to remain mum. But why? What could he stand to gain by not spreading such a provocative rumor? The man lived for the salacious tales and delicious gossip that greased the wheels of his precarious career. It made no sense. Robert could only conclude that he hadn't recognized Sarah and saw no point in antagonizing the duke over a minor indiscretion.

Lannister's peculiar behavior notwithstanding, the results of the night at Vauxhall were mixed at best. He had achieved his aim of testing the physical attraction he felt for Miss Watson and established that he did indeed find her alluring, damn near irresistible in fact. But her flight from him argued that she didn't feel the same. If she hadn't run into Lannister, he might have been able to salvage something from the evening, but as it was, the encounter had ruined all the ground he thought he had gained with her, and he was back at the starting line again. *Never had a knight struggled so much to win the hand of a fair lady,* he thought gloomily.

Buttonholing Ashford at the club over a late breakfast, he gave him a summary of the situation and said, "What do I do now?"

"What makes you think I can advise you?" Ashford cocked an eyebrow at him as he cut into his eggs.

"You're married—how did you persuade Caro to marry you?"

"We were in love; she didn't need persuading."

"So how did you make her fall in love with you?"

"I didn't *make* her do anything. She just did."

The duke sighed with frustration and sipped his ale.

"It ever occur to you, old chap, that you might be coming at this all wrong?" asked the viscount.

"Well, I'm certainly doing something wrong, but I don't know what it is."

"Tried talking to her?"

"What do you mean? Of course I've talked to her." Confused, Robert stopped with the forkful of ham halfway to his mouth.

"No, I mean really talked to her—about the things that matter. Your dreams and aspirations. Have you tried to find out what she wants? What she is interested in?"

"Oh." Robert frowned, chewing that over with the ham.

Ashford shoveled in some sausage and egg and watched him thoughtfully. When he'd swallowed his mouthful he said, "She's an interesting young woman. Have you talked to her about her family?"

"Not a great deal, no," Robert admitted.

"She's the eldest of eight. That ought to be something you have in common, eldest children and all that."

Robert nodded thoughtfully. "You're right. I've not been thinking enough about her, have I? I mean, I've done nothing but think about her, but not in the way you mean—from her perspective."

Ashford nodded. "Try to get off your high horse. Stop being a duke."

"I told you—"

"Yes, and I told you—be Robert, not Troubridge, when you talk to her. She'll be marrying *you*, not your bloody title."

Robert swallowed. That was the trouble, wasn't it? This was to be a marriage of convenience; it was his bloody title he was offering. Yet he desperately wanted to make it something else. But could he? Did she want that? He had to admit to himself that he hadn't a clue. He didn't know what she wanted, and he didn't know how to ask.

*But I'll bloody well have to learn, won't I? If I want a hope in hell of persuading her to view this as something more than a business transaction.*

"I'll take her for a drive in the park, talk to her. You're right, I'm an idiot."

"No just a duke," said Ashford with a smile. "You're not so bad when you forget your dignity."

SARAH HAD SPENT two days in a quake, waiting to be branded a harlot and chastising herself roundly for her behavior. She had not confided what had happened to Daphne, who seemed rather more taken with Ravenshaw than a respectable widow ought to be. Particularly remarkable considering the marquess was ten years her junior.

When the duke called late in the afternoon on the third day

to take her driving in the park, she was in two minds about refusing, but Daphne didn't give her a chance, accepting on her behalf and chasing her away to get her cloak, for there was a breeze out, and "It would not do for you to take a chill, my dear."

Returning back downstairs in her cloak and bonnet, she let the duke help her step up into his high perch phaeton, and when she was settled with a rug tucked round her legs he leaped up into the driver's seat, gave his groom the office to let go the horses' heads, and they were off. The pair he was driving were elegant greys, and he explained he had another pair for longer trips where four horses were required.

"I trust you have recovered from the other night?" he asked.

She nodded. "Yes, I should thank you because I am sure it was your idea, wasn't it, not Lady Ashford's?"

"It was," he admitted.

"The fireworks were spectacular."

"Even though your peace had been cut by what occurred earlier?"

She looked up at him, startled that he would so bluntly refer to what she had hoped to forget.

"Yes, I can only apologize for my silliness."

"Please don't, the fault was mine. We seem to have come off clean, however. Lannister must have taken my warning seriously." He looked a trifle grim at that.

"All the same, I should not have let you take me into that temple." She worried at her reticule, still uncomfortable with her own behavior. *It must have been the champagne and the masks.*

"Perhaps not, but in spite of everything, I cannot regret it."

Her heart skipped at the implications of that.

"You have mentioned to me that you are the eldest of eight. Would you care to tell me about your siblings?"

His abrupt change of subject took her further by surprise. "Why?"

"Is it such a stretch to believe I might be interested?" he asked, negotiating round a parked carriage.

She smiled thoughtfully. "No, I suppose not. You know, Your Grace, you are constantly surprising me. I'm not sure that I know you at all."

"I'd like to remedy that, and get to know you better, too," he responded. "Do you think we might start over?"

"And contrive not to insult each other?" she asked with a rueful smile.

"Something like that," he said, turning into Hyde Park.

"I don't know that I can," she said. "My tongue is disastrously blunt."

"Yes, I was warned about that. Perhaps I shall have to grow a thicker skin if I wish to pursue your society?"

Suddenly she was breathless and blushing. *Can I trust a word he says, or is it all my fortune?* She had fancied for a few giddy moments the other night that he was interested in more than her inheritance. But would he be so persistent as this if she weren't wealthy? She knew the answer to that.

"What have I said to put you out of countenance?" he asked, easing his team to a gentle walk.

What could she possibly say that wouldn't make her sound like an idiot? She couldn't admit that the mere notion that he might want her for more than her money reduced her to a puddle of longing. *I'm not even sure that I like him, yet I am prepared to let him drag me into temples and kiss me. More than prepared—I wanted him to.*

If she reviewed her suitors objectively, she liked Lannister more than the duke, and while Lannister flustered her a little, he didn't turn her inside out like the duke did.

"Who has been mortifying my character?" she asked after a moment, deciding attack was the best form of defense.

"Lady Sefton said you have a reputation for being direct."

She lifted her chin. "I suppose that is accurate. Mama is of a softer disposition; the children would run roughshod over her if I didn't intervene. Especially the boys. They all mind Papa of course."

"Your father is a strict disciplinarian?"

"No, not in the least. But he has high moral standards, and we have all been taught to value them. Papa places much more value on character, integrity, and hard work than on wealth, titles, or privilege."

"And he has taught you to value those things," he said quietly.

"Yes, he has." She looked down at her gloved hands clasped in her lap, her throat tight. She missed Papa's guidance and quiet common sense.

"Such sentiments do you a great deal of credit, Miss Watson, and I sincerely admire you for them. As a person of privilege, it is perilously easy to lose sight of what is truly important. Yet I have often wished my title and its obligations and privileges to the devil, for I know it separates me from much of what is of true value in life."

"That is an easy thing to do from your position, Your Grace."

"I know. It is a fantasy, no more. Take away my privileges and I would soon sing a different tune."

"You have probably not seen a great deal of what is like to live in a state of privation, have you?"

"I have not. Have you?"

"Some. I assist my father in supporting the parishioners, as does Mama, but with so many small children, much of Mama's time is taken up, so from the age of twelve I progressively took on more of Mama's duties as our family continued to grow. I find the luxury and frivolity of the London season somewhat trying. I miss my family and often just long to go home," she admitted in a rush. Talking of them always made her want them more.

"Tell me, Miss Watson, would you prefer marriage to a simple country parson, raising your own gaggle of children, than the role of a great lady?"

"It is what I always imagined my life would be until Great-aunt Agnes intervened. She is my godmother, you see, and I was always her favorite. She got the notion fixed in her head that she wanted to see me established with a titled gentleman. But I didn't take."

"Because you didn't wish to," he said shrewdly.

"Perhaps you are right," she admitted ruefully. "In any case, I would be at home now, stepping away to let my sisters take their turn, if I had my way. My next sister, Deborah, is the family beauty, although I think ultimately Hepzibah will outshine her. Zibby is only twelve and a bit of a hellion. Emanuel, the eldest of the boys, is her twin, and he leads the younger ones. Zibby tends to identify with the boys rather than us girls."

"And your other sisters," he prompted.

"Ruthy, bless her, is the plainest of us, but with the biggest heart. She loves animals and is always rescuing some stray or injured beast or bird. Mary is romantic and sweet and longs to be all grown up. She is just sixteen. Japheth is a determined little chap, quite the devil when he wants to be, and Zeke is the baby—he's six."

"Quite the brood."

"Yes, it is a joke in the village that Papa has his own cricket team. Not quite, of course, because you need eleven, but . . ."

"You know how to play cricket?" He appeared thunderstruck.

"Oh yes! We play cricket and croquet and all manner of games at home. When you have that many children cluttering up a house, there is a great deal of energy to be burned off. Outdoor games are a way to do that."

"Yes, I suppose so. We have the reverse pattern of gender to age in our family. The three boys are the eldest and followed by the three girls. Ingrid is the youngest—she is thirteen. Ava, the eldest, is about to make her debut. You'll no doubt meet her. I'm expecting her and Mama to arrive on my doorstep any day. They were supposed to be here three weeks ago, but Ingrid developed a fever and Mama would not leave her until she was better."

They had completed a full circuit of the park by now, and as they had progressed, she noted that the duke was hailed by a number of persons. He acknowledged them with a wave but did not stop. His attention, very flatteringly, was wholly fixed on her.

ROBERT RETURNED HOME to find that in fact his mother and sister had arrived, as the hallway was full of luggage. The duchess, who was a notoriously bad traveler, had retired to bed already, but Ava was in the sitting room eating afternoon tea with their brother Hereward who had been their escort.

Ava, who was a replica of their mother, being tiny, blonde, and beautiful, bounced up out of her seat at the sight of him and flung herself into his arms.

"We're here at last!" she said, her blue eyes sparkling. "I lived in dread that one of the girls would throw out a rash before we could leave! The journey took forever." Ava's come out had been delayed by a year due to their father's passing last year, and she had been waiting impatiently for this day to arrive. And patience was not one of Ava's strong suits.

"Mama *would* dawdle on the road. I should think, since she hates it so much, she would want it over with quickly. Instead, it took us three days to get here. Herey has the patience of a saint. I was about to tear my hair out!" She threw Hereward a beatific smile.

Hereward was the biggest of the Layne men, being an inch taller than Robert and broader through the shoulders and chest. He had brown hair and soft brown eyes and the most phlegmatic temperament.

He shook Robert's hand in greeting and slapped him on the back in a brotherly hug. "Thank you for bearing the brunt, old chap," said Robert.

Hereward shrugged. "I was coming to town anyway; I know Mama doesn't like to travel unescorted."

Ava broke in on this. "Creighton was complaining you have a cat, Rob?"

"Hm? Oh yes, her name's Emerald, Em for short. She was a stray and adopted me."

"And now, according to Creighton, runs the whole house. Where is she? I can't wait to meet her."

He smiled. "She'll come out when she's ready, all the kerfuffle of your arrival probably scared her."

"Is it true she sleeps on your bed?"

He nodded and Ava crowed, "You old softie!" Robert shrugged and turned back to Hereward, slightly embarrassed to be teased about his cat.

"Perhaps you can keep your eye on Kenrick for me, now you're here?"

Hereward snorted. "If you think he'll pay a blind bit of notice to anything I say—"

"I know, but at least you can give me some warning if he's about to do something harebrained?" Robert didn't mention the five-hundred-pound debt in front of Ava.

"I'll do my best," said Hereward, sitting down again and resuming working his way through the tray of cakes and sandwiches.

"So tell me, brother dearest, what have I missed?" asked Ava, resuming her seat.

Robert joined them and gave Ava an expurgated version of the start of the season. He did not, for example, mention Miss Sarah Watson at all. On the basis of today's drive around the park, he was ready to commit to a course that would see him end at the altar with Sarah, but he was miserably aware that she was far from sharing his view.

She may not be the woman he had once envisioned marrying, but with five-hundred-pound debts, the cost of his sister's debut, and all the expenses of maintaining multiple households, he needed money and fast. Sarah was acceptable on several levels for his purpose outside of her fortune—he liked her, he respected her, and he wanted her. Love would, he hoped, come in time. But not if he couldn't persuade her to accept him.

And what of his family? How would she appear to them? Would they like her? Would she like them?

Two days later, returned from his early morning ride, he found that the duchess had graduated from the couch and, accompanied by Ava, was busily penning notes to her acquaintance to inform them that she and Ava were in residence and at home to visitors.

"Mama," he said, entering the parlor and going to the desk at which she sat to kiss her cheek. "I am glad to see you restored to health!"

His mother was a diminutive woman whose pretty, blonde good looks had faded somewhat. He took after his father's side of the family as to height, build, hair coloring, and features, but he had inherited her blue eyes. She smiled up at him. "Yes, I am much recovered, love. You were up early. Riding in the park?" But she didn't pause long enough for him to answer that question. "You must take Ava the next time. You haven't forgotten that we will be hosting a ball for her in three weeks, have you?"

"No, Mama." He smiled at Ava, who rolled her eyes, and kissed her cheek. "I shall escort you to all manner of frivolities. Never fear."

"As soon as I've finished these letters, we are going to Bond Street. We still need several gowns for Ava, to say nothing of bonnets and slippers and all manner of things. Will you accompany us?"

"I cannot, alas. I have a prior engagement," he said hastily, his heart sinking at the prospect of how much his mother was about to spend. But it couldn't be helped. Ava's court dress alone would be several hundred pounds. The urgency of the situation grew more extreme with each day that passed.

Seizing the opportunity to float his plan to introduce Sarah to his family, he said, "However, I trust you are not yet engaged for tomorrow night?"

"No, why?"

"I am planning a trip to the theatre, and I would like you and Ava to come. I will invite the boys, too."

His mother blinked. "Good heavens, why?"

Taking a deep breath he plunged on, "There is someone I would like you to meet." He felt himself flushing, and his mother's eyes widened. "Her name is Miss Sarah Watson, I—well, suffice to say I would like you to meet her." He had issued the invitation to Sarah and Lady Holbrook and received a positive response with this morning's mail.

Mama looked at Ava and then at him and smiled. "Of course we would be delighted to come, wouldn't we, Ava?"

Ava grinned and, rising, gave him a quick hug. "How delightful. I am sure we will love her if you do, Rob."

He swallowed and felt his cheeks burning. Well, he had convinced his family that he was introducing them to a woman he had a partiality for. At least that part of the equation was settled. *All I need to do now is persuade her to have me.*

And he went off to the library to send two notes to his brothers, who did not live at Berkeley Square but had rooms in St James's.

FORTUNATELY FOR HIM, Lady Holbrook had received the invitation and sent an immediate acceptance on Miss Watson's behalf. By the time Sarah learned of it, there was nothing she could do about it. But she was thrown into a spin by the notion of being introduced to the duke's family. *He seems to be determined to pursue me, despite my disastrous tongue.*

After the drive in the park, she had been somewhat reconciled to receiving his attentions. He seemed to be genuinely trying to engage her interest and pay attention to her. Which made him increasingly attractive, she had to admit. She was beginning to think she might even like him a little.

# Chapter Eight

T HE PLAY WAS *Rob Roy MacGregor*, an operatic drama in three acts. The duke had his own box, naturally, but in the course of being conducted into it, Sarah began to understand for the first time what a proposal of marriage from the duke might entail, should she deign to accept it.

The role of duchess was a formidable one. Certainly not one a vicar's daughter was in any way fit for. *Could he be seriously contemplating offering for me?* Introducing her to his family would seem to indicate that he was. If she were any other young woman, she would be over the moon at the prospect.

"Mama," said the duke, bringing Sarah into the box, "I would like to introduce you to Lady Holbrook and Miss Sarah Watson."

"Your Grace." Both ladies curtsied.

The duchess, who was shorter than both of them, still managed to look down her nose at them, and Sarah's heart quailed.

"Lady Holbrook, I believe we have met before. But I have not had the honor of Miss Watson's acquaintance. Please let me introduce my daughter, Lady Ava Layne." A younger woman, who was clearly a replica of her mother, came forward and received their curtsies.

Lady Ava smiled, her blue eyes twinkling, and said, "I am delighted to make your acquaintance. Please come and sit by me.

I am dying to know all about you!"

Sarah blinked at this effusiveness, and the duke broke in upon it to introduce her to two young men who were taking up more than their fair share of space in the box.

"My brothers, Lord Hereward Layne and Lord Kenrick Layne." Both were bigger than their elder brother. Though Kenrick was the tallest, topping both his brothers by several inches in height, his physique was long and lean. Hereward was of a more solid build and the stockiest of the three. To Sarah's way of thinking, the duke's proportions were perfect. *He is also,* she thought, *better looking.* They certainly all towered over their tiny mother and equally petite sister.

Hereward gave her a neat bow and Kenrick went so far as to take her hand and smile, and she couldn't be certain, but she rather thought he winked at her. She smiled in return.

The lights were dimming in preparation for the curtain to rise on the first act, and they all shuffled around to take their seats.

Lady Ava was an expressive talker. She fluttered her hands while she chattered.

"So, tell me," she said in a confiding fashion, "how did you meet my brother? Was it at a stuffy ball or something romantic?"

"Very stuffy, I'm afraid. Almack's."

"Oh lud! Is it as bad as they say?"

"Worse!" said Sarah with a grimace. "The food and drink are appalling, the patronesses patrol the room looking for young ladies committing breaches of etiquette, and the gentlemen are bored stiff."

"Sounds perfect for Robert, I'll bet he fits right in!" said Ava with a giggle. Seeing Sarah's look, she placed a hand on her arm and said, "I must tell you he is not like that in private, but he is rather stuffy in public."

"Somewhat," acknowledged Sarah.

"Ah, if you haven't penetrated the ducal front yet, I pray you, don't despair, he is not as much of a lost cause as he appears. In fact, he's rather sweet underneath, he just lacks"—she paused, looking for the right word—"liveliness, I think. He is rather serious you see, because he has all these boring ducal things he has to do, and he takes his responsibilities very seriously."

"Yes, that is evident," said Sarah.

"He is very romantic, you know," said Ava. "Not that he shows that side to me of course, but I know he has been waiting and hoping to meet the love of his life for so long."

Sarah digested this in silence. He had told her as much, but she had discounted it because his behavior seemed to give it the lie.

"He is very fussy," went on Ava. "It seemed no one was good enough for the role. Mama was at her wits' end, for she has introduced him to countless young ladies over the years. None of them rose to his exacting standards."

Sarah swallowed the tightness in her throat and gripped her fan so tightly she felt the sticks bend. *So, he has lowered his standards to even consider me. Another mark of his desperation.* She glanced sideways at him in converse with his mother at the end of the row.

Daphne, she noted, was flirting shamelessly with Lord Kenrick, the one who'd winked at her. Really, she'd had no idea Daphne had such a partiality for younger men. Lord Hereward looked uncomfortable, perched on a seat that was obviously too small for his big frame and bored to boot.

With the first intermission, the box was inundated with visitors, all eager to note who the duke's guests were. *It will be all over London tomorrow that the duke is courting me!*

At the end of the intermission, the seating arrangements were reshuffled so that she was seated beside the duchess, and this time she was subjected to a much more pointed cross-examination.

"I understand, my dear, that you are the eldest of quite a large family?"

"Yes, Your Grace, there are eight of us," she lifted her chin, uncertain whether there was implied disapprobation in the question, but refusing to be ashamed of her family.

"That must be quite a challenge for your mother. You must be a great help to her."

"I hope so, Your Grace. I try to be."

"I'm sure you are. I have six children myself, of course. I know how much work little ones can be." The duchess patted her arm. "It may surprise you to know that Costin, that is Robert's father, was very involved with his children when they were young. I expect Robert will be the same. Costin never had much grasp of worldly responsibilities, but he loved his children fiercely." The duchess blinked, her face showing a momentary sadness. "I shall miss him to my last breath, my dear. I loved him with all my heart."

Sarah, at a loss for what to say, held her tongue as she watched the duchess visibly pull herself together.

"Robert has always aspired to a love match like ours, and I hope that all my children will find felicity in their marriages. Tell me, my dear, do you care for my son?"

The directness of the question took Sarah aback. With the duchess's blue eyes fixed upon her, she couldn't lie. "Very much, Your Grace," she said softly.

"Good. That is an excellent start. But you will have challenges, my dear. Robert is complicated, like and unlike his father. And he will expect you to fill the role of duchess flawlessly. He can be highhanded at times, but if you pull him up on it, he will bend. He's not as rigid and starched up as he appears on the surface. But if you hold his heart, my dear, he will do anything for you. He loves as fiercely as his father did."

Sarah's own heart sank at this, for she didn't hold his heart, did she? It was her money he principally wanted. She looked down at her lap where her gloved hands clenched her fan tightly.

"Robert has six establishments, you know," the duchess sailed on, oblivious to Sarah's discomfort. "Although his principle seat is in Leicestershire—The Castle. It's no such thing, of course, but the original building dates to the Conqueror, and the name stuck. The current building is largely Queen Anne with some modifications and additions made in the last century. We can sleep upwards of forty persons in the guest chambers, more if they share, which sometimes is necessary. The last house party we held, we had sixty guests.

"Don't look so daunted, my dear, I daresay you have not had much experience with such things, but I will teach you how to go on, never fear.

"When I married Costin, I too had little experience of managing a large establishment, and my mother-in-law was not welcoming. She wanted Costin to marry Lady Mary Hartley and was not happy that he chose me instead."

At the end of the second act, Sarah felt quite wrung out and thoroughly convinced that she had failed the test utterly. *What do I know of managing a large establishment and the number of servants that goes with it?* Despite the duchess's reassurance that she would help her, Sarah felt woefully inadequate to any such task.

Not that she cared, for she wasn't about to accept him anyway . . . was she? But still, pride made her feel rather low that she was indeed such a poor match for a duke. *I have not a clue how to be a duchess, and I will let him down if I try. Not that I'm going to.*

The second intermission was like the first except that they received refreshments as well as guests, and at the end of it the duke himself sat next to her at last.

"I trust you are enjoying the play?"

She suppressed the tart observation that if his womenfolk weren't such inveterate talkers she might be able to venture an opinion, but as it was, she had heard very little of it. Instead, she smiled vaguely and said, "Yes, delightful."

He wasn't fooled. "My sister and mother talked through the entire thing, didn't they?"

She nodded.

"Don't despair, they like you," he said with a smile.

She colored and said, "Good heavens, why?"

"Mama said that while you haven't a clue how to be a duchess, you were a lady and trainable." He stopped at her in-drawn breath and then went on with a wider smile. "To which I responded that of course you were a lady, as I wouldn't contemplate marriage to a woman who wasn't."

"This is all rather overwhelming, Your Grace," she said faintly, plying her fan vigorously.

"And my sister said that you were refreshing, and she couldn't wait to meet your siblings because they sounded like so much fun."

Sarah blinked eyes that suddenly stung with tears of pride. She missed her family with an acute ache of her heart. *It is for them that I am doing all this.* The reminder was timely. She really didn't have the luxury of considering her own preferences in this; there were larger considerations at play. She needed to remember not to be selfish. *After all, the duke is sacrificing himself for his family. Can I do less for mine?*

She turned her face away to hide the tears and fumbled in her reticule for a handkerchief.

"What have I said to upset you?" His voice had that stiff edge to it again.

"Nothing!" she said quickly. "I simply have something in my eye, an eyelash I think," she said, sniffing.

"Here, let me look," he said, lifting her chin. She blinked. "I think you must have dislodged it." He kept hold of her chin a moment longer, looking into her eyes. "If I said something to upset you, I'm sorry. I don't seem to be able to open my mouth where you're concerned and not put my foot in it."

"I am not upset."

"You're a very bad liar, you know," he said gently and with a smile to soften the mild rebuke. Her heart turned over and a shiver raced through her. For a moment she felt that frisson of intimacy from Vauxhall all over again. For a mad second she thought he was going to kiss her. His eyes darkened, his gaze dropped momentarily to her lips, then as if recalled to the reality of their surroundings, he let her chin go and sat back, his cheeks lightly stained.

Making a desperate recover, she said primly, "Lying is a sin," while restoring her handkerchief to her reticule.

"Then we shall not speak of this any further tonight. Tell me, have you read *Sense and Sensibility*? I believe you would like it."

"Yes, I have, and several others by the same author. My favorite is *Emma*."

"Not *Pride and Prejudice*?"

"Darcy is a prig!" she said tartly, and he laughed.

"Rather like me?" he asked in a teasing way that made her flush with another emotion than embarrassment altogether.

"I never said you were a prig, Your Grace."

"You came mighty close to it the other day," he said.

"It is not kind of you to remind me of my rudeness," she said with dignity.

"No, it isn't. I'm sorry," he said gravely.

"Now you are being ridiculously agreeable!" she said with a quiver of laughter in her voice.

"Well, I was being very disagreeable there for a bit, I thought I'd best turn over a new leaf."

"You're still teasing me."

"A little. I find it an—agreeable past time," he admitted.

"We really should watch some of this wretched play, don't you think?" she said desperately.

"If you insist," he said, taking her hand. They were both wearing gloves, yet she could feel the tingling heat of his touch even through the twin layers of fabric. Completely bereft of anything sensible to say, she turned her gaze to the stage and watched the rest of the play in glassy-eyed silence. All the while, she was horribly conscious of her hand still clasped in his, resting on his knee. It felt like the most intimate of acts, almost more intimate than the kiss they had shared at Vauxhall, and it completely overset her normally well-balanced state of mind.

AFTER ESCORTING LADY Holbrook and Miss Watson home, Robert returned to the ducal abode in Berkeley Square and found his brothers in the library, where he had bid them wait for him. Mama and Ava had already retired for the evening.

Kenrick was sprawled full length on the leather couch with a glass in his hand and Hereward in one of the large matching leather chairs, likewise with a glass, and Em curled up on his lap. A third glass stood mute, waiting for him on the table. He shut the door and joined them at the fireplace, taking the second chair and picking up his glass. The amber liquid sparkled in the firelight.

"She's delightful," said Kenrick, grinning at him, his lean, mobile features lighting up.

"I'm glad you think so," Robert leaned back in his chair and sighed. He glanced at Hereward who was the most taciturn of the Layne men.

"Aye," he said slowly. "She'll suit you well enough I'm thinking." He stroked Em absently and raised his soft brown eyes to his brothers with a frown. "Do you love her, Rob?"

Robert scrubbed his face with his hands. "I think I could, yes."

Kenrick threw Hereward a glance which Robert tried and failed to interpret.

"So, it's really about the money?" he asked.

Robert closed his eyes. "No, yes, I don't know! You know we need the money."

"Don't do it if it doesn't feel right, Rob. We'll manage somehow."

"We would manage better if you didn't insist on losing five hundred pounds on a racehorse!" snapped Robert.

Kenrick raised his head from the couch arm. "Sorry about that, but I was sure it would win! I tell you what, I'll marry the heiress, it doesn't have to be you who sacrifices yourself!"

"No!" Robert slammed his glass so hard on the table the whisky sloshed out of it and dripped onto the carpet. His sudden flare of temper took him by surprise, and he bit down on the possessive words that hovered on his tongue.

His brothers were both looking at him, startled. Then Kenrick grinned. "I think you like her more than you let on!"

"Yes," he admitted reluctantly. "But I'm not at all sure she even likes me at all. I keep putting my foot in it with her."

"Oh!" Kenrick chortled. "I never thought I'd see the day! Our perfect brother reduced to a fumbling, addlepated fool by a woman."

Robert flushed and threw a cushion at him. Kenrick caught it one handed and tucked it behind his head, grinning.

"What I feel is almost irrelevant at this juncture." He took a breath to steady himself and said more mildly, "I'm the eldest, it's my duty to provide for the rest of you, and I will. Mama and Ava liked her, too, so there really is no impediment beyond the lady's possible refusal of my suit."

"She won't refuse you, Rob. You're a bloody duke, for God's sake." Hereward echoed Pendrell's comment.

Robert's jaw tightened and he said shortly, "I'm aware." No, she would be unlikely to refuse him, her statement the other week notwithstanding. *How many vicar's daughters got to marry a duke?* In proper form he should apply to her father for permission, but she was of age, so legally it wasn't a requirement. She could make her own decision. Once he had secured her consent, he would seek out her father and make all tidy. He was unlikely to meet with opposition from her family, after all.

*I will call upon her tomorrow and settle the thing.*

# Chapter Nine

S ARAH SPENT A restless night and rose early to take a walk with her maid Esme. It was a daily habit that she had no intention of breaking while in London, and Daphne had long since ceased to remonstrate with her about it. James, the footman, followed them at a discreet distance. They walked to Hyde Park at a brisk pace, as the morning was chilly and a little cloudy.

Entering the park, she was surprised to see the figure of a gentleman in evening dress sprawled upon a park bench. She paused, considering whether to give him a wide berth, and then she recognized him. It was Lord Lannister. He was quite pale and appeared to be asleep. He also seemed to be in need of a shave. His neckcloth was undone, baring his throat to the collarbone, and his clothes disheveled. *Was he ill?*

"Lord Lannister?" she said tentatively.

He sat up with a jerk. "Hm?" Blinking at her, his eyes widened in recognition, and he got somewhat unsteadily to his feet and bowed. "Miss Watson, you find me at a disadvantage."

"Have you been out all night, my lord?"

"I have," he said ruefully. He ran a hand over his jaw. "I'm a sorry sight, I do most humbly apologize. Lost my way last night, or rather early this morning, and became overcome with fatigue. The bench beckoned."

"If you are quite well, I shall bid you good day, my lord," she said.

"Well as can be expected, Miss Watson. I shall hope to see you again when I am more presentable." He bowed to her, and she hurried on. She had seen men the worse for drink before during her work with the parishioners, despite her father's attempts to shield her from such sights.

Lannister was clearly no angel. She tried to imagine the duke in like case and failed utterly to do so. It was a mere step from there, however, to wonder what he would look like with his neckcloth undone. Her cheeks stained pink at the notion, and she quickened her steps as if she could outrun her wicked thoughts.

She returned to the house in time for breakfast. Not that she was hungry this morning. She was too churned up with indecision over last night. She toyed with a piece of toast and a cup of tea, paying little heed to Daphne's cheerful chatter about how wonderful the play had been and how kind and welcoming the duke's family were.

"Mark my words, he will be calling upon you soon, you lucky girl! To think of you landing a duke! After all this time. Agnes would be so delighted. And such a nice gentleman, too, so handsome and everything in his manner so proper and respectful. I hope you gave thanks for your good fortune in your prayers last night. Nothing could be better." She broke off to peer across the table at Sarah.

"My dear, are you unwell? You look a little peaky. Perhaps you should return to bed and rest. You want to be looking your best when he calls. As I am sure he will."

"I had a slight headache, but it is passing. I am perfectly well, Daphne."

Daphne frowned. "I don't understand you, Sarah. This is the best possible match you could have made. Why are you not happy about it?"

"I should be, shouldn't I?" she said, stirring her tea. She sighed. "You must own, Daphne, that if it weren't for Aunt

Agnes's fortune he would not have looked at me twice."

"What of it? You will get to be a duchess. It seems like a more than fair exchange to me. This is how things are done, you know that. Why this attack of missishness now, Sarah? If he were old or infirm or hideously pockmarked, I could understand some squeamishness on your part, but he is none of those things. On the contrary, he is young and handsome and in the best of health. He will treat you kindly, too, I warrant; even your sainted papa could not object to him as a suitor for you."

"You are right of course." Sarah swallowed her tea, trying to push down the ache in her throat. If she hadn't developed such a tendre for him, perhaps she could enjoy this for all the pragmatic reasons that Daphne pointed out. Listening to his womenfolk sing his praises last night had fed the traitorous part of her that desperately wanted to think well of him. The part that was dazzled by his good looks, seduced by his kisses, and gulled by his sincerity. For of one thing, she acquitted him: duplicity. He might be prickly and wrong-footed as he put it. And stuffy and proud in his manner. But he *was* sincere.

*If I could believe that he actually cares for me . . .* her heart leaped at the notion. *Could he care for me? Or is it all just my fortune, after all?*

"This will also ensure that your family wants for nothing going forward, too. Surely that consideration must weigh with you."

"It does." Sarah gave herself a mental shake. "You are right," she said again, attempting to smile and slough off her megrim.

"There then!" said Daphne with a smile.

After that, the morning dragged and Sarah's nerves began to wear thin. She was about to beg Daphne to accompany her to the shops just to get out of the house, when Daphne's butler Latham entered with a deprecatory cough.

"The Duke of Troubridge is here to see Miss Watson, my lady. May I show him up?"

Daphne smiled and threw Sarah an *I told you so* look. "Absolutely, Latham."

Sarah's heart thudded and skipped in panic, and she smoothed her hands over her gown nervously. *This couldn't really be happening, could it?*

A step on the stair and Latham opened the door wider and said, "The Duke of Troubridge, my lady."

He stepped into the room, looking perfectly splendid in a navy coat of perfect cut, a grey satin waistcoat and alabaster-colored pantaloons. He was shaved, his hair immaculate, his linen impeccable. The contrast between him and Lannister could not be more stark. Sarah and Daphne rose to curtsy.

"Your Grace."

He bowed, "Ladies."

"Would you care for some tea, Your Grace?" asked Daphne, positively beaming at him.

"I was hoping that I might have a few words with Miss Watson alone?"

Sarah, who up until this moment had clung to the faint hope that there was some mistake, and he didn't actually intend to propose, felt the world tip slightly on its axis. A faint whimper escaped her, but fortunately it was masked by Daphne's reply.

"Of course! I won't be far away, Sarah. I will give you ten minutes, Your Grace." She left the room, very properly leaving the door ajar.

The duke took her hand and smiled at her, his eyes looked more grey than blue today. Perhaps it was the light, for the day was a little overcast.

"Miss Watson, you must know what I have come to ask, I've made no secret of my intentions. You must also know that my circumstances have dictated my course of action. I cannot pretend to be offering you more than a marriage of convenience, but I hope that it is one of mutual benefit?"

His pragmatic words dashed all her hopes. *Foolish Sarah! Could I really think he would develop feelings for me in the space of a week?* Sarah swallowed, she felt sick and was unable for the moment to utter a word.

In the face of her silence, he went on doggedly. "I hope also that I have demonstrated that you will be treated with respect and kindness by me and my family. I assure you that I look forward to meeting your family and finding harmony in joining both our houses as one."

The mention of her family brought a lump to her throat, and she looked down trying to swallow it. She felt wretchedly torn in two. *What can I do?*

"Miss Watson?" he prompted. "This cannot have come as a surprise to you, surely?"

She swallowed again and cleared her clogged throat. *I should accept.* Everything pragmatic screamed at her to do so. The needs of her family also. But then her father's image rose up in her mind's eye, and she recalled his words to her: "If anything ever feels wrong in your heart, my dearest Sarah, no matter how much your head may tell you to do it, do not. For if you do not listen to your heart, you will never be happy. And the last thing I want is for my children to be unhappy."

Papa's words hammered in her head, and her heart clenched. The truth of the lies she had been telling herself burst in upon her. On the one hand, she had secretly hoped, foolishly, that an offer would mean he had some partiality for her, something that might burgeon into love with time. On the other, she had pretended to herself that she could accept his offer and do her duty because her family required it of her. Both she realized now were fallacies. *I am weak and selfish. I can't do it.*

"Your Grace—" she stopped and took a breath. "I am sensible of the honor you do me, but—" His eyes widened in surprise and her heart skipped and thudded again. "I cannot accept your kind offer."

His expression darkened into a frown. "Can I ask why not? I can see no impediment to our union, unless"—a fiery light came into his eyes that she had not seen before—"unless your affections are already engaged?"

She swallowed desperately, her heart thudding wildly. She snatched at this excuse for her wayward behavior. "Yes! Yes, they are—so you see—I—cannot. I'm so sorry!" For it was true her affections were engaged, by him, and she could not—she just could not—marry him, knowing he didn't care for her in return. Tears scalded her eyes and ran down her cheeks as she looked away, tearing her hand out of his grip.

"I see." His voice was grim, and she flinched as she moved away to stand with her back toward him. "I think you might have alerted me to this circumstance earlier, Miss Watson!"

"You are right, I should have done so. I am sorry. I"—she wiped her cheeks with the handkerchief from her pocket—"I-I have only just recently realized the full magnitude of my feelings."

"I see," he said again. "Well, I will not trespass on your time any longer, Miss Watson. I wish you well. Good day!" She heard the door snip behind him and the sound of his feet descending the stairs. She turned back to the couch and sank down, giving full vent of her feelings in a hearty bout of tears.

Daphne came in a moment later.

"My dear, what is it? What happened?" She came at once to the couch and sat beside Sarah, putting an arm around her.

"He—proposed and I refused—him!" sobbed Sarah into her sodden handkerchief.

"Good God, why?" wailed Daphne.

"He d-doesn't l-love me!"

"Well of course not, you silly girl! Good heavens, you know that love has nothing to do with marriage! Did you think I loved Lord Holbrook when I married him?"

Sarah sobbed harder.

"My dear," Daphne rubbed her arm comfortingly. "Love is something that comes later, if you're lucky, and I would think your chances of finding love with His Grace are high. In any case, he would be a considerate and kind husband, which is much more than many women can say they have." She sighed. "Your parents' marriage is the exception not the rule, my dear. I thought you understood that."

"Yes!" said Sarah soggily. "I know, but when it came to the point I just c-couldn't!"

ROBERT LEFT THE house in Brooke Street in a state of bewildered agitation and repaired to his club, by far too troubled to show his face in Berkeley Square. Flinging himself into a chair in the corner of the room and demanding a drink, he stared fuming at the fire and tried to make sense of what had happened between last night and this morning.

He had debated whether to hint at his burgeoning feelings and decided against it in the face of her fleeing from him at Vauxhall and his uncertainty whether she nursed any nascent feelings for him. He'd decided to be pragmatic, offer her the marriage of convenience he had begun this odd courtship with. He had thought that based on their discussions she would understand and accept that. But now it appeared that it was a moot point because her feelings were engaged. *By someone else.* Which would neatly explain his inability to gain her affections.

He wasn't sure what was making him more upset, her refusal or the reason for it. He only knew that the moment she uttered those words—*I have only just realized the full magnitude of my feelings*—an anger the like of which he could never recall feeling before seized him.

*Who? Who was she in love with?* He took the proffered glass from the waiter and swallowed a sizeable mouthful of fiery liquid. He tried to recall any gentlemen that had been paying serious court to her, but he had been so engrossed with his own pursuit of her and the mistaken belief that he had no genuine rivals, he had taken little notice.

He snorted at his own hubris. *It serves me right for being such a coxcomb*, he supposed. *She accused me of unconscious arrogance, and by Jove she is right. What a set down!* He swallowed the last of the whisky and rose—he was too keyed up to sit. He left the club to attend Gentleman Jackson's boxing saloon to work off some of the fury tying his muscles in knots.

Two hours later he was leaving the establishment, feeling marginally better but still with a knot in his stomach, and ran into Ashford in the street, who dragged him back to the club for a meal. Not that he felt like eating.

"Out with it," said Ashford, tucking into his bloody steak. "You're like a bear with a sore head."

Robert sipped his red wine and toyed with a gravy-covered mushroom. He glanced around to ensure they couldn't be overheard and said quietly, "I proposed to Miss Watson, and she refused me."

Ashford paused in the cutting of his steak and raised his eyebrows. "Really? Did she give you a reason?"

Robert swallowed some more of the wine to dislodge the mushroom, which seemed to be stuck. "It appears the lady has a prior attachment of which I was completely unaware! God damn it all to hell, why didn't she tell me? I would never—" he stopped, finished his glass, and waved the waiter over to refill it.

After the waiter did so and stepped back, Robert stabbed again at his steak viciously. "I would never have pursued her had I known. I've lost another three weeks! Who would have thought it would be so damned difficult to find a wife?"

"A rich wife," corrected Ashford, spearing a potato.

"Damn it, I hate this business!" He chewed a piece of steak which tasted like sawdust. He swallowed and sipped more wine to wash it down. It plunked into his stomach like a lead weight.

He pushed his plate away and took a bigger swallow of the wine. "The puzzling thing is, I cannot for the life of me think who it might be. Who else has been pursuing her?"

"Half the fortune hunters in London. Reynolds for one, Pocock, Lannister . . ."

"My God, not Lannister. She couldn't be foolish enough to fall for his oily charm, surely?"

"You know as well as I do that the ladies adore him."

"I refuse to believe she is so lacking taste as to entertain a tendre for that blackguard!"

"Did it occur to you it might not be anyone in London? Might be some childhood sweetheart from home."

"She said it was of recent date."

Ashford shrugged. "Could be anyone. Who was the next chit on your list?"

"The Grenfell girl," he said absently, his mind still full of Sarah Watson. "No, damn and blast it, we had a connection, I know it. After Vauxhall I wasn't sure . . . of her feelings, only my own. And yet . . ." He sighed. "How do you tell if a woman likes you?" he asked despairingly.

"Generally, it's in the eyes, I find," said the viscount.

"I'd swear she was ready enough to accept me last night. Or why the devil would she even accept the invitation to meet my family?"

"Lady Holbrook?" hazarded the viscount.

"Even so, I cannot believe she would lead me on so. What the hell happened between last night and this morning?"

"She got cold feet?"

"Yes, but why?" Robert frowned fiercely at the salt cellar, as if it were to blame for his troubles.

"What did you say to her exactly?"

"I told her that what I was offering was a marriage of convenience. It was on that basis that I approached her in the first place."

"And she had given you to understand that she would accept you?"

He opened his mouth to say yes and stopped. "Well, no," he admitted reluctantly. "At the Levington ball she told me that if I was to offer, she would decline."

Ashford raised his eyebrows as if to say *there you go, then.*

"You need to understand the context. She was angry with me,

she thought I had insulted her. It was a misunderstanding." He rearranged the salt cellar on the table. "Besides, we had moved on from that. At Vauxhall . . ." he rubbed his face. "I thought there was a spark, something . . . but I don't know. It might be all on my side. I was unsure of her feelings, so I presented a pragmatic offer. I thought it would be the one she would accept."

"I see." Ashford set his cutlery on his empty plate and pushed it aside, taking up his wine instead. "Why are you so upset?"

"I've lost another three weeks—"

"Apart from that?"

"Wounded pride, I suppose."

"Seems to me like you might be a little envious of the other fellow, whoever he is."

"I'm not envious. I'm annoyed! She deceived me. I thought she was free to pursue a contract when clearly she is not. If her affections are truly engaged, then there is no question—damn and blast, I *like* her!" *I want her!* The thought, fierce and disconcerting, made itself felt.

"Well, there's been no announcement of an engagement yet. Did she say she had an understanding with the fellow?"

"No." He drained his glass and waved the waiter over again. When both glasses had been topped up, the man stepped back again.

"Faint heart never won fair lady," said Ashford with a smile.

"You're right, but how do I pursue a woman who has made it so clear she doesn't want me?"

"I don't want to give you false hope, Rob, but I'd hesitate to put that construction on her refusal."

Robert's eyebrows lifted and his heart leaped. "You think I used the wrong tack?"

Ashford shrugged. "I don't know. Perhaps, if you're right about there being a spark between you. That kind of thing is hard to mistake." He paused and added, "You did kiss her?"

"I did," Robert flushed. "She ran from me," he admitted.

"Ah, well, that does rather put a different complexion on things."

"I know," said Robert miserably.

"Do you want her?"

"Desperately!" said Robert, pushed into admitting the truth. The wine had clearly loosened his tongue.

"Hm, I thought so."

"You thought—"

Ashford smiled.

"Stop that!" said Robert.

"Stop what?" asked the viscount innocently.

"That—that smirk!"

The viscount's grin widened. "Well, you can take your bat and ball and go home, or you can try again . . ."

"You think I should?"

Ashford swirled the wine in his glass and smirked. "For what it's worth, I think you should try, yes."

"I'm not about to push myself on an unwilling woman!"

"Not suggesting you should. Just test the water, see if she is *willing* to let you kiss her again."

Robert eyed his friend thoughtfully. *That kiss at Vauxhall had been so fleeting* . . . perhaps a second kiss would prove more successful? A thorough, proper kiss?

"Just saying, if you want her, you need to make an effort to attach her. If her feelings are truly engaged elsewhere—" he shrugged to finish the thought. "But if it's just a ploy to make you jealous . . ."

"But why would she do that?"

"Females like to have some power, too." Ashford finished his glass and asked the waiter for a whisky.

He blinked his greenish hazel eyes over the glass, and Robert wondered for a moment if the shine in them was caused by the light or something else.

Robert shook his head, "Miss Watson isn't like that."

"If you say so," Ashford swallowed the whisky and topped up his glass from the bottle on the table.

Robert reached for his own glass, his thoughts consumed by

Miss Watson. Her behavior was inexplicable. It behooved him to make one last effort to change her mind. If that failed, he would be forced to retreat and try the Grenfell girl. He shuddered. *For good or ill, I want Miss Sarah Watson, and damn it all, I'm not giving up without a fight.*

# Chapter Ten

ROBERT RETURNED HOME and slept off the uncustomary amount of alcohol he'd consumed with lunch, then he rose to wash and change for the evening's entertainment. He had promised to escort his mother and sister to a recital that evening at Convent Garden, followed by supper at the Piazza.

His valet, Bridges, who had been with him for ten years, laid out his evening wear and handed him his neckcloth. Some gentlemen allowed their valets to tie their cravats. Robert wasn't one of them. Bridges knew better than to interrupt him during the process, but when he was satisfied with it, Bridges held out his waistcoat of silver satin to slip over his white linen shirt and cleared his throat. A sure sign he had something to say. Robert buttoned up his waistcoat and raised an eyebrow, as Em jumped up onto the dresser and began rubbing her face around the edge of the beveled mirror, tail lashing.

"Something on your mind, Bridges?"

"I'm not one to gossip, Your Grace, but something has come to my hearing that—" he flushed, looking uncomfortable.

"Out with it, man." the duke frowned, thinking Bridges had got wind of one of Kenrick's more outrageous pranks.

"Well, Your Grace, we couldn't help but know about Miss Watson . . ."

Robert stiffened. "This concerns Miss Watson?" he said ominously.

"Aye, Your Grace," said Bridges, looking rather wretched. "It was one of the footmen who brought the tale to the hall," meaning the servants' hall. "He had it from one of Lady Holbrook's footmen, you understand. The two of them are friends from the same village."

"Get to the point!" said the duke, sliding his arms into the coat of a navy silk so dark it was almost black.

"Well, it seems that James, that's another of Lady Holbrook's footmen, accompanies Miss Watson and her maid on a walk each morning to Hyde Park and back."

"Yes?" Robert adjusted his sleeves, glaring at Bridges in the mirror as the man stood behind him.

"It seems that Miss Watson met Lord Lannister this morning in the park," he said miserably.

Robert's world tipped off its axis for a minute, and he actually had to reach out to the dresser to steady himself. After a moment he said, "I see." He cleared his throat and went on, "No doubt it was a chance encounter. Please make it clear below stairs that Miss Watson is not a suitable topic for gossip. On pain of dismissal. Do I make myself clear?"

"Yes, Your Grace."

"And if you hear anything further, bring it straight to me."

"Yes, Your Grace."

"Thank you," he frowned and then said, "I appreciate your candor, but there is nothing in it. Clear?"

"Yes, Your Grace."

Robert turned on his heel and walked out the door and downstairs, trailed by Em. He was to meet Mama and Ava in the front parlor, but he went to the library first and poured himself a brandy and swallowed it in two gulps. Em settled herself in his favorite chair and blinked at him.

Nursing his glass, he said aloud to the cat, "I refuse to believe she is carrying on a clandestine affair with Lannister. She wouldn't do such a thing . . . would she?"

Em made a *mrrp* noise and stuck out a leg, washing her flank.

"I'm glad you agree. So, the meeting was by chance?"

Em stopped licking to look at him and opened her mouth in a wide yawn.

"Thank you for your confidence," he said, finishing off the brandy and setting down the glass. He scratched Em under her chin and left the library to find his mother and sister.

The queasy feeling of unease in his gut was not assuaged one bit.

*Unless your affections are already engaged?* His own words reverberated in his head and her response *Yes! Yes, they are—so you see—I—cannot. I'm so sorry!*

His mind thoroughly elsewhere, Robert conveyed his ladies to the theater and settled in the box for the opening of the performance, and it wasn't until the curtains were about to rise that he looked across to the row of boxes on the other side of the theatre and saw that Ravenshaw had guests, just being seated. The lights were beginning to dim as he recognized with a shock Lady Holbrook and Miss Watson.

His plan to circumnavigate the theatre at the first intermission and visit Ravenshaw's box was stymied at the outset by the sheer number of visitors inundating his box, and the impropriety of leaving his ladies alone was borne in upon him. Instead, he watched with gathering fury as a number of gentlemen entered Ravenshaw's box and spoke with Miss Watson.

Miss Watson had been upset when he left her this morning, but there were no signs of that now. Indeed, she seemed well amused by her other beaux and oblivious to him, despite his staring at her in the rudest way possible. He should stop, but each time he dragged his eyes away, he found them creeping back.

He would be having a word later with Ravenshaw about what the hell he thought he was doing. Damn it, the man knew of Robert's interest in Miss Watson. What was he playing at?

But watching the silent mummery of action in the box, for he could hear nothing of what was said at this distance and over the general hubbub of conversation in the theatre, he concluded that the reason for their presence wasn't Miss Watson but Lady Holbrook. It seemed the acquaintance struck up at Vauxhall had continued. It was Ravenshaw's business whom he chose to conduct affairs with, but damn it all, he could have chosen someone other than Miss Watson's chaperone!

Halfway through the intermission, Lannister entered the box, much to Robert's horror. *Could this morning's meeting have been to settle an assignation for tonight? Was it indeed Lannister who had secured her affections?*

He watched in impotent frustration the array of emotions chasing themselves across Sarah's face as she spoke with Lannister—*Sarah! When did I start thinking of her as Sarah and not Miss Watson?*—from smiles to the flirtatious waving of her fan to more serious looks exchanged between the two of them, and at the conclusion Lannister took her hand and kissed it. The troubled look with which she watched him leave smote Robert to the heart.

*Was it indeed Lannister who held her affection?*
*Why do women fall for wastrels and rakes?*

SARAH SPOTTED THE duke the moment she entered the marquess's box, and panic made her want to turn tail and run. But of course, she couldn't do that, so she did the next best thing: try to pretend he wasn't there. If she didn't look at him, she could conduct herself with equanimity. She certainly had plenty to distract her in the intermission, as she was besieged by half a dozen of her suitors, and she tried to be glad that the duke made no move to come and see her. Of course he wouldn't, and she was glad of it. For it would be so mortifying to have to face him again after this morning.

When the Earl of Lannister entered the box and came straight to her side, she wasn't sure what to feel. He looked a great deal better than he had that morning.

Bowing, he said with a droll smile, "Miss Watson, I came to beg your pardon for my disreputable appearance this morning. I hope you can overlook it, and I can assure you that I am not in the habit of falling asleep on park benches in the wee hours of the morning."

His smile was so infectious and inviting her to share the joke on himself that she found herself smiling back. "Well, I should hope not, my lord. I daresay it is vastly uncomfortable."

"It was," he admitted. He moved his jaw. "My neck is still sore. May I?" he asked, indicating the seat beside her.

She waved him to it with her fan, and then plied it gently, for the theater was warm. "Are you fully recovered, my lord?"

"I am. Coffee is a wonderful restorative, as is several hours of sleep in a bed."

"It is to be hoped that you don't find yourself in such straits again."

"I don't intend to. It was a delight to wake and see your face, Miss Watson, and I cannot tell you how salutary a lesson it was to me. People have been trying to reform me for years. I think you may have done it with a simple look of concern for my welfare."

"I have seen many lives ruined by an addiction to strong liquor, in my father's parish, my lord," she said quietly.

"Ah, then you are a ministering angel."

She shook her head. "No such thing, merely a dutiful daughter helping her father."

"You are in serious danger of bringing me undone, Miss Watson. I must say something flippant and droll to turn the conversation into lighter channels or I risk unmanning myself before a lady."

His tone was light, and he smiled, but she saw a flicker in the back of his eyes that caught quite suddenly at her heartstrings. This man was dangerous precisely because he was broken, in a way that the duke was not.

As if her thought had communicated itself to him, he went on, "I cannot help but notice that His Grace is glaring at this box. Forgive me, it is none of my business, but that, coupled with the fact that you were fleeing from him the other night, makes me wonder if you are in need of protection?"

*He did recognize her, yet he had said nothing?* "From the duke? No indeed."

"And yet he has upset you?"

She colored and plied her fan more vigorously. "It is, as you have already observed, the duke who is upset."

"Indeed, he could never have made you an indecent proposal, for he is too upstanding for that. I wonder then, has he made you a decent one?"

"My lord, that really is none of your business!"

"Ah ha! He has, and you have refused him! What a set down for His Grace."

She bore his scrutiny in silence, for what could she say? To confirm what he said as the truth would be the worst breach of etiquette, but to deny it would be to lie outright, and she was an appalling liar. He would see through her immediately.

"I shall not tease you further, for I can see that *I* have upset *you,* for which I beg your forgiveness. You may trust me not to betray your secret. As you have not betrayed mine."

"I am not a gossip, my lord."

"You *are* an angel, I think. Sent to tempt me into reform. Can you succeed, I wonder?"

"It is not up to me, my lord. Only you can reform your way of life."

"True, but you could inspire me."

"To what end, my lord?"

"That I might aspire to your hand?"

"And would I inspire you if I were penniless, my lord?"

"Ah, a direct hit! Yet if you refuse a duke, and one of upstanding character and considerable moral fiber, what could one such as I offer you? Nothing, I fear." He shifted position and took her hand, the one not holding her fan. With a wistful smile and fixing her gaze with his, he said, "Let me leave you with this thought. I would redeem my fortune and my character and lay both at your feet, Miss Watson, along with my heart, if you would have it." On which he kissed her hand, rose, bowed, and left the box.

Sarah, much discomposed by this passage, sat through the next half of the recital with her mind in a whirl. Her instinct was to dismiss the earl's avowals as practiced lies to entrap her. He was right, if she had refused a duke, what could he possibly offer to tempt her to take him instead? Nothing. Yet he played upon the feminine desire to reform a rake. She would not fall for it. She would have neither the duke nor the earl.

# Chapter Eleven

T HE NEXT DAY, having spent a restless night worrying over what had passed between Lannister and Sarah at the theater, Robert attempted to call upon her only to be denied. He came back two hours later with the same result. Frustrated, he went home to discover that his duties that evening were to escort Mama and Ava to Lady Castlereagh's ball.

The ballroom was stuffed to bursting with London society, and it was obvious this was going to be a squeeze, which was a compliment to the hostess but less pleasant for the guests. Finding chairs for his ladies in a nook picked out in ferns and flowers, they soon found themselves swamped with gentlemen eager for introductions to Lady Ava Layne.

Three who did not require such an introduction were his friends Ashford, Ravenshaw, and Pendrell, who had all run tame at The Castle since their days at Cambridge together and knew Ava from when she was in pinafores. Ravenshaw, much to the chagrin of other gentlemen, earned the right to the lady's first dance and swept her off with the smooth aplomb for which he was well known.

If Robert hadn't been so preoccupied with looking for Sarah and Lady Holbrook, he might have been alarmed by this, as none knew Ravenshaw's reputation better than he. He had still not found them when the marquess restored Ava, flushed and sparkling to her seat. The practiced air with which Ravenshaw kissed her hand and gave her an extravagant compliment, and his sister's blush and coquettish laugh in response, gave him a jolt.

Little Ava was grown up and, damn it, Ravenshaw had no business encouraging her to form a tendre for him, particularly after the way he'd been disporting himself with Lady Holbrook. He threw the marquess a disapproving look to which his lordship responded with an urbane smile and a single raised eyebrow. Blast! He didn't have time to be keeping an eye on Ava and chasing Sarah—no, Miss Watson, for she hadn't given him leave to use her name, had she?

Pendrell took her out next, and since Robert had no qualms about Pendrell keeping the line—he wasn't interested in females as his only passion was his fusty antiquities—he was able to relax for a few minutes and look about for the object of his preoccupation at this cursed affair.

He spied Miss Watson joining a set just forming with Greathouse, Ashford, and Caroline. At least there appeared to be no sign of Lannister. It was to be hoped that he hadn't received an invitation. Lady Castlereagh being a patroness of Almack's, that seemed likely. As much as he wanted to approach Sarah, he thought he needed an ally in his quest, and Lady Holbrook might fit the bill.

Lady Holbrook he found seated with the duennas in the corner near the entrance to the gardens. He made his way there and bowed to her. "May I steal you away, Lady Holbrook?" he asked, breaking in on her conversation with Lady Pierce.

"Of course, Your Grace," the lady appeared startled and slightly flustered.

He guided her out onto the terrace where a seat away from the main throng gave them some privacy.

"You will be aware that I made Miss Watson an offer a few days ago and was refused," he began abruptly.

"I am, Your Grace, and I am terribly sorry!"

He wanted most desperately to ask her if what Sarah had told him, that her affections were already engaged, was true, but felt that to ask would put the lady in the difficult position of breaking Sarah's confidence.

Instead, he said, "I had hoped that if I could have some further speech with Miss Watson, I might persuade her to reconsider. Would that be a futile endeavor, Lady Holbrook?"

The lady's light blue eyes widened. She seemed to be considering his words, or perhaps she was just shocked. Whatever it was, she appeared to come to a conclusion and, leaning in, put a hand on his arm and said softly, "I do not. I do most earnestly encourage you to try again. Sarah has been a little emotional lately. She misses her family, you understand, and—and the prospect of assuming the role of your duchess overwhelmed her."

"I see, that is understandable." His heart lifted, this made perfect sense. Perhaps he had been mistaken in thinking Lannister had anything to do with her refusal. This put quite a different complexion on matters. Sarah had given him an answer she thought would drive him away because she was afraid. In fact, he had given her the lead by asking if her affections were already engaged.

He kicked himself for not reassuring her more. But her air of capability and intellect had fooled him into thinking her more worldly than she was. All the warm feelings he had been nurturing came back in a flood.

"Sarah has led a less sophisticated existence in a simple country vicarage. Her family is perfectly respectable and of good birth, but somewhat rustic." Lady Holbrook echoed the direction of his own thoughts.

"I understand, thank you."

"If you wish to have speech with her, go to the second room off the gallery at eleven fifteen. I shall contrive that Sarah will meet you there. I trust to your address, Your Grace, to persuade her."

"Thank you, Lady Holbrook." He rose and offered her his

arm to return her to the ballroom. He had just over an hour to wait until the appointed time of the rendezvous, and while it was tempting to request Sarah to dance, he did not. Instead, he returned to his mother and sister's side with the intention of keeping a glowering eye on Ava's partners.

He took the opportunity to have a word with Ravenshaw, who was propping the wall, watching the dancers.

"I'll thank you to stay away from Ava," he said abruptly.

Ravenshaw eyed him with his characteristic lazy smile and said, "Keep your shirt on, Rob, there is no harm in a little light flirtation, she has to try her wings sometime. Better me than some unscrupulous type."

"Since when have you had scruples?" demanded Robert, realizing belatedly he was being a curmudgeon. *What has got into me lately? I am not usually so testy.*

Ravenshaw stiffened slightly. "She is your sister, Rob, I've known her since she was a lass. I might be all sorts of a blackguard, but absolve me of that, please!"

Robert flushed and apologized. *Damn it, I am not myself. The sooner this business with Sarah is resolved the better.* Bethinking himself of last night he added, but rather more mildly than he had originally intended, "What were you doing squiring Lady Holbrook and Miss Watson to the recital last night?"

"Daphne had a fancy to hear the performance, so I obliged."

"Daphne, is it? I know it's none of my business—"

"You're right, it isn't," Ravenshaw cut him off.

Robert raised his eyebrows at him, and Ravenshaw flushed faintly. "Don't get your tails in a twist, it's just a harmless flirtation, nothing more. You wanted me to keep her entrained at Vauxhall, I did. She's a lonely widow, I've done nothing more than make her feel young again."

With that slight assurance, Robert returned his attention to Sarah who danced every dance. Not once did she appear to glance in his direction or even be aware of his presence, much to his chagrin. When she and Ava were in the same set, they talked in a friendly fashion, and he longed to ask what she had said but was afforded no opportunity to ask Ava, as she was barely back at her mother's side before she was whisked off again.

At the appointed time for the promised rendezvous, he made his way to the room indicated by her ladyship and entered. The chamber was lit by one candelabra on the mantelpiece, and a small fire burned in the grate. It was furnished with a couch and a side table and had a window embrasure that gave onto the gardens with thick curtains in red velvet hung on either side of tall windows.

"Daphne?" Sarah entered the room looking about and stiffened at the sight of him. "Where is Daphne?" she asked.

"Lady Holbrook? Were you expecting to find her here?"

"Yes, the servant told me she was feeling faint and had come in here to lie down."

"She is not here," he said, stating the obvious.

"No, you are, which I find most odd," she said. "I will bid you good evening, Your Grace."

"Please, Miss Watson," he said, coming forward and pushing the door gently shut behind her. "Grant me a few moments of your time, I beg you."

"We can have nothing further to say to each other—"

"Lady Holbrook explained. I understand perfectly."

"You do?" her eyes widened, and a pretty flush crept into her cheeks. He took her hands and led her gently over to the couch where he eased her down beside him, keeping a hold of her hands. They were both wearing gloves again, and he knew a moment's irritation. It would be nice, just for once, to touch her skin.

She was lovely tonight in a gown of sapphire-blue satin. Her soft brown eyes stared up at him as her lips parted slightly on a faint gasp. A waft of roses and her natural scent teased him, and all the pent-up desire aroused from Vauxhall came flooding back in a rush.

"I do. Your trepidation is natural but unfounded, I assure you.

You will make a magnificent duchess." He let go of one of her hands to raise his to her face and cup her jaw gently. "I realize with hindsight that I went about my proposal in the wrong way. I led you to think that my only motive in making it was mercenary. Please let me show you that it wasn't."

"I don't think I understand," she said, her breath coming in short pants, her eyes wide. *Is she going to flee from me again?*

"Sarah, if I frightened you at Vauxhall, I'm sorry, but I thought, perhaps mistakenly, that when we danced you wished me to kiss you? Tell me I was wrong?"

She swallowed visibly and licked her bottom lip nervously; the sight sent a pulse of desire through him. "Sarah?"

"No," she whispered. "You weren't wr—"

He cut her off with a swift, decisive kiss, breaking it only to dive back for a longer, deeper kiss, hauling her slender, delicious body tighter against him.

As he moved his lips over hers seeking a response, she made a noise in her throat, *encouragement or protest?* He nudged her lips with his, a flick of his tongue on her lower lip to encourage her. He ached for her response. *Kiss me, Sarah, please!*

A gasp parted her lips, and he took full advantage, invading her mouth with his tongue, teasing and persuading her with his lips. *And there. The response I have been after.* She moved her lips, kissing him back, taking his tongue and replying with her own. Desire surged in him, making him pull her closer, kiss her with deepened fervor. If she had doubts, *he* did not—he unequivocally desired her. *Miss Sarah Watson should be in no doubt that I want her for more than her fortune.*

THE PRESSURE OF his mouth on hers shocked her to the core. She had read his intent in his eyes as he leaned toward her, and her every instinct screamed at her to pull away. But something mesmerizing held her in its grip, and instead she leaned inwards and pressed her lips to his. The explosion of tingling delight that radiated outward from the touch of his lips robbed her of breath and sense.

The kiss at Vauxhall had just been a taster. Since then, she had fantasized about him kissing her properly, but her imaginings were nothing to the real thing. As his lips moved over hers, she felt a languorous heat pervade her limbs and settle between her legs. Her heartbeat kicked up and her breath came short.

He let go of her other hand and wrapped an arm round her waist, pulling her closer against the hardness of his chest. He angled his head to kiss her more deeply, his tongue teasing her lips, and she parted them instinctively. This kiss was so much more than the brief tantalizing brush of his mouth at Vauxhall. Nothing in her experience had prepared her for this avalanche of feeling and sensation. Her hands slid up his chest to his shoulders. He was big and solid and masculine, and his taste and smell made her dizzy with delight.

She pressed into his kiss, losing herself in the pleasure of his mouth and his hands on her body. *I am wicked, but oh I want more . . .*

"Sarah!" Daphne's shocked accents broke into her reverie, and she and the duke sprang apart guiltily as she turned to stare at the doorway where three ladies stood. Daphne and, horror of horrors, Lady Castlereagh, their hostess, and Mrs. Drummond-Burrell, two of the highest sticklers among the patronesses of Almack's.

The duke rose immediately and bowed, his color high and a look of barely concealed fury on his face.

"Ladies," he said.

"Your Grace, what is the meaning of this?" asked Lady Castlereagh.

He pulled Sarah gently to her feet, and he said, "You must be the first to congratulate us, Lady Castlereagh, Miss Watson has done me the honor of accepting my hand in marriage."

Sarah stiffened, her heart thudding. He squeezed her hand

gently and glanced down at her. His expression seemed to say *it will be all right.*

*Easy for him to say! He has what he wants now, doesn't he?* She threw a furious glare at Daphne. *He has conspired with her to spring this trap.* Tears stung her lids and she blinked rapidly to clear them. Betrayal cut her to the quick. *I will not cry like a ninny.*

Daphne came forward wreathed in smiles. "Your Grace, how glad I am to hear it." She glanced over her shoulder at the other two women. "A newly affianced couple can be forgiven one kiss, can they not?"

Lady Castlereagh's lips twitched. "I think we can forgive His Grace a little ardor, can we not, Clementina?"

Mrs. Drummond-Burrell sniffed. "I suppose so, Amelia."

# Chapter Twelve

Madeleine was sipping her tea when her eyes alighted on the announcement in the morning post.

*. . . the betrothal of the Duke of Troubridge to Miss Sarah Watson . . .*

The tea went everywhere and the wave of nausea she had been battling all morning sent her flying for the chamber pot.

Madeleine sat clutching the chamber pot, tears running down her cheeks, as the fantasy she had been nurturing for months was well and truly punctured.

She really did need to find another protector, because the duke had indeed found a wife as he had said he was going to do. He wasn't coming back to her as she had hoped, even persuaded herself, that he would.

"Robert, you cannot be serious! It will be impossible to pull together a wedding in only a month, and besides, it is the middle of the season. What of Ava's come out ball? It is scheduled for next week! Are you trying to ruin your sister's debut?"

"Not at all. We can still hold her ball before we leave for The Castle. You know very well that the wedding will become an event of the season. Any of Ava's beaux worth their salt will make the trip just for the chance to steal a march on his fellows."

The duchess regarded him with an arrested expression. He could see the thoughts ticking away behind her eyes as she considered his comment.

"You are perfectly correct!" Mama's eyes lit up with a sparkle. "In fact, we will make it *the* event of the season." She touched his arm. "It will be so exclusive that everyone will want to be invited!" She clapped her hands, taking a pace about the room. She turned back to him. "But a month is still not long enough!"

He smiled. "That's the dandy, Mama. You will contrive to manage it—you have an army of servants to do your bidding. And it will also give you the opportunity to put Sarah in the way of things, introduce her to the staff, and get her comfortable with her responsibilities, by being able to observe how you pull together a big event without her being responsible for any of it."

"That is very thoughtful of you, Robert." She paused and sighed. "If you are set on its being held in a month's time?"

"I am."

"Why the haste?"

"I do not wish to wait," he said, flushing.

His mother eyed him thoughtfully. "You do realize that such unseemly haste will cause gossip, don't you?"

"Yes, but we can weather that."

"Very well, I shall make it happen, somehow." She patted his arm again. "I am pleased you have at last found the woman you've been looking for, my dear. I had almost given up."

"So had I, Mama," he said awkwardly. He cleared his throat and went on, "You will be patient with her, won't you? Remember, she is not accustomed to the kind of pomp and ceremony we take for granted. And she has no worldly ambition—she didn't set her cap for me. In fact, she was deuced hard to convince," he admitted.

"I knew that first evening that I liked her. And if you love her, my dearest, I will learn to love her, too."

Robert flushed again and squeezed her hand. "Thank you, Mama."

Mama was a gem to accede to his desire to push forward with the wedding so rapidly, for it would mean a great deal of work for her and would be a distraction from Ava's season though Ava was far too fond of him to object to the interruption. It seemed he had fooled his family into thinking he had formed a strong attachment to Sarah, for which he was grateful. The truth was not so sanguine.

His fury over being entrapped by Lady Holbrook, was nothing to Sarah's. He'd had no moment alone with her to discuss it, but the daggers she threw at him and her cold manner told him that she believed him to have been complicit with Lady Holbrook in the affair.

The fact of the matter was he'd had no choice but to make their betrothal a reality upon being discovered in such a compromising position with Sarah. His reputation, as well as hers, was at stake. The last thing he wanted was a scandal, particularly in the middle of Ava's come out season, nothing could be more ruinous to her chances than to have her brother embroiled in a scandal. They had managed to avoid one at Vauxhall, though he was still not quite sure why or how. The fact that the alliance suited him was almost irrelevant.

SARAH WAS LIVID. Sarah wasn't sure who she was more angry with, Daphne or the duke. That they had conspired to entrap her she had no doubt.

Being perfectly aware of the terms of her great-aunt's will, she knew the benefit that would accrue to Daphne in orchestrating Sarah's marriage to a duke. It was a significant jointure that would see her comfortable for the rest of her days. And Daphne's refusal to apologize was even more galling. She stuck to it hammer and tong that she had acted in Sarah's best interests, and she would thank her for it one day.

Sarah was so flabbergasted by this she just stared at her duenna. "You cannot be serious!"

Daphne dabbed at her eyes and sniffed. "I am perfectly serious. The duke is an absolute gentleman, and he most sincerely esteems you—anyone with eyes can see that. He will make you a splendid husband, you just haven't the sense to see it yet, but you will!"

Sarah turned and left the room, unable to support a moment longer with the woman she had once thought her friend.

And as for the duke, she was so angry with him she refused to receive him. She kept to her room entirely for the first day after the announcement of the engagement, only emerging the next morning to resume her early morning walks.

She felt his betrayal, if anything more keenly, because it cut to the quick of her burgeoning affections toward him. She had assumed, wrongly, that he was a man of integrity. She now felt that she didn't know him at all and that every construction she had put on his behavior was false. He cared only for money and consequence.

Her thoughts thus were quite dark as she entered the gates of Hyde Park trailed by Esme and the faithful James. It was a gloomy day, which suited her mood, and she hunched into her pelisse against the cool breeze, her eyes on her feet.

"Good day, Miss Watson." The familiar voice brought her head up with a start and her steps to a halt. It was the Earl of Lannister again. But this time he did not appear to be the worse for drink. He was impeccably dressed in a jacket, breeches, and top boots under a caped greatcoat, shaven and quite bright-eyed.

He bowed. "I understand congratulations are in order," he said with a quizzical smile.

Feeling entirely unequal to dealing with the earl's double meanings and bantering manner, she tried to assume the demeanor of a just-engaged lady who was happy about it.

Acknowledging his bow with a curtsy and a nod of her head, she said, "Thank you, my lord."

"Will you let me take a turn about the park with you?" he said, taking her hand before she could protest and slipping it into the crook of his arm. Esme and James had fallen back a bit, although they were still in sight, as the earl tugged her gently along the path. There were few people out this early, and the air was still misty with dew upon the grass.

"What are you doing here, my lord?"

"Waiting for you. I waited yesterday, too, but you didn't show."

"I-I had the headache yesterday," she said, flustered.

"Did you?" He looked down at her. "Forgive me, Miss Watson, but you look like you still have the headache."

"What do you want, my lord?"

"I wanted to ascertain if you were happy with your new circumstances. From the look of you, I can only conclude that you are not."

She didn't respond, for what could she say?

"I must say that I am surprised at the duke. I would not have thought he would stoop to underhanded means to obtain what he wanted."

"You are mistaken, my lord," she said in a strained voice.

"Am I? I don't think so. In any case, he cannot compel you to marry him, and I wanted you to know you have an alternative if you choose to take it."

"My lord, this is outrageous!"

"No more outrageous than forcing a young woman into a marriage not of her choosing. I am a blackguard, Miss Watson, and even I would balk at that."

"Thank you, my lord. I'm sure your offer is kindly meant, but I cannot accept it."

"No? Very well, you can't blame a man for trying." He reached into his waistcoat pocket and removed a small card. "There is my direction. Should you change your mind, a note to that address will bring me swiftly to your rescue. I suspect that henceforward it will be virtually impossible for me to have any conversation with you. You are about to be swallowed up by the ducal machine." He doffed his hat, bowed, and strolled away.

Sarah watched his back for a moment or two, unsure of what she was feeling. Even if she loved him, which she didn't, marrying him would cause such a scandal it would ruin her sisters' chances and defeat the purpose of her marrying anyone at all. Angry as she was with the duke for trapping her, she recognized that to spurn him would ruin her. She was a vicar's daughter, and he was a duke. The unevenness in their stations would ensure that.

WHEN ROBERT RECEIVED the intelligence from Bridges that Sarah had met with Lannister that morning in Hyde Park, he was stupefied.

"Find Lannister's address for me immediately!"

"Yes, Your Grace," said Bridges with a bow.

An hour later, the duke knocked on the door of a narrow multi-story building in Ryder Street, where Lannister was reputed to have rooms. The landlady, much flustered when she learned the duke's identity, let him into the building and directed him to the second floor. The door was opened by Lannister's man who informed the duke that the earl was not at home.

"I believe he has gone to his club—Boodle's, Your Grace."

"Thank you," said the duke with punctilious politeness masking his growing fury.

He repaired from there to St. James Street and entered the club. He found Lannister at the gaming tables, of course. He approached the man and, leaning down, said quietly in his ear, "May I have a word with you in private?"

Lannister looked up at him with a raised eyebrow. He pursed his lips a moment and then threw down his hand. "Gentlemen, if you will excuse me?"

He rose to protests and grunts from the other men and followed Robert to a small antechamber. Shutting the door, Robert rounded on him.

"I'll thank you to stay away from my affianced wife!"

Lannister smiled, which irritated Robert even further. "You have excellent sources, Your Grace. But I believe you are overreacting. It was only a walk in the park, and her maid and footman were in attendance. All the proprieties were observed."

"Was it an assignation?"

"If you're asking whether Miss Watson was a party to planning it, no. I simply laid in wait for her, since I knew it was her habit to walk in the park at that hour."

"What possible reason could you have for doing so?"

"That, Your Grace, is my business."

"If it concerns my fiancée, it is my damned business!"

"You needn't concern yourself; I've retired from the lists. I made one last bid; she turned me down." He looked down ruefully at his boot. "A pity, but there it is."

Robert felt as if he would explode. "You have the temerity to stand there and tell me that you made Sarah an offer *after* she became engaged to me?"

"Yes, well, if you'd seen her face this morning you might understand. She looked dashed unhappy. I'm a scoundrel, I'll be the first to admit it, but even I draw the line at entrapment."

"Entrapment! It is no such thing!"

"What do you call it then? Forcing a woman to accept your suit when she has already rejected it?"

"She told you that?"

"Of course not, she is not that vulgar. I guessed. The fact is that she is unhappy but resigned to her lot. Many would fail utterly to understand her discontent. After all, she is to be a duchess—that should be enough to make her happy, shouldn't it? Except she is not in the least little bit worldly and doesn't care about your coronet."

"I'm aware of that!" said Robert stiffly.

"Are you? Do you also know that she is a warm, vital, loving creature, with a soft heart and caring nature?"

"She has many estimable qualities, yes."

"By God, you don't deserve her if that's the best you can do!" Lannister flung away from him in disgust.

Robert struggled with himself for a moment and finally admitted, "You may be right. But in the circumstances, there was no choice but to offer her the protection of my name, and frankly, it was what I desired in any case."

"But not what *she* desired! You're such a self-satisfied, self-centered, sanctimonious prick!"

"If we're to exchange insults, my lord, I think I can construct a longer list of your faults than mine!"

Lannister looked at him with contempt and shook his head. "You're missing the point!"

"No, I'm not. I'm simply a different stamp of man to you. For which I will not apologize. Your question is 'Do I care for Sarah?' Of course I do. As I do for every member of my family and my household. Her happiness and safety will become my chief concern."

"She's not one of your assets, man, she's a woman! With thoughts and feelings and aspirations and desires of her own."

"I know that."

"Do you? Then bloody well show it." He stared at Robert for a minute. "My God, you don't know how, do you? You've got a stick so far up your arse it's protruding through the top of your head!"

"I think this conversation has gone far enough. Stay away from my wife in future or I'll demand satisfaction."

"You can try! I'm accounted quite a good shot myself, Your Grace."

Lannister opened the door and left, and Robert slumped into one of the overstuffed leather chairs in the room. He was shaking, not from rage or fear, but a sudden and overwhelming self-loathing. He felt sick with it, and the kind of shame invaded his gut that he hadn't felt since he was a boy and his father had reprimanded him for cheating. But this was far worse than that. Lannister, with a few well-chosen words, had ripped the ground from under him and torn his worldview to shreds.

The evidential fact that Lannister knew and understood far more about Sarah than he did gouged a painful hole in his chest. His description of her as *a warm, vital, loving creature, with a soft heart and caring nature . . .* he felt the visceral reality of that strike home in his vitals. He realized with a shock that he had been viewing Sarah as if through a veil. As if he were one step removed.

He had allowed himself to feel a burgeoning physical need for her, but for all his talk of wanting to find love, to love some mythical woman who didn't exist outside his imagination, when confronted with a real woman, a woman of quality and kindness, who valued things that mattered, who gave herself to her family and her father's parishioners with unstinting care, he remained frozen behind a shield.

*How did this happen?*

Somewhere along the line in becoming the duke, he had lost the ability to feel. Emrys was right, he had lost Robert the man.

# Chapter Thirteen



*Dear Sarah,*

*I shall be meeting with your aunt's solicitor this afternoon at three o'clock in Berkeley Square to finalize the settlements for your family, Lady Holbrook, and your dowry. I would very much appreciate your attendance at the meeting to oversee and agree to the settlements. I will naturally apprize your father by letter of what is agreed upon for his approval also.*

*I will send my carriage for you just before three.*

*Yours sincerely,*
*Robert Layne*

Sarah read the note with wide eyes. She had not expected such consideration, and it somewhat disarmed her anger, which had not abated in the five days since their betrothal was announced to the world. She had kept to the house for the duration of that time and declined every one of his invitations to attend a social function in his company, claiming a feminine weakness that forced her to remain sequestered. It galled her to do so, but she simply couldn't face him.

The note jolted her out of her self-pity and anger to think of the people for whom she was doing this. So, she put on her best bonnet and a new walking dress and was ready for the duke's carriage when it appeared.

Arriving at Berkeley Square for the first time, she mounted

the steps of the four-story mansion with trepidation. The door was opened to her by a middle-aged butler of very superior bearing. However, as soon as he clapped eyes on her, he unbent considerably, smiling and bowing.

"Miss Watson, welcome to Layne House, Mr. Creighton at your service. May I convey the sentiments of the whole staff, how glad we are to welcome you to the house and family. I and the entire staff look forward very much to serving you as the new duchess."

Sarah blushed, taken aback by such a fulsome welcome. "Th-thank you, Creighton. I believe the duke is expecting me?"

"He is. Let me take your bonnet and cloak, and I will take you to him straightaway."

Divested of bonnet and cloak, she followed Creighton to a door on the left side of the house. He opened the door and announced, "Miss Watson, Your Grace."

Sarah stepped over the threshold and caught her breath in surprise. The room was of generous proportions and was lined floor to ceiling with books on three of the walls. The front wall had two window embrasures flanked by red velvet curtains, and a fireplace with the generous fire splitting the bookcases was on the far wall. There was a huge desk at the other end of the room and between were strewn several comfortable looking leather couches and chairs. The floor was covered in an expensive looking carpet of eastern design. The whole effect was both sumptuous and cozy.

The duke stood before the fire, dressed as always with taste and elegance. Today he wore a bottle-green jacket and buff-colored pantaloons which showed his excellent legs to advantage. As always, his cravat and waistcoat were of impeccable taste. It made her glad she had chosen to wear the new walking dress in Pomona green.

"Your Grace," she curtsied as the door closed behind her and the duke came toward her. She had expected the solicitors to be here, but they were alone.

"Sarah, thank you for coming," he said, taking her hand and kissing it formally.

She retracted her hand, trying to ignore the little tingle that ran up her arm from his touch. "Where are the solicitors?" she asked, unable to keep the note of accusation out of her voice.

"They will join us shortly. I wanted to allow you time to peruse what is being proposed. If you will sit?" He indicated the desk where some papers were spread out. She moved to take the seat behind the desk and looked over the papers there.

"You will see your aunt's will, which you should be familiar with," he said, indicating one multi-page document. "Here you will see set out the amounts I propose for settlements on your family, for Lady Holbrook, and your dowry. Please review them and make any amendments you see fit."

With a fast-beating heart, she ran her eyes over the amounts laid out. Allowances and dowries for her sisters, annuities for the boys' education and larger, individual sums to be paid on their reaching majority. An income supplement for her parents with a significant sum held in reserve for her father's retirement or payable to her mother should he die before then. The amount for Daphne was likewise generous and practical, payable for her lifetime or payable in a sum to the value of twenty years should she choose to marry again, as her dowry. And for herself a very generous dowry and allowance.

He waited by the fire in silence while she read through the paper and made a couple of minor changes.

"You are most generous, Your Grace," she said stiffly, feeling quite awkward and uncomfortable in the circumstances. She handed him her amendments, and he took them with a glance.

"You should know also that I intend to use part of the principle to revive the estate at The Castle, my primary seat. It has been sorely neglected and requires an input of funds to restore it to working order so that it may begin to pay for itself and the family's other expenses. I intend also to divert some of the income to members of my family in the interim and use a portion of the principle to clear an accumulation of debt.

"Once The Castle is in good heart I will look to improve the condition of my other assets. I will keep you fully informed of the financial status of each property, and when I am able, I will transfer ownership for life of one of the houses to you. I can't will it to you outright, as everything is entailed. Everything will go to our eldest son upon my death, but this arrangement will ensure that you are never without a home or income should something happen to me."

"You are very practical, Your Grace. Thank you."

He nodded and seemed to be about to say something else when the door opened and Creighton announced, "Mr. Benson and Mr. Harley, Your Grace."

Mr. Benson was short and round and Mr. Harley tall and thin. With the introductions out of the way, the gentlemen sat down to business and Sarah listened. At each point a decision was made and committed to paper, the duke asked her directly for her assent. At the end of the process, her signature was requested alongside the duke's.

Through the execution clauses of the new contract, he had ensured that he could not spend the principle, nor redirect the income from her fortune, without her written approval. Furthermore, he had no control over the monies settled upon her outright, which she could spend as she saw fit, and he could not take them back should he wish to.

The solicitors had looked at him very oddly when he insisted on this clause, and Sarah suspected that if she hadn't been present, they would have argued strongly against it. As it was, they didn't dare with the duke looking at them grimly and herself sitting there with her hands in her lap feeling quite overwhelmed.

The business concluded, Messrs. Benson and Harley left, and she prepared to do the same, but inevitably the duke stayed her with a hand on her arm.

"Sarah, please, we need to talk."

"You have been exceedingly generous, Your Grace, I don't

know what to say," she said, looking anywhere but at him.

"You could look at me to begin with," he said, touching her chin lightly to bring her face round to his.

She glanced up at him and away, her heart clenching in her chest. His generosity to herself and her family had gone a considerable way toward puncturing the ball of anger in her stomach, but she felt the gulf between them keenly.

"Sarah, I felt that you needed to understand that I would not abuse the financial advantage that you bring to our marriage and to reassure you that you will not be left unprotected should something happen to me. Having got that out of the way, we need to address the other aspects of this union."

"Indeed, Your Grace."

"Will you please call me Robert?"

She compressed her lips. "You cannot buy my affection, Your Grace."

He sighed with a tinge of frustration. "I wasn't trying to."

She looked at him run a hand through his hair, a gesture she had noticed before that expressed agitation.

"Sarah, what can I say? I am at a loss."

"You could try starting with an apology!" she blurted, her anger flaring up again.

"You believe me complicit in Lady Holbrook's deception?"

She nodded, her back ramrod straight and her hands clenched tightly before her.

"I wasn't," he said baldly.

"How can I believe that when you stood to gain everything from it?"

"If you can believe I would stoop to such tactics as that, you know nothing of my character. I don't know what else I can do to demonstrate to you that I am a man of honor and integrity, two traits that I thought would weigh with you."

His words pierced her angry defenses, yet she turned them off. For if she weren't at outs with him, she would fall victim to his charm again, and it would *hurt!* Gathering her anger around her again, she was about to reply that she didn't know what to think of him when he said stiffly, "Very well, if it is an apology you require, you shall have one." He cleared his throat. "I do most sincerely apologize if anything I have done or said has caused you distress."

She listened to these words with her heart beating fast. They were obviously uttered reluctantly and did little to assuage her anger. He must have seen that in her demeanor for his stiff posture collapsed and he reached out a hand toward her, saying with far more sincerity, "I'm sorry, Sarah. Please, I cannot bear it if you're angry with me."

She stared at his hand, not sure if it was a viper or an olive branch. Her traitorous heart wanted to think of it as the latter. But before she could react, the door opened, and the duchess came in.

"Sarah, my dear, how lovely to see you! I do hope you're feeling better." She advanced on Sarah and kissed her cheek. "Robert, why didn't you tell me Sarah was here? You must join us for afternoon tea," she said, sweeping Sarah off upstairs to the parlor where she found not only Lady Ava but Lords Hereward and Kenrick, who were all delighted to see her and enveloped her in hugs and kisses—and from Ava, a pelting of questions. She wanted to be angry with the duke, but it was impossible to be angry with his family.

ROBERT CURSED UNDER his breath as his mother bore Sarah off. *Had she been about to accept my apology or not?* Em emerged from a bookcase and jumped to the ground with a thud, prowling over to rub round his legs. He bent and patted her, running her tail through his hand.

"It's a tricky one, Em. What do you think I should do?" Green eyes blinked at him, and she uttered one of her *mrrp* noises, butting his hand with her head.

"Thank you for the vote of confidence," he said. "I'll keep trying."

Straightening, he followed Sarah and his mother upstairs to the parlor. Joining Sarah on one of the sofas, he took a cup of tea from Ava and hoped Sarah would not show his family that there was discord between them. They needed to finish their conversation on their own. The talk was all of Ava's ball which was set for tomorrow night.

Sarah, to her credit, participated in the conversation with all signs of enthusiasm. She was not allowing their disagreement to color her behavior in front of his family. He was conscious of a sudden surge of pride in her composure, despite his frustration with their situation. *She has the maturity and self-control required of a duchess, and in fact she puts me to shame for my lack of it,* he reflected in a moment of insight. He was having rather a lot of those lately, and none of them reflected well on him. When the opportunity presented itself, he sought her left hand discretely where it lay in the folds of her skirt and squeezed.

Startled, she glanced at him and flushed faintly, he smiled and raised her hand to his lips. While public displays of affection could be considered vulgar, he felt that it was worth whatever blow his dignity might take in letting his family see this bit of discreet affection between them. Sarah stared at him a moment and lowered her gaze with becoming maidenly confusion, a disguise he suspected for her latent hostility toward him, though he was pleased to note that she didn't try to snatch her hand away.

He caught a smirk on his mother's face and a positive grin on Ava's. Kenrick actually winked at him, and even Hereward showed mild signs of amusement.

The duchess put her teacup down. "Well, I have a dozen things to do before dinner. Sarah, you will stay and join us for dinner, won't you? We are having a quiet night in, because tomorrow will be so hectic. I'm sure Robert can keep you amused until dinnertime."

Sarah glanced at him helplessly and he smiled. "Of course I can, Mama. Perhaps you'd like a tour of the house, my dear?"

"What a splendid idea," said the duchess. "I'd do it myself, but as I said, I have a dozen things to do."

"Do you need some help, Your Grace?" asked Sarah.

"No, no, not today, but tomorrow perhaps if you come over around midday? Bring your gown and you can change here with the other girls. Ava's maid can dress your hair."

"You're most kind, Your Grace."

"Please, my dear, you must address me as Mama. I cannot tell you how delighted I am to have another daughter."

The duchess gave her a hug and Robert mouthed *thank you* over her head. The duchess shook her head at him and smiled. She then swept Ava off for more ball preparations, and his brothers sloped off to the billiard room, leaving him alone with Sarah. His family could always be relied upon.

"Thank you for agreeing to stay," he said, drawing her back down onto the couch.

"I hardly had the opportunity to refuse."

"Mama is somewhat of a force of nature," he said. "She knew I wanted you to stay."

"To continue our quarrel?"

"To resolve it, I hope. Will you accept my apology, Sarah?"

She looked down and then up, swallowing visibly. "Yes," she smiled tentatively, and he was tempted to kiss her, but there was one other matter he needed to address with her. It was burning a hole in his breast.

"I also wanted you to know that I have taken steps to ensure that you will no longer be bothered by the Earl of Lannister. If he should approach you again, I want you to advise me at once."

Her cheeks flamed, and she jerked her hands from his grasp.

"What do you mean?"

"I am aware that he importuned you in the park two days ago. I regret that you were put to such distress and that I was not able to prevent it."

"So, you're spying on me as well?" Her eyes flashed, and his heart sank. She was angry with him again, but this time he felt as if he was on firmer ground.

"No, servants' gossip. I was informed, that is all."

She rose and walked to the window, so he perforce rose also and followed her. She was clearly agitated.

"I'm sorry to upset you," he said again. "But it is my duty and privilege to protect you from such blackguards as Lannister. He is not a proper person for you to know. It upset me greatly that he had the audacity to offer for—" he broke off as she turned to face him.

"How do you know what he said to me if you were not spying on me?"

"He told me himself when I confronted him."

"He made the offer out of kindness, nothing else. He could see I was unhappy."

"My dear, you are surely not that naïve? If you think me a fortune hunter, Lannister is far worse. And his reputation is shocking, his morals no better."

"Yet I believe he was more sincere in his offer than you, Your Grace."

Her words were a kick to the gut. Struggling to maintain control of his temper, he said in shaking accents, "In what way?"

"He was motivated by care for me, which you were not!"

"I was motivated by the need to save your reputation, and"—his innate honesty forced him to add—"in some small measure my own. The last thing Ava needs right now is for her brother to be embroiled in a scandal. But that aside, I had already offered for you before being discovered at the ball and renewing that offer. It was you who turned me down!"

He recalled the reason she had given him for her refusal in the first place and a sick feeling of dread entered his stomach.

"Am I to understand that the person who had engaged your affections was Lannister?"

"That is a moot point now," she said, her back still toward him.

"Yes, because once the announcement of our engagement was made, it would cause a monumental scandal if you threw me over for Lannister, wouldn't it? And that would as surely ruin your sisters' chances as any scandal I could have caused. Worse in fact."

"Exactly."

He found he was shaking now with something other than anger, and there was an ache in the region of his heart the like of which he had never felt before. "Damn it, Sarah! You can't love him. He is the worst kind of man, a liar and a cheat, a libertine. I tell you he has no moral compass whatever."

"You cannot tell me who to love and who not to love, Your Grace. Although it is just like you to try. You are so accustomed to having everyone do your bidding, you cannot fathom why it is you cannot control me!" Her voice cracked on a sob and something inside him cracked with it.

"Sarah, Sarah, don't." He wrapped his arms round her, pulling her back against his chest. "Don't cry." He squeezed her tight and kissed her hair, getting a lungful of orange blossom scent. Her hair was so soft and lush. He closed his eyes. He felt like something had stabbed him in the heart. *Is this what it is like to love someone? It is nothing like I had thought it would be. Or is it just hurt pride? Jealousy?*

He was so confused he didn't know what to think, except that having her cry was tearing him apart. He had to do something to make her stop. "Sarah, please, don't cry. Don't cry over him, he's not worth it. He doesn't deserve your tears." He kissed her hair again and murmured, "I'm sorry. I'm sorry, my dear. If I could make it right, I would."

The notion that she could shed tears over Lannister was eating a hole through his stomach. If he had disliked the man before, he loathed him now. What he was apologizing for he had no clear idea of, only that he wanted her to stop hurting.

She turned within his arms, her face resting against his chest, which he rather liked the feel of. She sniffed and said, "That's the first nice thing you've said to me."

"Is it?" he asked, appalled.

She nodded, pulling away from him and searching in her reticule for a handkerchief. She blew her nose and wiped her eyes.

"Am I so abominable?"

"Yes," she said, putting her handkerchief away. "You don't mean to be. I've grown somewhat accustomed to your barbed comments and your complete lack of consideration of others' feelings."

Her words left him speechless.

"But I've seen you with your family and I admit you're much nicer with them."

"Oh God! You're the third person in three weeks to tell me I'm an inconsiderate"—he stopped short of using the word on the tip of his tongue and instead said—"person."

"I was infatuated with you once. But that was before I knew you. Before I understood that the only things you care about are appearances and money."

He fell back a step, gut punched yet again. "That isn't true, Sarah."

"Isn't it? Yet everything you say and do convinces me that it is."

"Then I shall have to endeavor to convince you otherwise, though I'm at a loss to know how to do so at the moment," he said stiffly. He felt bruised, battered, and confused. As if he had been picked up by a whirlwind, tossed about, and dropped carelessly on the sidewalk. She turned aside and he ruffled his hair again. "You seem determined to paint me as some kind of monster."

"We are perhaps ill-suited, Your Grace."

"No. I refuse to accept that. We have had moments of accord, have we not?"

"Yes," she agreed somewhat reluctantly.

"Well then, that must give us a basis for something. Please, Sarah, I cannot face the prospect of being in a state of discord with you for the rest of my life. The thought is untenable." When she didn't respond, he said awkwardly, "Unless you find me so abhorrent that you cannot stomach me . . ."

She turned then and said, "No, you are right. We must make the best of it. There are others who are impacted by our decisions, who do not deserve to be punished for our—mistakes."

"That is true. Both our families would suffer."

"I would do anything to save them hurt."

"As would I. We have something in common then," he said with a hopeful smile. His chest still hurt. He wanted her back in his arms. Things seemed better when they touched. He stroked her arm. "Sarah?" He turned her gently to face him. Lifting her chin, he bent his head and kissed her, desperately trying to evoke something of what they had shared before.

She stiffened initially but didn't pull away. He slid his arms round her, pulling her closer and deepening the kiss, that tingling delight he had experienced before overwhelming his senses. Her mouth moved under his, responding to his kisses in a way that gave him heart. They might struggle to communicate verbally, but this, this was something else.

He had bedded several women in his life, but none had inspired the level of longing and, he had to admit, outright lust as Sarah did. What it was about her, he didn't know, but his thoughts had grown increasingly lewd where she was concerned. To have her back in his arms confirmed that it was where she belonged, and he wasn't giving her up without an almighty fight. She may have developed a tendre for Lannister, but it was he she was going to marry. And damn it, he would win her elusive heart or die in the attempt.

He pressed her closer, his body hard and hot for her soft curves, his mouth greedy for her kisses. His lips wandered from her mouth to her jaw and her neck, his hands sliding over her back and only by sheer force of will avoiding wandering lower. He wanted to, but he also didn't want to shock her.

He found her mouth again and was rewarded by her arms

sliding up round his neck and her head titling to give him a better angle to kiss her. She leaned into his kiss and returned it, sending shocks of pleasure through his body that made his pulse race and robbed him of breath.

He pulled her closer, kissing her more deeply, unable to stifle the noise of longing in his throat she aroused in him. *God, I want her.* She was going to be his wife and he would find a way to win her heart, he would.

A noise made him look up and let go of Sarah abruptly. Ava stood in the doorway, her hand over her mouth. "I'm so sorry!" she said, grinning widely. "I left my book in here." She dove across the room to get it and fled. "Please carry on, don't mind me!" she said, halfway down the hall.

Sarah was flushed, her eyes bright and her lips slightly swollen from his kisses. And his eyes couldn't fail to pick up the slight protrusion through her bodice of her nipples, which told him all he needed to know of her reaction to his lovemaking. That at least was a comfort in the face of their previous conversation.

He smiled at Sarah. "Ava enjoyed that far too much. Would you like that tour of the house now?" Any more kissing at this point would be dangerous, but he would renew his assault on her senses every opportunity he got.

*Lannister be damned. I am the better man, and I'll prove it.*

# Chapter Fourteen

AVA'S BALL WAS, as should be expected, a raging success. And Sarah had her first taste of what her new life would be like, participating with the Laynes in greeting their guests. Standing beside the duke and receiving the congratulations of the *ton* en masse was intimidating. For the first time, she thought Robert's idea of holding the wedding at The Castle might have some merit. It would at least limit the number of people she would have to deal with.

She was in part still reeling from Robert's kisses the previous afternoon. And that had come on top of their tumultuous conversation, which had put her through so many emotions that by the end of it she didn't know what she was feeling. She had managed to avoid being alone with him again after that, not a very difficult task as she was caught up with the preparations for the ball, and he, like his brothers, beat a retreat from the feminine chaos.

She had been rather brutal toward him, and he'd taken it better than she would have thought he would. Her anger found outlet in a bluntness that she would never have thought herself capable of previously. He had apologized, and his kisses had devastated her, leaving her more alarmed than ever over her loss of control. It seemed he only had to touch her for her to lose all sense and reason.

She did feel guilty about one thing. She had led him to think she had a partiality for Lannister, which wasn't true. She did like the man, and she was grateful for his kind offer to rescue her from her circumstances, but she wasn't in love with him.

She hadn't been able to resist feeding the duke's ire in regard to him because he seemed to be jealous, and God forgive her, she liked the idea of being able to arouse any such emotion within him! Though she had berated herself quite severely for that lapse. *But if he is jealous, doesn't it mean he cares a little?* her heart prompted. *It's just his possessive pride!* countered her head, determined to think the worst of his motivations. *That doesn't excuse me deceiving him in the matter,* objected her conscience, and she winced internally, ashamed of herself.

Released from the receiving line, she found herself paired with Kenrick for the first dance, as precedence demanded that Robert lead the duchess out, and Hereward therefore Ava, leaving herself for Kenrick.

Kenrick, she had decided, was as audacious as he was charming. This impression was consolidated by the first few minutes on the dance floor with him.

"You're the perfect fit for my brother, you know," he said, twirling her neatly.

"In what way?"

"Well, you're a vicar's daughter, a good girl. Robert is the good one, and I'm the bad one. Hereward is somewhere in the middle."

"I see."

"Rob's the most honorable, upstanding man I've ever met. Irritates the hell out of me that he's my brother, because I can't ever quite measure up. I've made an art form out of doing the wrong thing, and he's the opposite. You know he can't even tell a lie?"

"Oh." Sarah digested that in silence as they moved round the dance floor. If his family were to be believed, Robert was incapable of the sort of duplicity she had accused him of. The evidence was mounting that she had misread his character. *If that was the case* . . . her conscience pricked her further about misleading him as to her feelings for the earl.

"He's a bit pompous and far too serious, but I suppose that is because he's been saddled with looking after the rest of us since he was in short coats. Our father was a charming but rather feckless rogue, a bit like me!" He grinned. "Mind you, he stopped being a rake once he met Mama. Never strayed after that, but his other ways didn't mend much. Still, there's hope for me yet. If the old man can be reformed by love, maybe I can, too?"

She smiled up at him. "I'm sure you can."

"Well, perhaps you have a sister who could take me in hand?"

"I have four sisters."

"Four? I look forward to meeting them," he said with a wicked smile.

"The youngest two are but children yet, Hepzibah is twelve, and Mary is sixteen. Ruth is eighteen, and Deborah is twenty. Deb is the beauty of the family."

"She cannot be more beautiful than you," he said gallantly, turning them in the dance.

She shook her head. "Deb is very sweet, but she is also very practical. She will give you short shrift, I assure you."

"Will she? I can't wait," he said, grinning broadly. It made his eyes dance which would, she reflected, make him very attractive to a certain type of female. She hoped ardently Deb wasn't one of them. She might need to warn Deb against Kenrick. He was dangerous by his own admission.

THREE DANCES LATER, Robert claimed Sarah for the waltz. While he had been busy about his hosting duties, he had been constantly conscious of where she was in the room and itching to get to her side. He was hopeful that he had clawed his way back to a semblance of equilibrium with her, but he was not sanguine as to its lasting.

He had spent quite some time last night tossing and turning, worrying over her feelings for Lannister. The notion filled him with a mixture of fury and a kind of despair. The idea was painful in the extreme. It made his heart ache whenever he thought of it.

He'd risen in the morning with an even stronger determination to win her heart from that worthless rake. He could not believe that when she knew him better, she could fail to see the difference between them. *Surely, she would recognize I am the better man?*

Following Ava's interruption yesterday, he had taken her on a tour of the house and maintained appropriate decorum despite the promptings of his baser instincts. They parted before dinner on amicable enough terms. He hadn't spoken to her again on anything more than commonplace topics until they were ready to receive the guests tonight, when he took her hand and squeezed it encouragingly. He understood it was daunting for her, but she did really well, and he was proud of her and had said so.

Leading her onto the floor now, he said, "Ashford has Ava, thank God. It's dashed taxing having a sister to keep an eye on, and I've got three! Ava is a handful, and I suspect Ingrid will be just as bad. Heather at least should be less of a worry."

"Tell me about them, Heather and Ingrid," she prompted.

"Heather is sweet, though I might be biased. We have always had more of an affinity for each other. Not that I don't love Ava and Ingrid equally as well, but Heather inspires fewer headaches. Ingrid is a little rebel, and Ava just has too much vivacity for her own good and my peace of mind. Heather on the other hand is restful and sweet tempered, gentle."

"Your womanly ideal?"

"I used to think so, but not since I met you," he said ruefully.

"Meaning I am not restful, sweet tempered, and gentle?"

"At the risk of saying something intemperate, no."

"How would you describe me then?"

"You were described to me as a warm, vital, loving creature, with a soft heart and caring nature. Which I have come to think is a fair description."

Sarah flushed with pleasure and smiled. "Whoever said such a lovely thing of me?"

"That I am not prepared to tell you, but I do agree with it." He certainly wasn't going to tell her Lannister had said such a thing. Her reaction might confirm her partiality for him. He pulled her a little closer and wished he could whisk her off into an alcove and kiss her. She looked lovely tonight in a pale-lavender silk gown with lace cap sleeves and a bodice low cut enough to be distracting. Not that it was extreme—Sarah was by far too modest to adopt the very fashionable bodices that were nearly indecent.

He smiled down into her face and their eyes locked.

For an endless moment, time stood still. Her eyes widened slightly, and he felt a surge of something warm pass between them, something like the communion of souls he had so longed for. His chest filled with that warmth, and he forgot to breathe. It seemed to last forever and be over in a moment.

Her cheeks flushed, and she broke the connection by dropping her gaze, and the wrench of it actually made him stumble. His heart thudded hard and the pain beneath his sternum was sharp enough to make him gasp.

"Sarah?" he murmured, his mouth close to her ear, as he fought to recover the rhythm of the music. He glanced up, the movement of the dance had brought them close to a curtained-off alcove. On impulse, he swept her behind the curtain. It was a small space occupied largely by a damaged alabaster statue that was due for repair, hence the curtain to hide it.

He wrapped his arms around her, his hand coming up to cradle the back of her head and press her face into his chest, where his heart thumped and ached. His eyes stung. *What the hell is wrong with me? Am I ill? Having some kind of seizure?*

She leaned against him in silence, her hands resting against the lapels of his jacket. He kissed her hair gently, careful not to disturb her elaborate coiffure of curls and combs.

"Sarah?" he said again softly.

She raised her head, her eyes glinting in the dimness of the alcove, and irresistibly he bent his and kissed her, a soft touch of his lips, trying to recapture that moment of connection. When she responded, his heart lifted, and he deepened the kiss, pulling her closer against him. Heat surged behind his breeches and his body ignited, hot desire flooding his senses.

If he didn't end this soon, he wouldn't be in a fit state to appear in public. But the last thing he wanted to do was end something that felt so good, so right.

As she wrapped her arms round his neck and gave him back kiss for kiss, he lost his head a little and pushed her back against the wall, the kiss escalating to something hungry and devouring. His late-night lewd impulses threatened to break free as desire consumed him in a tingling hot rush. He was hard, burning and aching with desire. For her. He tried and failed to stifle a groan in his throat as he ground himself against her belly. *Oh, Sarah, I want you!*

Her body jerked with what he assumed was alarm, penetrating the fog of desire clouding his mind. He realized with horror what he was doing and pulled back. *Damnation! I have no control where this woman is concerned. What in Hades is making me behave this way?* He stepped away fighting for composure.

"I'm sorry."

The dance was drawing to a close, someone was going to notice their absence. *And here I have been worrying about Ava causing a scene!*

"Please," he waved to her to leave him. "I'll rejoin you in a moment."

She eyed him with a look he couldn't interpret and slipped from the alcove, leaving him to rearrange his breeches and try to think about bills and agriculture. Thank God the wedding was only three weeks away. He was getting eaten up with wanting her and all they'd done was kiss, he'd not touched her anywhere inappropriate. *How the hell am I going to manage the wedding night if I lose control at the smallest provocation?*

Thinking about that didn't help his current predicament. *Bills! How many acres can we put under corn by the middle of the year?*

A few minutes later, order restored to his breeches, he left the alcove looking for Sarah and spotted her with his mother. He would not go there right now. He was still shaken by the events of the last few minutes, and he didn't need his mother's sharp eyes ferreting out his business. It was a shock to realize that it *was* only a few minutes. It had seemed like an eon.

The event felt seismic to him, as if the whole world had shifted around him.

*Did I imagine it?* He began to wonder. Could he have imagined that moment of connection? *Do I want it so badly I am making things up, or did she feel it, too?* He would have sworn in the moment that she did. He fervently hoped that it wasn't his imagination. The moment seemed so fragile, in retrospect, as if it could be blown away in a puff of wind, destroyed by sound or movement. By the infinitesimal ticking of the clock.

*Or by my blundering passion . . .*

Sarah was so innocent; his lack of control frightened her. He was such a beast. And if he started thinking about that, he would have to go behind the curtain again.

FOR THE NEXT three hours, Sarah watched Robert prowling round the ballroom avoiding her. At least she could only conclude that was what he was doing. Each time she thought he might come in her direction, he veered off somewhere else to talk to a guest, to solicit a lady to dance, to talk to his mother or Ava or one of his brothers, or have a discreet word with a servant.

She was rattled by whatever it was that passed between them on the dance floor and then behind the curtain. She had felt a surge of warmth in her breast and something that she could only describe as affinity, as if they clicked in some way. She shook her head, unable to find words to capture the feeling adequately. She desperately wished she had a friend to talk to, to try to make sense of what was happening.

And when he'd swept her behind the curtain and held her in his arms, kissed her hair and whispered her name in such a reverential tone, she'd just melted against him. It was akin to the magic she had felt when they were at Vauxhall, and yet it was different.

At Vauxhall, everything had felt slightly wicked, but this had felt more divine, almost like the feeling she got in church when she prayed.

And then he kissed her, and things were deliciously wicked again.

When he pushed her against the wall, and she could feel the hard heat of him, his body trapping her, his mouth demanding, taking and giving in a way she'd never experienced before, it exhilarated her. The heat and tingling pleasure, the press of his body, the invasion of his tongue, the touch of his lips provoked, carried her to a point she had never been before, a state of desire, where she began to understand why women were often lured into a fallen condition. If Robert had asked her to do something truly wicked just then, she would probably have done it. Not that she really understood exactly what that meant, only that he could have done anything to her, and she would have let him.

Instead, he'd stopped. Pulled away and sent her away. Logically she knew he was protecting her, being a gentleman, yet it had felt like rejection. And now he was avoiding her. *Have I given him a disgust of me by responding so wantonly?* She felt wretched. She so wished she had someone to talk to.

Since her falling out with Daphne, that avenue of confidence was closed to her, and there really wasn't anyone else. She had no close female friends in London, all her friends were at home. Not that they would be any use anyway, all her single female friends would be as clueless as she was, and the married ones had all moved away. The notion of talking to her mama about any of this made her blush with embarrassment.

There was Lady Ashford, she supposed, but really, she was the merest acquaintance. She didn't feel an affinity with her the way she did with Lord Ashford. *Was that wrong?*

As if summoned by her thoughts, Lord Ashford appeared at her elbow with a glass of champagne and a plate of food. "Rob is so busy he sent me to feed you," he said, holding out his offerings.

"Oh!" she said, startled, accepting the glass and plate and finding a seat on a couch against the wall. Ashford joined her. "Thank you," she said jerkily. Her gaze trailed wistfully over Robert, who was standing on the other side of the room, talking to a group of men she knew vaguely by sight but couldn't recall the names of.

"He sent his apologies; he's been caught in a political debate. It's the sort of thing I avoid like the plague, but there is a bill coming up in the house shortly and it's something Robert has an interest in."

"Oh," she said again, realizing that she'd had no idea Robert had political interests, nor what they could be. It wasn't something they had discussed. One more thing she needed to add to her list of wifely or duchess-ly duties.

Turning her attention to the plate he had brought her, she took a sip of the champagne, set the glass on the side table beside the couch and took up the fork on the plate. "Have you eaten, my lord?"

"Yes," he said with a smile. "Tuck in, please."

She forked up a bit of lobster patty for the look of it, although she wasn't really hungry.

"What's wrong?" he asked gently.

She looked up, startled. "Nothing!"

Ashford raised a single eyebrow but said nothing. She set the plate aside with a sigh and picked up the champagne glass. She couldn't confess her premarital troubles with Robert to his best friend. But perhaps she could put a hypothetical to him?

"C-can I ask you a—hypothetical question, my lord? In confidence?"

"Of course. I don't know that I'll be able to answer it, though. But I'll try," he said with a quizzical smile.

She took a large swallow of the champagne to fortify herself.

"If a lady were to—to kiss a gentleman with—enthusiasm, would that give the gentleman a—disgust of her?" she asked in a jerky rush. Her cheeks in flames, she sat twisting the champagne glass nervously.

"Miss Watson—Sarah, if I may?" he said. She peeked at him and nodded. "If the lady were you and the gentleman were Robert, I can tell you, most unequivocally, no. In fact," he added, "at the risk of breaking his confidence, he would most assuredly welcome it."

"Then why is he avoiding me?" she asked wretchedly.

"Ah. I would hazard a guess that he is in duke mode." He went on carefully. "Robert is a very private person; he doesn't share himself easily with other people. There are but a few of us who truly know the man behind the ducal facade. It's a shield of sorts, one he is barely conscious of, I think. I suspect you have pierced that shield in some way, and he has retreated behind it."

"Oh."

"If the two sides of himself have been brought into conflict in this, a public arena, he would instinctively have retreated into ducal mode."

She nodded. "I see. That explains why he was so different at Vauxhall," she murmured. "Wearing a mask, he perhaps felt freer to be himself?"

"Undoubtedly. But to say 'to be himself' is probably not entirely accurate. He is the Duke of Troubridge as much as he is Robert Layne. They are two sides of the same coin. He manages them by having one at the fore in the appropriate situation. He runs into trouble when both surface at the same time or one surfaces in a situation that is inappropriate for it."

"Thank you, Lord Ashford," she said with a smile, proffering her hand.

He took it in both of his. "Please call me Emrys. There is nothing to thank me for. I am his friend and yours, too, if you'll have me."

"Indeed, you are a good friend!"

"He is a good man. Give him a chance, Sarah."

# Chapter Fifteen

T HE BALL RAN very late, and Sarah and Daphne were pressed to stay the night, for the sake of propriety perforce to share a room. Which, given the nature of their strained relationship, was decidedly uncomfortable.

Based on the information Sarah had gleaned this evening, it seemed more and more likely that she had been wrong about Robert and that the blame for her entrapment lay squarely at Daphne's feet. Her fury with the woman had abated not one whit, was in fact more surely stoked. It hurt that someone she had thought a friend should betray her so. It hurt even more because she felt so in need of a female friend to help her sort through her very confused emotions about Robert.

She rolled onto her side away from Daphne and tried to get comfortable. Light from the candle flame on the bedside table danced against the wall. She was tired, her feet and back ached, yet she couldn't sleep.

"Will you never speak to me again, Sarah? It's not very Christian of you."

Sarah bounced up in indignation, her tiredness forgotten. "How dare you invoke Christian principles over me after what you did to me!"

Daphne sat up, pushing her night cap back off her face. "I did it for your own good!"

"You did it for your own benefit! I know exactly to the *shilling* what you stand to gain from it, so don't you dare try to make this about me!" said Sarah.

"With you refusing him in a freak of distemper, what else was I supposed to do? Vicar's daughters don't refuse dukes when they propose! It's unheard of!"

"Well, I did, and you had no right to interfere!"

"It is what Aunt Agnes wanted for you! I cannot believe you would throw over a fortune and the prospect of marriage to a man of Troubridge's quality for some absurd notion that he doesn't care for you! Particularly when it is obvious to the blindest of fools that he is more than a little enamored of you."

"He doesn't care for me!" Sarah's deepest fear burst out. For whatever he said or did, that was the truth she always came back to. *It is my money he wants. He is trying to make the best of it by being nice to me, and heaven help me it is working. I can feel myself falling for him all over again, but what will happen when he gets tired of pretending?* "He isn't enamored of me at all!" she insisted. *Is he?* Unable to resist asking, she said, "What makes you say so?"

"He is a very reserved gentleman, he is not going to wear his heart on his sleeve, Sarah." Daphne retied the strings of her night cap. "Jerome says he truly esteems you, Sarah. He wouldn't have made you an offer if he didn't. He is notoriously fussy."

"Jerome?"

Daphne looked coy. "Ravenshaw."

Daphne's flirtation with the marquess had progressed if they were on first name terms. It was a scandal. Papa would surely not approve of Daphne carrying on with the marquess under Sarah's nose. Which just added to the weight of things she shouldn't forgive Daphne for. But there was no one else to seek guidance from, and she desperately wanted some right now.

"I am aware that the duke has lowered his standards to offer for me," said Sarah stiffly.

"Sarah, that is nonsense!"

"Is it?" Sarah wiped her eyes with the sheet. "Then why did he ignore me for most of the night?" Despite her conversation with Ashford, she wasn't reassured.

"As the host, he was busy with his guests, you couldn't expect him to dance attendance on you all night."

"I didn't—it's just—" she stopped.

Daphne took her hand and patted it. "What? Did something happen between you that has made you think all these dismal thoughts?"

She had never missed her father so much in her life. He would know the right thing to do. She suspected he would prompt her to forgive Daphne, too, even though she wasn't quite ready to do that yet. But she did need her advice.

"He kissed me! And things got a little heated!" said Sarah, blushing furiously. "And then he stopped and sent me away and didn't come near me again all night!"

"Oh, Sarah!"

"Does he have a disgust of me, do you think?"

Daphne smirked, her eyes dancing. "Not at all, you silly girl! He's protecting you of course, and himself, from temptation. The duke is not the sort of man to anticipate his vows."

"Anticipate his—" Sarah broke off, scandalized. "He wouldn't. I wouldn't."

"Of course not, which is why he left you alone. My dear, this is even better than I had hoped for you. Sarah, there really is no need for this long face, I assure you."

"I don't understand what you mean." She had an inkling, but she wanted more plain speaking. She was tired of dancing round the point.

"My dear, hasn't your mama spoken to you about these things?"

Sarah flushed and shook her head. "Mama said that things might be a little painful at first, but that if my husband was considerate, things would be vastly better with time and even enjoyable."

"Did she explain the mechanics at least?" asked Daphne.

"Um, in the broadest terms." Sarah hesitated and added, "Being in the country, I have, um, observed farm animals. Mama said it was similar."

Daphne swallowed, and Sarah just knew she was trying not to laugh, which was mortifying but also funny. She giggled, partly with nervous embarrassment. Which gave Daphne permission to laugh also.

"So, you're in possession of the basic facts but not much else," said Daphne, wiping her eyes.

Sarah plucked at the sheet and took a deep breath. "Yes, I feel as if there is much more to know. Is there?"

"A great deal, my dear, much of which I can't tell you because I don't know myself. My experience is not vast, but I do talk to other ladies, and I do know it can be a great deal better than it was for me at first. Things did improve."

Sarah looked at her slightly puzzled. "Can you explain what you mean by that?"

"Gentlemen have a requirement for regular physical—release. It is considered a wife's duty to provide the means for that. In so doing we may, if so blessed, conceive also."

"So, the duty is double—to provide release as well as children?"

"Indeed. Hubert, my husband, was kind and quite patient with me, but the first time was not felicitous. We eventually reached an accommodation that was satisfying for us both, but it took some time and, ah—experimentation."

Sarah looked at her helplessly. "I still don't know what you're talking about."

Daphne, pink cheeked, waved a hand to cool her cheeks and said, "Well, it turns out that ladies can experience this—ah, release, too! I didn't know that when I was a bride. I thought it was all on the gentleman's side and that ladies were supposed to—endure, I suppose." Sarah widened her eyes and Daphne went on. "The release, my dear, is extremely pleasurable."

"Oh."

"And" she added, as if conveying a deep secret, "it is possible to achieve it alone as well as with a gentleman."

"I don't understand."

"I know, and I'm not going to give you the details. It will be the duke's privilege to introduce you to those pleasures, as I am sure he will."

"Why do you think so?"

"Gentlemen prefer it if the lady participates in the pleasure. It heightens it for them, too."

She recalled the viscount's words: *he would most assuredly welcome it.* That would seem to support Daphne's statement.

"So, you think R—the duke is leaving me alone because he finds me too tempting?"

"Yes."

"Oh. But I'm not the pretty one, that's Deb!" she protested.

"You don't have to be beautiful for a man to find you desirable."

"No?"

Daphne shook her head. "Physical attraction is governed by more than symmetry of features."

"But it surely helps?" Sarah thought of her infatuation with the duke, provoked almost entirely, originally, by his considerable good looks. She was beginning to feel very shallow.

"Certainly. One has to find the other person desirable, and beauty can enhance that likelihood, but there is a factor that cannot be calculated for, an instinctive thing." Daphne flushed again. "It can overwhelm one in an instant and be very powerful, and have nothing whatever to do with the other person's appearance."

"Oh." Sarah considered that moment in the duke's arms when she felt that rush of warmth, that instant of soul connection. And then moments later, the rising desire that made her want to do wicked things. She still wasn't sure what those things were really, she only knew the feel of his body pressed against hers had made her frantic for something more. More kisses, more touches, more of his hard heat and something to assuage the aching tingle between her legs.

She began to understand that if she felt that way it was not beyond the realm of possibility that the duke felt the desire to *put* something between her legs. She flushed all over with that notion. That hot, hard something she'd felt pressing into her belly.

"Thank you, Daphne, I think I understand a little better now." She sank back against the pillows. "But does any of this have anything to do with love?"

"In the best of all possible worlds, yes, but regrettably it often does not. At least not for gentlemen. Men," said Daphne with emphasis, "require regular release and will often seek it wherever it is available. Emotions frequently play little to no part in that process. That is why many gentlemen keep a mistress, for that very purpose."

"I–I see. Does the duke have a—"

"Mistress? I believe so. She is rumored to have a house in Clarges Street, paid for by the duke naturally. Her name, I understand, is Madeleine."

"Do married gentlemen keep a mistress also?"

"Some do, some don't."

"I see."

"Don't ask him, my dear. It's not the done thing for a wife to acknowledge that she knows about her husband's mistress."

"And yet the wife is expected to tolerate this?"

"Yes. In marriages of convenience, it is quite common for both partners to seek pleasure outside the marriage, once the wife has done her duty of course."

"Her duty?"

"Ensured the succession."

"I see," Sarah clenched her hands on the sheet. He had offered her a marriage of convenience—in his own words! *He no doubt assumed I knew what that meant!*

"I only tell you this to save you from the shock later, should it turn out that the duke . . ."

"Yes, I see. Thank you, Daphne," said Sarah, her voice shaking. "I cannot believe that Papa keeps a mistress."

"Oh, I shouldn't think so. He is a man of the cloth, after all, and a devout one. He is quite devoted to your mother." Daphne patted her hand. "It is much more common among the upper classes, where the gentlemen can afford it. Keeping a mistress is expensive."

"Expensive."

"Yes, there is the house, servants, a carriage, clothes, jewelry, all paid for by the woman's protector. But I shouldn't think it is something you need concern yourself about in the immediate future, Sarah. The duke strikes me as the sort of man who will keep his vows at least until he has an heir and the succession is properly secured. By that time, you may have snared him deeply enough that he won't stray at all."

"But if he still has a mistress now?"

"That is only a rumor, I don't know if it is true."

"It is a quite specific and detailed rumor for an untruth."

"For all I know, he may have given her up. Given her a congé."

"Congé?"

"Farewell gift. A substantial payment to secure her comfort until she can find another protector."

"I see." Sarah felt ill and very weary. "I think it is time I went to sleep," she said, sliding down the bed and rolling onto her side.

"Good night, my dear, and try not to worry so much about the duke. I believe all the signs are very positive that he esteems you highly. I am confident you will find great felicity in your marriage with him, Sarah. He is a good man." For the third time that night, she heard that term applied to the duke.

But he had offered her *a marriage of convenience*. She swallowed, her throat tightening. She would not cry, could not, for if Daphne heard her, she would demand to know what was wrong.

And Sarah was too ashamed to tell her that she was so hopelessly in love with the duke that the notion he wanted a marriage of convenience made her ill.

In the morning she slept very late, but then so did the rest of the household. Daphne was still asleep when she went down to breakfast, and she met only the servants, being informed that the duchess and Lady Ava were having trays in their rooms and the Layne men had all breakfasted earlier and gone riding in the park.

After a light breakfast, she went in search of some quiet reading to soothe her troubled heart and ventured into the library. She found a book and curled up on one of the sofas. A few minutes later, she became conscious of a purring noise and looked down to see an exquisite little black cat with a torn ear and emerald-green eyes rubbing herself against the sofa.

"Gosh, where did you spring from?" she asked, bending to pat the creature. The little cat uttered a *mrrp* noise and leaped up into her lap where she proceeded to knead and circle, rubbing her face against Sarah's hand.

"Sarah?" The duke's voice behind her made her start. She looked round and he came toward her. "I trust you slept well?" he asked, bending to kiss her cheek before she could react. "Ah, I see you've made Em's acquaintance."

"Em?"

"Emerald," he said, petting and scratching the cat under her chin.

"I didn't know you had a cat."

"She is a fairly recent acquisition." He picked her up and cuddled her, she even let him roll her onto her back and pat her tummy. Sarah stared at this side of him she had never seen before. "She found me on the steps of the Levington's house waiting for my carriage and inveigled me into bringing her home."

"She's a stray?"

"Yes, poor thing. She had this ratty ear and was thin as a rake. No longer so skinny now though, are you madam?" he said, rubbing her tummy.

Sarah gaped at him. After the revelations from Daphne last night, she was in a muddle about how she felt about him. And this was just another piece of the puzzle to confuse her more.

He sat down beside her still holding the cat. "Mama and Ava will be leaving for The Castle in a few days to get the wedding preparations underway. I thought that would be a good time for us to visit your parents. I've already written to your father. Do you think you could be ready to travel on Thursday?"

"I suppose so," she said, feeling winded.

"If we leave early, we should be able to make it in one day. It will be tiring but better than staying somewhere overnight, I think. My carriage is well sprung, and with a team of four we should make good time. What do you think?"

"Ah—yes. Yes, it will be wonderful to see my family." The thought of seeing them again made her heart surge with joy.

"Good." He put down the cat and kissed her hand. "I look forward to meeting them very much." He said it with such a warm smile, her heart turned over in her breast. *He is doing it again! Charming me into falling for him, and I must not!* She needed to remember this was a marriage of convenience. She was giving him her money. He was giving her a title—not that she wanted one—but that was all he was offering. She thought about the faceless Madeleine and felt sick.

# Chapter Sixteen

ROBERT STEPPED DOWN from the carriage and turned to help Sarah to alight, followed by Lady Holbrook, who had accompanied them on this journey into Hampshire so that he could meet Sarah's family.

The trip into Hampshire had taken a full day, and it was just on dusk as the duke's carriage drew up outside the vicarage. The church, dedicated to St. Catherine, stood to the right of the vicarage. Both buildings were at least sixteenth century or earlier by the look of them. The vicarage door opened and out poured three young ladies, a little girl and three little boys.

Within moments, Sarah was surrounded by this vociferous herd, all of them talking at once, it seemed to Robert's overwhelmed senses. Added to the confusion was a white fluffy dog of indeterminate pedigree, whose excited barks, leaps of joy, and wagging tail created even more chaos. He tried for a moment to work out who was who from Sarah's descriptions of them, but he soon gave up. Looking over Sarah's head toward the vicarage doorway, he spied a middle-aged man and a woman who must be her parents. Making his way around the Watson brood, he approached the front entrance of the thatch-roofed, stone-built house.

"Mr. and Mrs. Watson?" He offered his hand. "I am very

pleased to make your acquaintance. Robert Layne at your service."

"Your Grace," Mrs. Watson curtsied, obviously flustered, and the vicar, a little more collected than his wife, inclined his head, shaking the hand that Robert offered.

Sarah resembled her mother, with brown curls and eyes and a comely face. Mrs. Watson showed the thickening of figure to be expected of a woman who had born at least eight children. The vicar was of medium height and spare frame with thinning hair, grey eyes, and a rather beaky nose.

"Will Your Grace be joining us for supper? It is only plain fare—"

"I will be delighted to accept your hospitality, Mrs. Watson, and well pleased with whatever is put before me," Robert hastened to reassure her. The last thing he intended was to play the grand duke for his future in-laws. "You need not be concerned about where to put me, either. Lady Holbrook and I will both be staying at the Blue Boar for the night."

Mrs. Watson's sigh of relief was audible. "Thank the Lord for that, Your Grace, I was at my wits' end, for with eight children we haven't the room for guests."

He smiled and glanced back at Sarah whose welcoming committee was bearing her inexorably forward toward the door.

"Watsons!" said the vicar sharply. This command had a magical effect, for all the children stopped talking and lined up from eldest to youngest, even Sarah with the dog in her arms, and chorused, "Yes, Papa."

Robert's lips twitched. Mr. Watson might look mild-mannered, but he clearly still held sway over his brood. "Introduce yourselves to His Grace."

At this command, Sarah stepped out of the line and joined him with a shy smile, murmuring, "They are a bit overwhelming. I'm sorry."

"Don't be," he murmured back as he turned his attention to the children.

"I am Deborah," said a striking young woman with dark ringlets and blue eyes, dropping a graceful curtsy.

"I am Ruth." With her father's unfortunate nose and pale blue eyes, she was less comely than her sisters, and her curtsy was awkward.

"Mary," said the next one, whose rounded face and burgeoning figure suggested she was on the cusp of womanhood.

"Hepzibah!" said the youngest of the girls with a certain air of world weariness. "But please call me Zibby, for I hate Hepzibah!" She was still a child, and she was the fairest in coloring with blonde curls and the same pale blue eyes as her elder sister.

Next came the three boys who each gave him a neat bow as they rattled off their names.

"Emanuel." Brown hair and brown eyed like Sarah.

"Japheth." Dark like Deborah.

"Ezekiel." Blonde like Hepzibah.

The biblical nature of their names wasn't lost on him.

"I am very pleased to meet you all," he said gravely.

"Are you really a duke?" asked Ezekiel with a wide-eyed look.

"I am."

"You don't look like one," Japheth said skeptically.

"Shut it, you two!" said Emanuel, flushing with embarrassment for his younger brothers.

"Are you really going to marry Sarah and take her away to live in your castle?" This from Zibby.

"Yes, I am." He glanced sideways at Sarah who was smiling slightly tearfully. He took her hand and squeezed it gently.

"I think it is very romantic," said Mary softly and blushed bright crimson.

"That is enough, children. Go and wash up. Supper will be on the table in fifteen minutes." Their mother intervened before any more embarrassing questions could be asked.

The children filed into the house and the younger ones ran noisily up the stairs. He suspected none of them did anything quietly. With the children out of the way, Mr. and Mrs. Watson greeted Lady Holbrook and ushered their guests into the house, followed by the eldest two girls who were clearly adults. *Hadn't Sarah said they were twenty and eighteen?* They bore Sarah and Lady Holbrook away upstairs to put off their bonnets and traveling cloaks and wash up, while Robert was conducted to the vicar's study, and Mrs. Watson disappeared toward the back of the house, no doubt to see about supper.

"Would you care for a drink, Your Grace?"

"Yes, thank you."

Robert accepted the glass of sherry handed to him and took the seat he was waved to near the fire.

"This is certainly an unexpected turn of events," said the vicar, taking his own seat and nursing his drink. "While we always hoped our Sarah would make a good match, we never expected one of this magnitude. You'll forgive us if we appear a little stunned."

"I understand, sir. It has all transpired rather quickly."

"Indeed." The vicar took a sip of his sherry and cleared his throat. "In addition to your letter, I have received communication from my aunt's solicitor regarding the settlements. The settlements are far more generous than I anticipated."

"It turns out that the amounts were tied to the degree of Sarah's husband's title, and I'm a duke. Short of a royal prince there isn't a higher degree, therefore the maximum amounts have been settled on your family, Lady Holbrook, and Sarah, or they will be once the marriage is deemed legally binding. At that time, I will, as Sarah's husband, also receive access to the remaining principal and income from the estate."

"Hence the rapidity with which this process is being put into effect."

Robert winced internally but simply nodded. *What could he say?*

"Tell me, Your Grace, do you care for my daughter at all, or is it merely her fortune that you covet?" The vicar eyed him with a grim look. *Easy to see where Sarah got her directness from!*

"I will not pretend that her fortune wasn't a consideration. My circumstances made it imperative that I secure a bride with a significant income. However, I had a choice, and I chose Sarah for a number of reasons that have nothing to do with her fortune."

"Which are?" The other man leaned forward, spearing Robert with a look that reminded him strongly of Sarah.

"Unusual in someone of my station, I had always the intention to marry for love. When my circumstances forced me to consider a marriage based on more worldly grounds, I was resigned to the prospect that love might not be an option." He paused and took a sip of the sherry, looking down at the dark liquid, whose color reminded him of Sarah's eyes. He looked up again and met the vicar's gaze firmly. "I have, however, on becoming better acquainted with Sarah, formed the opinion that it is not impossible that we might find felicity in each other's company. I do most sincerely esteem and respect her; she is an extraordinary young woman, and I will be proud to call her my duchess."

The older man regarded him in silence for a moment, appearing to deliberate on what he had said. The vicar inclined his head.

"Thank you for your honesty, Your Grace."

"Please call me Robert. I do not wish to stand upon ceremony with you. I can assure you that Sarah will meet with only kindness in my house. My family already like her and are prepared to welcome her with open arms. Her comfort and happiness will be my highest priority."

The sound of a bell ringing made the vicar rise. "Supper is ready. Again, I thank you for your honesty, Robert. You have gone some way to allaying a father's concerns, but I will speak to Sarah and ensure myself of her acquiescence to this plan for her future."

Robert bowed and opened the door for his prospective father-in-law, his heart sinking a little. While he and Sarah had achieved a better accord over the past two weeks than they had initially, following that disastrous event at Lady Castlereagh's ball, he was by no means certain that she was completely reconciled to the situation.

Things had become strained between them again following Ava's ball. He had pulled back from any further intimacy with her due to his fear of losing control of himself again, and she had seemed to withdraw also, perhaps in response. Her withdrawal gave him that by now familiar ache in his chest that seemed to afflict him almost perpetually where she was concerned. He had found the gap created was difficult to bridge. He hoped that perhaps here, or once they were home at The Castle, he could begin to repair the damage.

There was also the matter of her feelings for Lannister. As much as he tried to tell himself that she couldn't possibly entertain any, he couldn't rid himself of the fear of it, which also left him with a sick feeling in his stomach and it made him uncertain in approaching her on the subject. If he were really honest with himself, he didn't want to find out if it was true. Every time he thought of it, he suffered an internal flinch.

What he did know was that they had a powerful physical connection, which he was constrained from pursuing for fear of overstepping the bounds of propriety and frightening her. That she was exceptionally innocent, he had no doubt, which roused protective instincts in him and also made him uncomfortable about his own level of passion toward her. He couldn't touch her without entertaining lewd thoughts, her very scent aroused him, the aching longing to take her in his arms and devour her with kisses was a constant desire.

And to make matters worse, he still had no real idea of how she felt about him, Lannister aside. *If she told her father that she wasn't a willing party to this marriage, would he encourage her to break off the engagement, despite the social risks to the family and the financial costs?* Watson was not materially driven any more than Sarah was. Robert could see he was idealistic enough to sacrifice his family's material wealth for Sarah's happiness.

# Chapter Seventeen

For Sarah, to be home again was bittersweet and made her heart ache. She was happy and sad at the same time. She had missed them so, and to know that she could no longer call this house her home sent a pang through her that robbed her of breath.

Her initial fury with both the duke and Daphne had been tempered by discussions with each one. It had been born in upon her that her assumption that the duke was complicit with Daphne in entrapping her was likely not the case. According to his family, he wasn't even capable of that kind of duplicity. That Daphne was, and for such mercenary purposes, still galled her.

Daphne's revelations about the existence of the duke's mistress and her realization that his intention all along was to offer her a marriage of convenience—now that she understood what that meant—had put a different complexion on things again. If Daphne was to be believed, the duke's physical attraction to her was nothing more than a normal male response to an available female for whom he felt a certain degree of physical attraction. It did not denote burgeoning feelings for her.

In short, he didn't love her and likely never would. He would treat her with courtesy and respect, kindness even. But he would not love her. She did not resemble the mythical, ideal woman of his dreams. He had quite bluntly told her so. She was not restful, sweet-tempered, and gentle.

"Are you happy, Sesi?" asked Ruth, breaking in on her dark thoughts. Her sisters had conducted Daphne to another room to refresh herself from the journey and rejoined her in her own room.

Deb perched on the bed and regarded her with a frown. "You don't look happy."

Sarah wrung out the cloth she was using to wipe her face and pushed down her instinct to confide in her sisters. They stood to benefit from this marriage significantly, and what was done was done, after all. She couldn't change it now; her fate was sealed. So she said as brightly as she could manage, "I am happy. It is wonderful to be home, I am just a little fatigued from the journey."

"Well, he's very handsome," allowed Ruth.

Sarah smiled perfunctorily. *Yes, he is.*

"Does he treat you kindly?" asked Deb, watching her like a hawk.

"Yes, he does," she had to admit.

"Do you love him?" asked Mary from her place by the door. Mary was sixteen and romantic.

"This is a marriage of convenience, Mary. Love has nothing to do with it." Deborah spoke firmly.

"He looks just like a storybook hero," said Mary defiantly. "And he squeezed your hand. I saw it!"

Sarah dropped the cloth back into the water, picking up the towel to dry her face and neck. "He knew that I was happy-sad to be home. He was trying to comfort me, I think," she admitted, surprised by the evident truth of that. He *was* considerate of her feelings in many ways. *Now that he has what he wants . . .*

"Are you sure you can go through with it?" asked Deborah, rising and seizing her arms to scan her face.

"Oh, yes," said Sarah calmly. "His family have been very nice to me. I shall manage quite well once I become accustomed, I daresay." She swallowed the lump in her throat, but it didn't stem the tears that spilled over, and Deborah folded her in her arms.

"Don't do it if it's going to make you miserable, Sesi!" she said fiercely.

"No, it isn't that. I shall just miss you all so much, not living here anymore!" Sarah gulped on a sob and tried to wipe her eyes as her sisters crowded round her and Mary offered her a handkerchief.

⇛⇚

SUPPER WAS A boisterous affair, which Robert surmised was normal for the Watsons. Lady Holbrook seemed unperturbed. As the vicar's cousin, she was presumably used to it. The small fry were vastly entertaining, but most of his attention was on Sarah, who was seated beside him.

The redness of her eyes told him she had been crying, and he was anxious as to the reason. *Was she thinking of crying off in spite of all? Or was it an excess of sensibility at being home again?* He must contrive to get her alone and seek to comfort and reassure her. The thought of her distress made his chest ache.

Following supper, however, he was frustrated by Sarah disappearing with her father. *Will she tell him she doesn't want to proceed with the wedding?*

⇛⇚

PAPA SHOWED HER into his study and waved her to the couch. She sank down on it and he joined her, taking her hands.

"Now, Sesi, I want the truth. Are you happy? Because you don't look it," he said, fixing her with his familiar stare, both kind and piercing. It was too much, and despite her resolve to tell him everything was fine, she burst into tears.

"Oh, my darling girl." He drew her close and comforted her.

161

"There, there, sweetheart, you don't have to do anything you don't wish to. You know that, don't you?"

"I've missed you so, Papa!" she sobbed into his shoulder. "And I've been so wicked!"

"Now that I don't believe," he said, rubbing her back as if she were five and had scraped a knee. He fumbled in a pocket and produced a handkerchief for her as she sniffed and tried to wipe her eyes.

"It's true!" she bawled into the handkerchief.

"Well, I'm not a Catholic priest, but I'll listen to your litany of sins if you wish to unburden yourself, my dear."

She sniffed, wiping her face, and blew her nose. "I have been so angry, Papa, and suspicious and unforgiving. And I've told lies!" she added conscientiously.

"I see. Anything else?"

"Yes, Papa," she whispered.

He waited, and she gathered her courage and, blushing furiously, her eyes on her lap, said, "I've been tempted by desire."

"Well, let us take each of those one at a time, shall we?" he said, letting go of one of her hands and tilting her chin up so she would look at him. She blinked wetly at him and nodded, sniffing.

"Firstly, what have you been angry about?"

"I was angry with Daphne and the duke. I thought he had done something to deceive me, but I've since learned it probably wasn't the case. I'd rather not reveal what Daphne did, but it made me angry, and I wasn't able to forgive her for days. In fact, I still haven't completely."

"I see. Well, anger is a normal emotional reaction to being wronged by others. It is not wrong to feel anger, child. It's what you do when you're angry that makes the sin. And to continue to nurse anger and unforgiveness indefinitely often hurts the angry person more greatly than the person it's directed at."

She swallowed and nodded, wiping her eyes which were still leaking. "This is why I've missed you, Papa—your wisdom. You always set me straight."

"Very well, then let us take the next thing—lying. What have you lied about and to whom and, more importantly, why?"

"I led the duke to think I may have a partiality for another when I do not, because"—she looked down at this and whispered, because she felt so truly ashamed of this one—"I wanted to make him jealous just a little."

Silence greeted this, and she eventually peeked at Papa to see what he was doing. His lips were curved in a slight smile.

"Why are you smiling?" she asked, half accusing, half baffled.

"If we were all sent to hell for that one, my dear, there would be no one in heaven."

"Truly, Papa? But it was wrong!"

"Yes, it was wrong, my dear, but I have to ask, did it work?"

"I think so, yes," she admitted reluctantly, remembering Robert's show of possessiveness. Even if it was just driven by a proprietary sense within him, it still made her feel wanted and protected.

"Now we get to the serious one," he said. "Ah, no hiding." He nudged up her chin again. "What has he done?"

She flushed. "Nothing but kisses, Papa, I promise. The duke is very proper, and he has treated me with nothing but respect."

"I'm glad to hear it. So what are you concerned about?"

She squirmed. Really, discussing this with a parent was so uncomfortable. "I think I understand now why girls become fallen women. Kisses feel so nice, Papa," she admitted in a rush.

"Well, yes, they do, with the right person. If you've come to that realization, you can advise your sisters and warn them what to be careful of. Your mother, bless her, is not up to the task. Been worrying me terribly having you exposed to all that corruption in London and no one to advise and protect you but Daphne and your own common sense." He smiled and hugged her.

She hugged him back and sniffled.

"Which brings me to one final question, Sesi. Do you want to marry him?" He waited a moment, and when she didn't answer, he went on, "If you do not, you have no need to worry about what it means for the family. I won't have you sacrificed for worldly gain. Do you want to be a duchess, Sarah?"

"Not—not especially," she admitted.

"Well then, there is nothing more to be said." He prepared to rise, and she grabbed his arm.

"I don't especially wish to be a duchess, but I think I do want to marry Robert," she said quickly. Papa didn't know about the incident at Lady Castlereagh's ball, and he probably wouldn't understand the ramifications, either, of her calling off the wedding, the social ruin that would follow. For good or ill, the die was cast. She'd made her decision, and she did want to see it through, not least for her family's sake.

And confessing some of her transgressions, if not all of them, to Papa had relieved her conscience somewhat, and just talking to him had made her feel better about everything. She really had missed him dreadfully. The prospect of being separated from him on a more or less permanent basis going forward made her heart ache, but her marriage to the duke was for the best and perhaps not as awful as she had previously thought it might be.

He smiled, and this time his eyes teared up. "My baby girl is truly grown up now. Dearest girl, I do so wish you every happiness." He hugged her again. "I believe the duke will make you an admirable husband. He seems a fine upstanding fellow.

"I've done a little research on him, you know, as soon as I received his letter informing me of your betrothal. I couldn't find anyone with a bad word to say about him. Except that he is a little formal and proud, which is to be expected of someone of his social standing. And I have to say that the little I've seen of him so far has shown him to be far less high in the instep than I expected."

She smiled tearily at him and hugged him. "Thank you, Papa." The last thing she was ever going to tell Papa was about Robert's mistress. *If he knew about that . . .*

SARAH AND THE vicar were gone for a good half hour, during which time Robert made awkward conversation with Mrs. Watson, Lady Holbrook, and the two eldest girls.

He rose as soon as Sarah entered the room with her father and noted with alarm that her eyes were red. *More tears!* He took a step toward her but addressed Mr. Watson. "May I have a few moments alone with Sarah?"

Watson glanced at his wife, and then nodded.

"The back parlor is unoccupied," said Mrs. Watson.

He looked at Sarah. "Will you?"

She gave him a small, painful smile and turned back toward the door. He accompanied her down the hall, noting the slightly threadbare nature of the runner. Everything was spotlessly clean, but he couldn't help but notice the worn furnishings and scratched and battered furniture.

They entered the back parlor which was lit by a single candelabra on a side table. There was no fire, so the air was chilly, and Sarah pulled her shawl more tightly round her shoulders. He closed the door and turned to take her hands.

"You're upset. What is it?"

"This is the last time I will live in this house; I had not expected—I shall miss it and my family." She avoided his eyes.

"You will still see them any time you wish. You don't think I would keep you from them, do you?"

She looked up at him, blinking in the poor light. "I don't know. Once we are married, I don't know what level of autonomy I will have, if any. The role of duchess is demanding. This has all happened so quickly, I am not sure of anything." The expression of confusion in her eyes smote him in the chest.

"Sarah, I would never—" He stopped, his throat suddenly tight with emotion. "My family is very important to me, and I would have to be blind and insensitive to an extraordinary degree not to see how important yours is to you. I would never seek to separate you from them."

She lowered her eyes. "Thank you."

He nudged her chin up with a finger so she would look at him. "Why would you think I would do such a thing?"

She shook her head, her throat working and the ready tears spilling over.

"Oh, Sarah!" He gathered her into his embrace and held her close, his cheek resting against her hair. "I know we got off on the wrong foot, but surely we can do better than this? I hate to see you so upset, especially if I am the cause. Tell me what I can do to rectify it."

"N-nothing!" She wiped her eyes. "I just didn't understand why you stayed away from me at Ava's ball after—after—" She flushed.

"Ah!" Comprehension dawned on him, and he flushed, too. "You're too much temptation, Sarah, and I was afraid I had frightened you," he confessed.

"Oh!" She looked down and then up. She smiled shyly, and the expression was so sweet he couldn't resist dipping his head and kissing her. He meant it for a comforting kiss, a quick and gentle kiss and hug. It quickly degenerated into something else as she leaned up into his kiss and his arms tightened round her.

His tongue delved beyond the barrier of her lips to explore her mouth more deeply as she responded to him, inching her arms up round his neck and enabling him to pull her closer against him. *Sarah. Sarah. My beautiful Sarah.*

A groan in his throat came involuntarily as his body ignited once more with a flood of heated desire. His senses melted into tingling, delicious, aching need. This happened every time he touched her. He could feel every curving, soft, delectable inch of her body through her clothes as this time she molded herself to him, and his own hard heat responded fiercely.

*Is she getting accustomed to our heated kisses?* As he plundered her mouth with his tongue, he shifted his hold on her to pull her even tighter against him.

He pressed his hard cock into her belly, and he groaned in delight when she pressed back. *Yes, Sarah, yes.* Her breath was coming in quick pants, little noises in her throat, like whimpers of need, as he kissed her and kissed her, losing himself in her mouth.

His hands ran over her body, unable to keep as chaste as he had before. He wanted her closer, he wanted her naked beneath him, with her legs spread. He wanted to touch her and pleasure her and make her explode . . .

He groaned, panting. *Fuck, I have to stop, or I'll be the one doing the exploding.*

He finally broke the kiss reluctantly, diving back in for one more, and one more. Breathing heavily, he scanned her flushed face. *God, she is so exquisitely beautiful.*

"I want you, Sarah," he said, husky voiced and panting. "I hope that is ample evidence of the fact that you are more temptation than I can easily withstand."

She blinked at him as if surfacing from a dream, her breathing as ragged as his.

Getting control of himself, he pulled back a fraction and stroked a curl off her cheek. Smiling, he cupped her jaw and planted a soft kiss on her forehead.

"As much as I want to, I can't ravish you in your parents' parlor. Whatever else you believe, I hope that you now understand that my desire for you is not feigned?"

She nodded. "Yes," she said huskily.

"It is my sincere wish that we deal together better than we have to date. I want our marriage to be a success, Sarah. Will we rejoin your family now?"

She nodded and they left the room together, her hand tucked into his arm.

They found a game of spillkins in full flight and the duke got down on the floor to join in, much to the delight of the children and, judging from Sarah's expression, her surprise. He grinned and winked at her. The game lasted until the vicar intervened and sent the small fry off to bed, leaving the adults to conversation. After the tea tray, he took his leave with Lady Holbrook and repaired to the nearby Blue Boar for the night, not unpleased with the way the day had ended.

# Chapter Eighteen

S ARAH RETIRED TO her room, hugging the intensity of his kisses and the desire he aroused in her body to herself. Whether he had a mistress or not, he'd made it amply clear he meant to share her bed when they were married and that he was impatient for that moment to arrive. She had to admit she was growing impatient for that, too. His kisses were so addictive.

It would be so tempting to think this meant he had stronger feelings for her, but she was mindful of Daphne's warning that it wasn't the same for gentlemen, that they could feel all this desire without it meaning they cared for the person who aroused it. For herself, it was becoming more and more difficult to resist caring for him. In fact, if she was honest, it was a losing battle. Her feelings threatened to swamp her.

It took a long time for her to go to sleep. Her body was keyed up in a way that made her restless and achy. The tingling desire between her legs gradually subsided, but she still felt as if she needed something and didn't know what it was.

She dreamed of something that made her body tingle and explode with pleasure, but the memory faded before morning.

ROBERT HAD SENT Bridges, Esme, and Fleur, Lady Holbrook's maid, on ahead to The Castle in a separate carriage with the bulk of their luggage, so he was forced to undress and dress himself, but as he was trying to cultivate a casual and relaxed air with the Watsons, he was not too concerned about his appearance. Lady Holbrook had stayed at the Blue Boar today, nursing a headache.

The kissing session with Sarah necessitated a session later with his hand, and after attempts to avoid thinking of Sarah failed, he gave in and did think of her, in lewd detail. The sooner they were married the better.

Breakfast with the Watsons was as chaotic as supper, and afterward he found himself drawn into one of those backyard cricket matches Sarah had told him about. It was a fine day, perfect for a game, and memories from Eton came tumbling back. But those matches had been played entirely between teams of boys. It was a different experience to have teams half made up of girls and all with such a variety of ages. With six players a side, and three of the neighbor's children joining the fray, he was appointed captain of one team and Sarah the other. So much for ducal dignity.

Sarah won the toss and elected to bat. Advancing to the crease with her bat, dressed in a plain cotton gown with her hair bundled up under her sun hat, she waited with the relaxed air of a veteran for him to bowl. He had to admire her sangfroid. His first impulse was to bowl wide so he would be sure to avoid hitting her—it felt wrong to pelt a ball at speed toward a defenseless woman—but it was obvious that Sarah expected him to throw the ball so she could hit it, and he had to assume she could.

With his team distributed around the field—they were playing on the open lot behind the vicarage—he wound up to bowl and launched the ball toward the wicket standing behind her.

She hit the ball square on with a crack and sent it flying to the trees.

"Run, Japh!" she shouted. She and Japheth made four runs while his team scrambled to retrieve the ball and get it to

Emanuel, his wicket keeper.

Fronting up to the crease again, she grinned at him and said, "Didn't think I could hit it, did you?"

Almost breathless with admiration, he made a recovery and retorted, "You're on notice, Miss Watson. The Layne honor is at stake—watch your wicket!"

He kept her scoreless for the rest of the over, but by the time he managed to bowl her out, she'd scored twelve runs in total and Japh three. Mary replaced Sarah at the crease and proved almost as good as her sister. He surrendered the ball to Emanuel to let him get his brother out, and when little Zeke stepped up to bat, Sarah helped him. Once he'd got Mary out, the batting side collapsed, and they stopped for lunch.

Mrs. Watson brought out pies, sandwiches, and cake to feed the hoard under the trees, and he sat beside Sarah on a rug and tried to remember when he had enjoyed a morning more in his life. She was very different in her home surroundings. More relaxed and confident, happier. She smiled a great deal more and laughed a lot.

"You're very good," he said, toasting her with lemonade.

"Admit it, you were surprised I could hit the ball at all!" she teased.

"You're right, I was. I will never underestimate you again."

She smiled and was going to say something else when an argument between the boys distracted her.

"Japh, apologize, please."

"But he took my piece of cake!"

"Emanuel?"

Emanuel sighed, rolling his eyes. "He wasn't eating it!"

"I was saving it!"

"In that case, return his cake and you can both apologize."

The boys obeyed her with a show of reluctance, and peace was restored.

She then spent the next several minutes ensuring all the children had their fair share of food and drink, that Mary put her hat back on to protect her complexion, and stopped Emanuel from pulling his twin, Hepzibah's, hair.

He was conscious, lying on his side, propped on an elbow, of a very strong desire to pull her close and kiss her. It was impossible of course, but the impulse was distractingly difficult to shift. She had never appeared more attractive or desirable to him than she did in that moment, and he was reminded of Lannister's description of her again with a pang. *Vital and warm.* She was that in abundance, and he'd not really seen it in London. The formality of the *ton*, which he took for granted, stifled her natural vivacity.

The game was abandoned for the rest of the day because the elder girls had visits to make to parishioners and errands to run.

As he helped Sarah pack away the luncheon things, she said with a rueful smile, "I would normally be doing that, but Mama says I must stay and entertain you."

"Of that I am very glad," he said.

"Perhaps I can show you round the village?" she said, handing him the folded rugs to carry. "Littledon is not large."

"I'd be delighted," he said, happy for her to dispose of his day as she saw fit. As long as he got to spend it with her, he didn't mind what they did.

She took him on a loop of the village commencing down Church Lane toward the river and the mill. From there they walked along the riverbank under the trees. It was very peaceful with the trickle of the water over the rocks, much quieter than the loud rush of the mill race they had left behind. The occasional call of a bird or buzz of an insect disturbed the drowsy afternoon. She picked up a flat stone and skipped it across the surface of the water. It got halfway across before it disappeared.

"We used to see how far across we could get the stones to go before they sank when we were children," she said, picking up another stone and trying again. "I'm out of practice. I used to be able to get it all the way across."

He picked up one, and it hit a rock and bounced into the

water. "It would be easier if the surface of the water were entirely flat. Why do it here where there are so many exposed rocks?"

"That's part of the challenge, avoiding the rocks. We started with flat water and worked our way up."

"I see." He picked up another stone and tried again. He did better this time and got halfway across, but she was still beating him. Another three goes, and he thought he could catch her. "Another go?" he said.

She nodded, "Best of three?"

They each found three nice flat stones and took it in turns. He beat her on the first, she beat him on the second.

"The decider," she said.

"Loser pays a forfeit," he said with a smile.

She cocked her head. "Very well. If you lose, Sir Knight, you must collect me a posy of wildflowers from the field over there."

"And if you lose, you give me a kiss and I will carry you all the way to that bridge." He waved to the stone bridge fifty yards ahead of them.

She blushed. "Carrying me hardly seems like a reward for you."

"It will be," he said, stepping closer. "I get to put my arms round you." He slid an arm round her waist, drawing her against his chest.

She raised her eyebrows. "You haven't won yet, Your Grace." She slipped out of his embrace and threw her stone. It got more than three quarters of the way across. "There, beat that!" She gave him a saucy smile.

He took careful aim and watched as his stone skipped and bounced artfully over the expanse of the river and dropped from sight in roughly the same spot as hers.

"A draw," she said. "Neither of us won, no forfeits paid."

"On the contrary, both forfeits should be paid," he said, determined to get his reward. "Stay there, I will fetch your posy."

He plunged off into the field full of wildflowers and picked her a generous bunch of purple, pink, yellow, white, and red blooms. Bringing it back, he presented it to her with a low bow.

She giggled and took it. "Thank you, Sir Knight."

"Now for my kiss," he said, wrapping his arms round her and drawing her close. She wrapped her arms round his neck, the posy clutched in one hand.

"I've been wanting to do this all day," he murmured, lowering his head and finding her lips. Determined to take his time and savor it, he took it slowly, brushing his lips lightly over hers, pulling her closer, teasing her lips apart and exploring with his tongue.

He couldn't suppress the groan in his throat, she was so delicious. His hands roamed over her back and lower to squeeze her bottom, pressing her belly against his hardening cock. He slid one hand upward, over her hip and up her side until he could cup one breast in his hand and fondle and squeeze. His thumb rubbed over a nipple through the fabric of her gown, and she gasped.

It was the first time he'd groped her so, but he could no longer hold off from touching her, and after last night her response assured him he wouldn't frighten her. He wanted all of her. When she arched into his touch and melted against him with a whimper and a moan, he groaned again with delight, deepening the kiss. His hips stirred against her belly, hot need coursing through him.

"Sarah," he murmured between kisses, his lips tracing down her neck and back up to her ear where he nibbled it, causing her to shiver and arch her neck for more with a little mew of delight. Every movement, gasp, and mewl from her sent more heat through his body. He found her mouth again and kissed her deeply. He could feed on her kisses for eternity and never be sated.

He wanted to lay her down on the grass and take her. The impulse brought him to his senses with a jerk. Reluctantly he broke the kiss, breathing quickly, as was she, he noted. Her face was flushed, her eyes wide and dark, her lips pink and swollen. He kissed her cheeks, forehead, chin, and nose, fighting to bring his raging lust back under control. His cock was throbbing and leaking in his breeches, and his whole groin ached. *Fuck, he wanted her!* The crude thought shocked him.

"Sarah, you are undoing me," he confessed.

She stroked his face with one hand, and he leaned his cheek into her touch. A warm tendril of an emotion he couldn't name, beyond the fact that he liked it, curled through his chest. Her expression was softened, and there was a light in her sherry-colored eyes he'd not seen before. It made his heart lift and beat more strongly. He turned his face to kiss her hand.

"A perfect day," he murmured.

She reached up and kissed him softly on the lips, a chaste, closed-mouthed kiss, but the imprint of her touch still tingled all the way to his groin.

"Yes," she said softly. Then an impish smile broke across her face, and she turned and ran, saying over her shoulder, "Catch me if you can!"

He gave chase with a growl and a wave of warmth washed over him for her playfulness. He caught her within six yards and swept her up into his arms. "I told you I would carry you all the way to the bridge, my lady," he said as she settled into his arms with a cry of delight and a giggle, her arms going round his neck.

HER HEART WAS beating so fast she wouldn't have been surprised if he could hear it. The flood of joy made her laugh out loud—she couldn't contain it.

"Robert, this is ridiculous—I can walk!" She felt she should protest, but she secretly loved it.

She had never flirted and played like this before with a man, and the duke's masculine strength, the hard lines of his body, his heat, his kisses, his obvious desire for her was making her drunk with happiness and an equally hot desire.

"This is your forfeit," he said with a grin, but the softened light in his eyes made her heart turn over in her chest. *Dear Lord, is there more to this than flirtation?* A surge of longing for that to be true warred with fear that she was reading more into this lightness of spirit than was there.

He carried her easily to the old stone bridge that crossed the river and linked Littledon with its neighboring village of St. Swithin. He set her on her feet gently in the middle of the bridge and wrapped his arms around her waist to keep her close to him.

He kissed her nose and loosed one arm so that he could turn and survey the length of the river before and behind them.

"That is where the Monastery of St. Swithin is located," she said, pointing to the other side of the bridge, and his gaze followed the direction of her arm. "The monks still make and sell wine, and very good wine it is, too." She leaned on the bridge rail and looked down at the water, her heart still racing. He tightened his arm round her waist, drawing her closer against his side.

"You're so different here at home, to what you are in London," he said.

"Is that a good or a bad thing?" she asked with some trepidation.

"Good," he said, bringing her chin round to face him. "I like big sister Sarah," he grinned. *Oh God, his eyes are so blue, I could drown in them.*

"Well, you're different, too," she said with a smile, trying for light and playful, despite the thudding of her heart.

He looked down ruefully at the rocks below them, where the water ran, eddied, and splashed with the current. "You don't like the duke much, do you?"

"I prefer you like this," she admitted.

"I can't get rid of the duke, you know. He's part of me."

"I know, but knowing there's another side, a warmer one, makes him easier to accept." She waited with bated breath to see how he took that. *Would he be offended?*

"I have a feeling you will bring out more of this side of me."

He leaned his chin into his hand, elbow propped on the rail, frowning abstractedly at the middle distance. "I never realized that was what I needed, but I think I do. Someone to balance me and challenge me. You do that."

She gasped, a big wave of emotion taking her breath at this admission. "Th-thank you," she said shakily.

He tightened his arm around her and then, straightening, pulled her round to kiss her. A light kiss, not the searing, knee weakening, devouring kisses of before. "Thank *you*," he said softly.

*Oh God!* She melted against him, burying her face in his jacket and he held her close in silence.

After a few moments, by common accord, they resumed their walk, making their way back toward the main street.

After supper that evening, Hepzibah very improperly begged the duke for a story. It was a family tradition on Saturday nights for someone to tell a story for the edification of the rest. The only stipulation was that it had to be a new story, not one the family had heard before. Sarah held her breath, hoping the duke wouldn't refuse and squash Zibby. He could be devastating when he got on his high horse.

He appeared flummoxed at first, but then something must have occurred to him because he said, "Very well, I shall tell you the story of my ancestor who was made a knight by William Conqueror for valor in the field of battle. How does that sound?"

This was greeted with shouts of glee from the boys and Zibby and murmurs of approbation from the girls.

The children gathered round his feet on the carpet and the rest of the family took up seats on the sofas and chairs in the front parlor. Sarah sat beside him on the couch beneath the window.

"My ancestor's name was Alain de Launde, which in English means Alan of the Forest Glade. Launde became anglicized as Layne in the twelfth century. Alain came to England with William of Normandy and fought in the Battle of Hastings in 1066. He was a part of William's personal bodyguard; his role was to protect the standard-bearer who held William's colors so that the troops would always know where he was on the field at any time.

"This was important for morale. The troops needed to know where their leader was and that he was still fighting, for if he went down or fled, they would also flee the field.

"Alain was young and fit and strong. In those days they fought in heavy chainmail, with bucket helmets on their heads, and they held great swords that took two hands to wield. I have some examples of these at The Castle that I can show you when you come for the wedding." He smiled at the reaction he got from the boys to this.

"Really, sir?" Emanuel leaned forward, his eyes shining. "Jolly good! You hear that, chaps—real swords and armor!" Japh gave a whoop, and Zeke, not to be outdone, bounced in his place.

Sarah smiled. The boys had been somewhat reluctant at the prospect of participating in a wedding, which to Emanuel's way of thinking was poor sport. Robert had just made the prospective trip exciting for them. She was grateful and reached surreptitiously for his hand to squeeze in thanks. He glanced at her and smiled, squeezing her hand back.

"The battle was thick and fast, for King Harold's troops were not giving up without a fight, even though they were composed mostly of infantry and archers, whereas William's had much more mounted cavalry. The French cause seemed to be hopeless until William gave the order to retreat. It was a feint, for once the French had the English broken up, chasing them from the field, they turned and annihilated them, the advantage of the cavalry being able to run down and trample the foot soldiers beneath the hooves of the French horses.

"It was during the mock flight that my ancestor proved his mettle. The English targeted William's bodyguard, and in particular the standard-bearer. Alain fought off three Englishmen who tried to bring down the standard-bearer and saved William's colors when the man was stabbed in the arm. He not only raised the wavering flag above the throng, but kept it up while he got the injured man to safety. And he was able to hand the flag to another man and continue his fight to protect the colors of the Duke of Normandy, who would be crowned King of England at Christmas that year."

The boy's noises of approval at this stirring tale of valor make the duke grin.

"Alain was knighted for his deeds that day and given the hand of an English duke's daughter. Her name, alas, is lost to history, but by all accounts, she bore him six children who lived, so it is to be hoped they were happy."

The boys had many questions, which the duke did his best to answer, then the children were sent off to bed and the adults settled to a game of speculation followed by a tea tray.

When the duke rose to take his leave, Sarah accompanied him outside for a farewell and was unsurprised to be kissed again under the moonlight on the front porch. It seemed Robert would take every opportunity he could to kiss her. She wasn't inclined to deny him after such a spectacularly successful day. Her heart was full.

"Thank you for that story. How much of it was true?"

"The bare bones are true as far as we know. It's folklore in the family, a story handed down from generation to generation. No doubt it's been embellished over the years and perhaps his feats of bravery have been exaggerated, but I like to think there is a grain of truth in it somewhere. He must have done something to earn his knighthood and the hand of the duke's daughter—that part at least is true."

"A pity we don't know her name. So many of the women are lost to history."

"Yes, that is a shame. Perhaps her name was Sarah, too?" he said whimsically. He kissed her again. "Thank you for a wonderful day, I have enjoyed myself immensely."

She tightened her arms round his neck. "I have, too," she admitted a little shyly. "I didn't expect to enjoy sharing my family with you. I thought you would consider us country bumpkins," she confessed.

"I may have done if they weren't your family. But I hope I'd be too polite to show it. Given they are your family, I was determined to like them, though I found no determination was required. They are like you, refreshing and delightful. I look forward to sharing The Castle with them."

She flushed with pleasure at this compliment. Even twenty-four hours ago she would not have believed they could be so in harmony as they were now. *Would it last? Or would they slip back to bickering and awkwardness?*

"You may regret that promise to show the boys your armory. They will plague you to death, you realize."

"Aye, but I was a boy once, too, you know. My brothers and I played with that armor and those swords, just as generations of Layne boys have before us."

"You had a happy childhood?"

"By and large, yes. I told you once that I was a privileged person, and I meant that in more ways than just my wealth and social standing. I have had precious little to complain of in my life. I have been very fortunate indeed."

"Yet you've borne the brunt of responsibility for your family for years."

"Who told you that?"

"Kenrick."

He raised his eyebrows in surprise. "Well, I'm gratified he's noticed."

"He said you were irritatingly good or something to that effect!" she said with a smile.

"Yes, part of the burden of being the oldest, but you would understand that."

"Yes, I do. We are surprisingly similar in that regard. I didn't realize that at first."

"Neither did I." He nuzzled her hair with his nose and kissed it.

She leaned her head against his shoulder. "Kenrick is like your father?"

"Yes, unfortunately. I loved my father, but he wasn't the best with money. He's the reason I was forced to seek a wealthy wife. And Kenrick is carrying on the family tradition of feckless behavior."

"Perhaps a good woman will save him?"

"Maybe, but he can't have you—you're taken," he said, his arms tightening round her. The slightly possessive note in his voice, coupled with the gesture, gave her a warm feeling in her belly.

A breeze picked up, rattling the leaves in the trees, and she shivered.

"You're getting cold," he said. "I'd best be going; I will see you in the morning. What delights have you got in store for me tomorrow?"

"It is Sunday, so we will be in church for most of it."

"Oh yes, when does the service start?"

"The first one is at eight, the second at ten and there's evensong at six. But we will have a big midday meal, usually a roast."

He smiled, "I look forward to it." he kissed her gently. "Goodnight, my sweet Sarah. Pleasant dreams." He gave her one more kiss and let her go reluctantly.

She watched him walk out into the street and turn the corner to take him down the main street toward the Blue Boar.

# Chapter Nineteen

DESPITE THE DUCHESS'S warning that The Castle was no such thing, and that the architecture was mostly Queen Anne, her cursory description did not prepare Sarah for the sheer size of the place. But then the duchess had also said they had bedrooms for forty guests, and that presumably did not include the family or the servants.

The main part of the house had three stories, plus attics, and the double story wings on either side stretched out and then turned back in L shapes to enclose three sides of a courtyard.

The entrance hall was wood paneled and rather dark, with a staircase that rose and branched on either side to feed both wings of the house. Despite the Queen Anne architecture, medieval touches abounded with suits of armor and swords mounted on the walls in the entrance hall and gallery on the first floor, where Sarah was introduced briefly to several generations of Laynes. There was no doubting the ancient lineage of this family.

"Robert will give you a proper tour of the house later," said the duchess, leading the way to the east wing, where she and Daphne were to be housed.

Her room was done out in rose pink brocade and velvet and was quite cloying to one accustomed to simpler furnishings.

"This is not the room you will have once you are married.

The ducal suit is situated in the center of the house overlooking the gardens." The duchess smiled. "I hope you like the decoration; I supervised it myself, but you may want to update it. If you do, I won't be offended, my dear. Every new bride needs to leave her stamp on the place, and I perfectly understand."

"I'm sure I'll love it—" said Sarah, overcome by this generosity of spirit. Really, the duchess was so kind to her.

"Don't be too hasty, my dear. You may think differently once you've found your feet. And you needn't fear I will be in your way here. Robert has assigned the Thornbury estate in Shropshire for my use. I will repair there with the girls after Ava's season is completed."

Her maid, Esme, who had arrived earlier with His Grace's valet in a separate carriage, along with Daphne's French maid, Fleur, had already unpacked her things, and she was able to wash and change into a fresh gown before joining the family for afternoon tea.

After doing so and entering the drawing room, she found seven sets of eyes on her.

The duchess, in charge of the tea tray, smiled at her. "There you are, I was about to send out a search party!" She hoped that she had not kept them waiting long, but no one seemed less than amiable at her arrival, and she resolved to be swifter in future.

The duke had risen on her entrance and came forward to conduct her to her seat beside him on the sofa. He murmured for her ears alone, "I trust your room is comfortable?"

She glanced sideways at him and nodded. "Thank you, yes."

Daphne, seated in an armchair to the left of the duchess, smiled at her, too, and she returned the smile perfunctorily.

Ava gave her a twinkling smile which seemed to promise secrets to be shared, and her heart warmed all over again to this sweet young woman who seemed determined to welcome her as a sister with open arms.

The three other females in the room had also risen when she entered, and the youngest two curtsied to her politely.

"These are my sisters, Heather and Ingrid. My fiancée, Miss Sarah Watson," the duke said, performing the introductions.

The elder most resembled him, having dark hair and blue eyes and a similar cast of features in feminine form. Sarah remembered his description of her as sweet-tempered, restful, and gentle. Holding out her hand, Sarah smiled, "I think my sister Mary is of an age with you," she said, clasping the girl's hand.

Heather's eyes widened and she murmured, "I look forward to meeting her, Miss Watson."

"Call me Sarah. We are to be sisters, after all."

"Sarah," Heather repeated obediently.

The younger was a little older than the twins, Zibby and Emanuel, and followed her eldest sister and mother in coloring. A little rebel, the duke had called her, which would make her fit right in with Zibby.

"I am very pleased to meet you, Miss Ingrid," said Sarah and received a big grin in response that quite surprised her. These girls seemed most inclined to embrace her warmly also. Really, she couldn't fault Robert's family for their warmth.

The third female could have been anywhere between twenty-five and thirty and was dressed in a plain, dark-blue gown and spencer made high to the neck. Her hair was confined to a chignon on the nape of her neck and her only ornament was a small brooch in the shape of a lover's knot, and decorated in seed pearls, pinned to her left breast.

"And this is Miss Pringle, the girls' governess," said the duke.

Miss Pringle also curtsied and murmured, "A pleasure to meet you, Miss Watson."

When everyone was seated, the duchess dispensed tea and cakes and began to outline the events of the next week leading up to the wedding. It was abundantly clear to Sarah that she was to have no leisure time at all. The duchess seemed bent on ensuring her new daughter-in-law was inculcated into the role she was soon to fill. Sarah reflected that she ought to be grateful. The duchess could have made her life hell. Instead, she seemed to be determined to be as helpful as possible. Sarah *was* grateful, but she couldn't help but be a little overwhelmed.

"When do you expect the boys?" asked the duchess of the duke, sipping her tea and selecting a biscuit from the array of delicacies on the tray.

"In the next couple of days," he replied.

"And your family is due to arrive tomorrow, is that correct?" she asked, directing her question to Sarah.

"Yes, Mama Duchess," Sarah said, using the more familial appellation the duchess insisted she address her with.

"Good, we will accommodate them in the west wing. There are nine of them, is that right?"

"My parents, four sisters and three brothers," confirmed Sarah with a slightly apologetic air.

"Servants?" asked the duchess crisply.

Thrown, Sarah looked at her bewildered.

"Are your parents bringing any servants with them?" elaborated the duchess.

"Ah—no, we only have a part-time housekeeper in the vicarage and the blacksmith's daughter who helps out in the kitchen. Neither of them will be coming."

The duchess raised her eyebrows. "Who is to look after the children?"

Sarah flushed and the duke leaned forward to select a finger of plum cake. "Mr. and Mrs. Watson will take care of their offspring."

"How peculiar," said the duchess with a shrug of one shoulder.

"They are quite housetrained, Mama," he said with a slight smile.

The duchess threw him a speaking look, and Sarah quailed at the thought of her brothers and Zibby running riot through the ducal demesne. She hoped fervently that Papa would keep a tight rein on them. It would be so embarrassing if they caused a rumpus.

"I understand Ashford is bringing his brood, too, so perhaps their nanny can help out," he said.

At the conclusion of afternoon tea, far from being able to rest, she was swept off by the duchess to meet the housekeeper and the cook for a discussion on the arrangements being made for the wedding guests and the wedding feast itself.

Her family's arrival the following day put Sarah in mind of a plague of locusts. She flinched seeing the duchess wince as the boys came roaring into the entrance hall only to be brought up short by a word from Papa. The duke then stepped into the breach, promising the boys a tour of the armory on the morrow.

Two days after that, the first guests began to arrive, among them, she was glad to learn, Viscount Ashford and his wife and offspring.

After shaking the duke's hand in welcome, he smiled at Sarah and said, "Let me offer my felicitations again, Miss Watson." He squeezed her hand slightly, his hazel eyes shining with his usual warmth. Really, he was such a nice man.

Lady Ashford smiled at Sarah and embraced her kindly. She leaned in to air kiss Sarah's cheek and Sarah stooped a little to accommodate her. Caroline was so very tiny she made Sarah feel inordinately tall. The lady smelled of roses, and her cheek was damask smooth, so beautiful.

Sarah noticed three children standing silently behind the viscount and his lady, two girls on either side of and holding the hands of a little boy. "And these are yours?" she asked, smiling at them.

"Lizzie, Charlotte, and Ewen," said the viscount with a proud smile. "Make your bows, children."

The girls curtsied and the little fellow who seemed a miniature of his sire bowed solemnly.

The viscount looked toward the duke, who was making polite conversation with Lady Ashford, and said apologetically. "I'm sorry, old man, but we were forced to come without the nanny. Wretched woman tendered her notice just before we left, and I haven't had a chance to get a replacement.

"We have quite a contingent of infantry. Miss Watson has eight siblings," said the duke with a rueful grin. "We had hoped your nanny would take on the smaller fry. Well, there are enough servants in the house, I'm sure we will manage somehow. Perhaps Miss Pringle can wrangle them."

"Miss Pringle?" asked the viscount.

"Governess."

"Hm, good notion."

The duke turned to the butler. "See that Lady Ashford and the children are shown to their rooms, Jardin, and their luggage sent up. Ashford, come and take a glass with me."

The duke swept Ashford off to the library and Sarah was left to enlist the help of the housekeeper, Mrs. Jardin, in getting Lady Ashford and her brood settled, the duchess being laid down with a headache that afternoon.

That evening after dinner, the duke found her where she sat talking to Miss Pringle and drew her out onto the terrace. It was a fine night; the weather had been unseasonably warm and dry, and the pattern was continuing. She had seen little of him except in company the last three days, and she was gratified he sought her out now.

The intimacy they had developed while at her parents' home had seemed to dissolve since they'd arrived at The Castle. He was absorbed into his daily duties of estate matters and host, and she was kept fully occupied by the duchess.

However, now he drew her away from the house to walk under the trees in the moonlight with his arm round her waist, and she rested her head against his shoulder feeling that harmony creeping back. It soothed the uncertainty in her heart.

"I feel as though I've barely seen you," he said.

"I feel the same," she admitted.

"Is Mama wearing you out?"

"There is a lot to learn."

"I'm sorry if I've been neglecting you," he said, looking down at her. His face was in partial shadow, devoid of color in the moonlight. They had reached a garden seat, and he drew her down onto it beside him. "I've missed you," he said softly and kissed her.

Her heart lifted and fluttered at this admission as his lips captured hers in a soft, warm, deep kiss. She kissed him back, her arms going round his neck. *Perhaps all my worries are unfounded after all?*

She lost herself in the heat and languorous desire of his kisses. Finally, he broke the kiss and said, breathing quickly, "I know it's only two more nights, but it seems like an eternity."

"Until the wedding."

"Yes," he kissed the side of her face and her neck. "Come sit on my lap," he said, tugging her closer. Somewhat shocked, she still let him pull her into his lap. He settled her, wrapping his arms round her. "That is better. I can kiss you and touch you better this way. Do you mind?"

She shook her head, slightly dazed.

"You've been driving me crazy, you know," he said softly, tracing a line along her jaw with his finger, it made her skin tingle.

"I have?" Her voice came out slightly husky. There was a heavy heat sinking into her limbs; she could feel the magnetic pull of it coming off him in waves. She shifted in his lap, feeling hard heat pressing against her flank.

"You're very innocent about some things, Sarah. It's daunting for a man, that kind of innocence. Do you understand that?"

She shook her head, surprised by him approaching the topic in this way at this time.

"I want you to know that I will try not to frighten or hurt you. Do you trust me?"

Her heart was racing. *Do I trust him? In this, I must.* He was the one with experience, and she knew virtually nothing of what to expect beyond the basic logistics as she had told Daphne. Daphne had indicated that it was the duke's responsibility to introduce her to—to pleasure. Was it that he alluded to? She swallowed and nodded.

"Good." He nuzzled her ear and her neck with his nose and lips. "You like it when I kiss you?"

"Yes," her voice cracked.

"Do you feel a—an aching heaviness here?" He cupped one of her breasts and ran a thumb across the burgeoning nipple.

She uttered a whimper and nodded.

He shifted his head and captured her mouth while his hand caressed and squeezed her breast. His tongue explored her and the aching heaviness he spoke of increased, and each time he touched her hardened nipple a shot of heat went straight to the burning place between her legs.

He broke the kiss, tracing kisses across the top of her bosom, exposed by the décolletage of her gown.

He slid his hand from her breast, down her belly to her lap. "And do you feel a wet, burning heat here?" he asked, his voice low and soft.

"Y-yes," she managed, blushing furiously in the dark. *How did he know to describe it so accurately?*

"Oh, Sarah!" his voice had an aching cadence to it that sent shivers through her and made the place between her legs throb.

"Let me," he whispered, "do something about that." His teeth grazed her neck lightly, making her gasp, and his tongue soothed the spot as his hand pulled up her skirts, until she could feel cool night air against her exposed thighs. She stiffened with embarrassment.

"R-Robert?" half question, half protest.

"You'll like this, I promise," he soothed, his hand tracing tingling patterns over her thighs.

She gasped, her breath coming in pants, her skin tingling, the aching heat, the wetness, getting stronger. He adjusted his arm around her shoulders to hold her more securely and slid his other hand higher, toward the apex of her thighs and that aching, wet place.

"Part your legs a little for me, Sarah," he murmured softly against her ear. The intimacy of it, the strength of his arm around her, made her feel as if she were wrapped up in a cocoon of pleasurable warmth and safety. She did as he said, leaning her head into his shoulder, her hand grasping the lapel of his jacket.

"Good," he whispered, and finding her mouth again, he kissed her. She lifted her head, pushing into the kiss, parting her lips and giving him access to her mouth as she did to the place between her legs.

The feather-light touch of his fingers gliding between her nether-lips made her gasp, such a searing exquisite pleasure took her breath away and made her whimper. Her flesh jumped and her hips jerked.

He made a noise in his throat that she recognized as a groan. He'd groaned before, kissing her, and she knew it denoted his own arousal, as it had been accompanied by the growing hardness in his breeches. She felt it now, pressing against her hip.

His fingers continued to slip up and down the channel between her lips and her breathing became erratic as an itchy restless pleasure took possession of her body. The achy desire built and built as she clutched at him more tightly, rubbing her face against his chest, squirming in his lap as her hips refused to stay still. Little noises escaped her, whimpers, mewls, moans as his fingers increased their pace, and moving them higher, he stroked a place where the pleasure was so intense she jumped nearly out of her skin when he first touched it.

"Robert!" she gasped.

"It's all right, I have you," he soothed. He swirled around that place, avoiding direct contact with it again, and the hot, hard desire built and built in her body once more. The intensity of it was like nothing she had ever felt before. Every fiber of her being strained toward something, she knew not what, as the feeling wound up to unbearably exquisite levels.

And then it burst, shattering her into a thousand pieces, her body going taut at the apex and then descending into a shuddering mass of quivering, throbbing pleasure. A groan tore from her throat and then her body collapsed back against him, in languorous peace, her face nuzzling into him as the throbs and tingles gradually dissipated, leaving her limbs heavy and her body limp.

He removed his fingers, cupped her briefly, and then dropped her skirts back into place, wrapping both arms around her and cradling her in a rocking motion, kissing her hair. "I have you," he whispered.

A sense of peace pervaded her as she leaned into his embrace, soothed by the calm and the comfort of his arms.

She stirred eventually and lifted her head, and he kissed her lips gently, a chaste closed-mouth kiss. "Recovered?" he asked softly.

She nodded. "I think so."

He smiled. "Good. There will be a great deal more on our wedding night, but I wanted you to experience something that would, I hope, allay your natural anxiety?"

She bit her lip and stroked his cheek. If she had been teetering on the brink of falling back into love with him, she had lost the battle entirely now. *To show me such consideration and care, such exquisite pleasure, and take none for himself?*

"Thank you," she whispered, her whole heart in the words. She flung her arms round his neck and hugged him.

He kissed her neck and stroked her back.

"We had best go back in before a search party is sent out to retrieve us," he said.

She stood up, and he rose and turned away, to rearrange his breeches she thought. Not surprising. She felt oddly light and buoyant.

As they approached the house, Robert felt a surge of satisfaction, he had achieved his objective, he thought, of preparing Sarah for their wedding night. She would now, he hoped, look forward to it with as much anticipation as he did. His groin ached, and he hoped there were no damp patches on his breeches. He would take care of himself later in the privacy of his room.

The key thing was that Sarah had achieved release and remarkably easily. He had been prepared for it to take much longer, but she seemed highly primed and even attracted to him. He had worried that she wouldn't be and what he would do if she weren't. But her reactions tonight made him hopeful that their wedding night could be one of mutual pleasure. He would certainly do everything he could to ensure hers. This was a step in the right direction, surely. He meant their marriage to begin on a good note. And perhaps he had done something toward atoning for his previous errors.

# Chapter Twenty

"OH SWEETHEART, YOU look beautiful," said Mama, wiping tears off her cheeks.

"Don't cry, Mama, you'll set me off," said Sarah, surveying herself in the full-length bevel mirror. Her wedding dress, which had been hastily ordered in London following the announcement of their engagement and sent straight to The Castle from the very expensive modiste patronized by the duchess, was a white satin and lace confection that made Sarah feel like a fairy princess.

Esme had just finished putting the finishing touches to her hair which was bundled on top of her head in a riot of curls held in place by combs and pins.

The door opened and the duchess appeared, followed by her maid. "Lovely, Sarah," she said approvingly. "And I have just the finishing touch." She waved the maid forward who held out a case with a string of milky pearls nestled in white velvet.

Sarah gasped at the opalescent sheen on the white globes.

"Mama Duchess, they are beautiful!"

"They are my bride gift to you, my dear." The duchess looped the long strand over her head and settled them on her bodice, where they complemented the white satin. "Lovely," she said again. "Now—" She turned and held out her hand, and the maid presented another, bigger box. The duchess lifted out a gold coronet set with diamonds and Sarah gasped, goggling at it. She had never seen anything so exquisite in her life. It was delicate, with a frame made of twisting vines of gold rising to a peak in the center and had an intricate design of leaves and flowers made of gold, each suspended on a thin wire so that they bobbed with the movement of the coronet. Each flower was set with tiny diamonds that glinted and glittered in the light.

"This is the duchess coronet, my dear, and yours by right now." She reached up to set it carefully on Sarah's head, making sure not to disturb Esme's handiwork. Sarah blinked at herself, stunned. If the past month had been a whirlwind of new emotions and experiences, never had the weight of her new position been brought home to her more strikingly than in this moment.

The duchess kissed her cheek and wiped away the tear that escaped from Sarah's eye. "You will do well; I am proud of you."

"May we come in?" Ava asked from the doorway. Followed by Sarah's sisters and soon to be sisters-in-law, they all spilled into the room like a flock of geese. Behind them came Daphne, who nodded to Sarah approvingly over the girls' heads as they all converged on Sarah to hug her and congratulate her and ooh and ah over her dress.

"You look gorgeous!" said Ava, sparkling. "Robert is going to be beside himself."

Zibby and Ingrid, who were her flower girls, pressed forward for their share of the glory, their baskets of rose petals clutched in their hands.

"All right, that is enough," said the duchess, clapping her hands. "Ava, go and tell Robert his bride will be arriving shortly. Out, all of you!" The duchess herded the girls out, and Daphne came forward to kiss her cheek and smile. She had such a look of cat-that-got-the-cream about her, Sarah had to bite her tongue. Summoning all her Christian spirit, she kissed Daphne's cheek and murmured, "Thank you."

Daphne grinned broadly and followed the duchess to the

door.

"I'm ready when you are, Sesi," said her father from the doorway, where he waited. Mama went to him, and he kissed her cheek and squeezed her hand. Mama cast her one last look before disappearing, and Sarah flew to her father, flinging her arms round his neck. "Papa!"

"My baby girl," he said, husky voiced and sniffing, hugging her tight.

"Oh, Papa, it's so daunting!"

"I know. But I have confidence you'll not let it go to your head. You're a sensible girl with your feet on the ground. This is all fluff and nonsense, and you know it. The important bit is your vows. Say them with your whole heart, my dear, and God will hear you and bless you."

"Yes, Papa," she said, sniffing and wiping her eyes. *My whole heart indeed!* Since the other night, she had been floating on a cloud. She collected her reticule and her fan and joined her father at the top of the stairs. Holding her skirts up with one hand, the other resting in the crook of her father's arm, she descended the stairs slowly. They reached the ground floor where The Castle's butler, Jardin, bowed to her with stately grace.

Passing outside, they traversed the front of the house and around the side to the chapel, on a red carpet laid out especially for her. Ingrid and Zibby went before them strewing rose petals in her path. The servants all lined the carpet to wish her well, and she smiled at them as they each curtsied or bowed as she passed. It was a fine, warm day for May. The weather so far this spring had been warmer and finer than usual.

They reached the entrance of the little chapel and her father stopped. "Ready?" he asked.

She took a deep breath, trying to still her nerves. Her stomach was flip-flopping and her heart skipping. She looked at him anxiously, and he nodded reassuringly. She smiled, it wobbled a bit, but it was a smile. *I can do this.* She nodded, stiffening her backbone and lifting her head. "Yes."

"Good." He patted her hand, and she lifted her skirts as they stepped up the shallow, worn steps of the chapel and entered the small building. It was full to bursting, and at her appearance the organ struck up and the chatter stopped. Her gaze flew to the front of the church where Robert stood waiting for her, and her heart turned over in a flood of warmth.

Since their encounter in the gardens two nights ago, she had seen little of him except in company. When he did see her, he smiled encouragingly and squeezed her hand or murmured something sweet, like how much he missed her or was looking forward to the wedding.

She was afraid to surrender to the happiness bubbling in her veins, yet it was too late to pull back from it. God had heard her prayer. She was marrying the man she loved, and she hoped that he loved her, too. He hadn't said the words, but his behavior suggested that he esteemed her highly, and he had demonstrated that he was intent on treating her with the utmost respect and consideration. *Can I ask for more?*

*What about Madeleine?* The niggling voice in her head teased her. She shoved the thought aside, determined not to ruin this moment with things she couldn't control.

She reached his side to the murmurs of the wedding guests. Her father released her and stepped back a fraction. She smiled up at him and glanced over at Mama who was still wiping tears off her cheeks. She was seated with all the children in her row and a vacant place beside her for Papa when he joined her.

She turned to face the altar and Robert, beside her.

"YOU LOOK BEAUTIFUL," he murmured and took her hand. She blinked up at him and tried to smile, it was a little awry. He smiled back, his heart thudding heavily. *This was it, no turning back now.* Within the hour he would be a married man and back in control of his family's finances. Never again would the Layne estates get into such a parlous mess on his watch. Careful husbandry would see Sarah's money put to good use.

And for Sarah herself, he was a fortunate man. The past week and a half had revealed to him what a treasure he had gained in Sarah. He was truly happy to be marrying her, and he thought—he hoped—she was happy to be marrying him. It might not be the love match he had originally envisioned, but he suspected she was what he needed. And she would grow into her responsibilities. She would become not just the wife, but also the duchess he wanted and needed. When he thought of her, which was often, he got a warm feeling in his chest—and lower down! For all that, anxiety nibbled at him. *Can I be the husband she wants and needs? The husband she deserves?*

The vicar cut across his thoughts, commanding the attention of all within the chapel.

# Chapter Twenty-One

ROBERT STOOD WITH his hand on the door to his wife's bedchamber and took a steadying breath. The other night had gone so much better than he had expected that anticipation had his body taut with need and wanting. He had relieved himself this morning, but it didn't seem to have made any difference. He had been carrying around a low buzz of desire since the kisses they exchanged at Ava's ball, and every encounter since had just fed that desire. Bringing her to climax had set the seal on his unslaked lust. Nothing was going to assuage it but having more.

He was shocked by his own need, he'd never felt such a strong desire for a woman before, and he was worried about his ability to control himself. It had taken every bit of his self-control the other night to focus on her and not his own lust. But it had been worth it, and it would be worth it again.

He pushed the door open and entered the room. It was done out in sky blue and white, a brighter version of his own that sported navy and white. The colors were currently muted by the glow of the fire and candlelight that cast the bulk of the room in shadow. He looked toward the big four-poster bed, but she wasn't there. Then he found her, curled up in a deep armchair by the fire, dressed in a blue silk robe over something white and filmy, her hair loose about her shoulders. It made her look more vulnerable somehow.

His heart squeezed. *His wife.* His to protect and care for as he had vowed earlier today. He swallowed the unexpected surge of emotion. Vows did make a difference. He hadn't expected them to—they were just words after all. But they were words he had sworn he would only utter to the woman who held his heart. *Can Sarah be that woman?* He wanted her to be.

Predictably, she had a book in her lap, although he fancied she wasn't actually reading, as her head was turned to the fireplace as if seeking something from the flames. *Insight, courage?*

She turned her head at his entrance. The fire cast her in a rosy glow. He moved toward her as she rose, the book and her spectacles slipping from her lap to the floor unheeded. He almost smiled. She made a habit of dropping books around him. He reached her and took her hands. "Alone at last," he quipped in an attempt at humor.

She looked up at him and tried to smile, but he couldn't help but read her hesitancy as anxiety—still?

He slipped his arms round her and brought her against his chest gently, "What's wrong? Are you afraid?"

"No. I just—" She paused as if trying to find the right words, and he waited patiently. This was important. "Nothing will be the same again after this."

"True, but it's a natural progression. Would you agree?"

"Yes." She took a breath and let it out slowly. "I don't really know why I'm nervous. You showed me the other night how pleasurable things can be. I suppose I'm worried I won't meet your expectations," she admitted with a wry smile.

"Oh, Sarah!" He tightened his arms round her, touched. "Haven't I demonstrated that you have exceeded them already? That is the last thing you should be concerned about."

She laid her cheek against his chest. "Thank you." Should he admit he was worried he wouldn't meet her expectations? A lifelong habit of hiding his vulnerabilities from others made him hesitant to confess this one. When you were the one everyone else looked to for leadership and to take charge, it didn't do to admit to anything that might be considered a weakness. He had never been able to afford the luxury of vulnerability, even when he was young. But she tempted him sorely to let his guard down. Perhaps when they knew each other better. When he felt more secure in the relationship. Marriages weren't built on vows alone. Ashford had made it clear that actions spoke louder than words.

"May I kiss you, Sarah?"

She nodded and bit her lower lip in such an unconsciously seductive gesture. It forced him to swallow a sudden groan.

That fierce wanting was back again with a vengeance. His hands splayed across her back, and he felt the warmth of her body through the slippery fabric. He wanted to run them all over her luscious shape, feel and touch and kiss and lick . . . He took a breath to steady himself and got a nose full of her scent, roses and something that was uniquely her.

"Sarah," he breathed, drawing her closer and lowering his head to kiss her. He intended the kiss to be slow and gentle, tender even. Intentions and reality rapidly diverged when she responded with unexpected ardor to the touch of his lips to hers. Her quick, fervent kisses pressed to his mouth. The parting of her lips and flick of her tongue undid all his good intentions and the kiss became devouring, hot, wet, and wild.

He crushed her to him, his hands sliding over her body through the fabric of her night attire, as the pent-up flames from weeks of tamped down desire took flight and threatened to consume him. She clung to him, pressing close and her mouth gave him back kiss for kiss.

She felt, smelled, and tasted delicious. She was all his, and he wanted her desperately. He was so hard it hurt. The throbbing ache in his groin urged him to get to the point swiftly.

He broke the kiss, panting, seeking to rein back to some semblance of control. Her face was flushed, her lips swollen, her eyes dark pools. Her breathing was as rapid as his. At least their desire for each other appeared to be mutual. Even so, he needed to find some restraint so that he didn't frighten her. In spite of what they had done the other night, she was still an innocent, her body still virginal. He would hurt her if he gave into the wild desire in his blood.

He eased the robe from her shoulders, and it fell in a puddle at her feet, leaving her arrayed only in the diaphanous folds of her filmy white nightgown. The rosy light of the fire turned it pink and limned her shape in shadow through the light fabric. He set his hands on her slender waist, and squeezing her warm flesh, he kissed her again, more gently this time.

Drawing her closer, one hand slid lower to squeeze her buttock. *God yes, a plump handful!* Pressing her closer still, she must be able to feel his cock, hard as a steel bar and twice as hot, pressing into her belly. She did not recoil from him. Instead, she molded her body to his with a little whimper in her throat that pushed his control to snapping point.

With nothing but his robe and her gown between them and his balls aching and hot, he bent and swung her up into his arms and strode quickly to the bed and laid her gently down upon the turned-back sheets. She lay with her hair splayed round her head like burnished mahogany on the pillows. Her breasts were rising and falling rapidly, the outline of pert nipples poking against the almost translucent fabric of her gown. Her eyes were fixed on his, questioning but not frightened.

He smiled reassuringly and shed his robe, letting her look her fill at his body. It was likely the first time she had ever seen a fully naked man, and conceit aside, he knew his figure to be trim and nothing to be ashamed of. It was primarily the state of his cock he was concerned about. *Will it alarm her?*

He doubted he was the biggest of men, but he also knew he was of a respectable size, and frankly he felt enormous just now with pent-up desire. What he wanted to do—ravish her, take her hard—he could not do.

He cleared his clogged throat, "You know what to expect?"

"Yes." She did that thing with her lower lip again and he

swallowed another groan. He stroked his cock with a distracted hand, trying to soothe the raging need that was making him tremble. *Perhaps I should relieve myself first before we commence?* He had no doubt he could be ready again once he had made her ready to receive him, but he was unsure if he could restrain himself to make her so in his current condition. *God, I am reduced to the state of an adolescent boy by this overwhelming need for her.*

As if sensing his hesitancy, she held out her arms to him, and that did make him groan aloud. "Sarah!" He climbed onto the bed and pulled her close, finding her mouth in a kiss that was both hot and tender. A hand sought one breast and he squeezed, finding and fingering the pert nipple. She arched under him at this treatment, giving another one of those irresistible whimpers. His lips traced kisses down her neck to the collar of her nightgown.

"May I remove your gown?" he asked, panting now. *God, I am a mess.* His cock was leaking fluid and twitching with desire.

She nodded again. He wished she would say something more. He reached lower and pulled the hem of her gown up, slowly uncovering her shapely legs, until the curly thatch of deep, reddish-brown hair at the apex of her thighs was revealed. He had felt the crinkly curls the other night with his fingertips but hadn't seen them. He couldn't resist running a hand up one thigh, squeezing the flesh and coming to rest on her hip. His thumb traced circles in the hollow of her hipbone and her stomach muscles visibly tightened, her hips undulating, a slight gasp escaping her.

Such a blatant sign of her arousal—*and I've barely touched her!* "Oh, Sarah," he whispered and, leaning forward, he pushed her gown up farther and pressed his lips to her lower belly below her navel and above the line of her pubic hair. He could smell her arousal, and it made his cock quiver and leak further.

She gasped louder and bucked her hips. "Robert?"

He lifted his head, catching the expression of longing in her eyes, and smiled. "My dear, Sarah . . ."

"That burning heat is between my legs again," she confessed, flushing.

"Sweetheart," he leaned in and captured her mouth again. "I've barely touched you yet!" he said hoarsely. He knelt up, "Lift your hips." She did as he pulled her gown upward, and she sat up to let him pull it off over her head, then she settled back against the sheets. Her body revealed to his sight was perfection. Creamy skin, small breasts with raspberry nipples, a slender waist and lovely curve from waist to hip.

"Beautiful," he breathed, lowering his head to kiss her lips, her neck and then those enticing breasts and nipples. As he took one in his mouth, she gasped, arching up into him. He held her breasts, one in each hand and fondled, while he licked and sucked on first one nipple and then the other.

His cock throbbed and his balls ached. He ignored them. Arousing his wife was his main focus, and he was damned if anything was going to distract him from that goal. *If I spend all over myself in the process, I don't care.*

He shifted to lie down beside her, finding her mouth again and running a hand down her belly to cup between her legs.

"Spread your legs for me, sweetheart," he murmured in echo of the other night, pushing a knee between hers to emphasize the point. She did so with one of those throaty whimpers and his cock jumped, leaving a sticky trail on her hip where the hot bar was pressed against her, in a vain attempt to assuage the ache. His hips ground him against her involuntarily, as his fingers sought the parting of her nether lips and encountered silky-wet, warm flesh. *So soft, so smooth.* He groaned. "Sarah, Sarah, you're so wet for me again!"

He had kept his touch very simple the other night, sliding between her lips and circling her bud to make her come. This time he ran his fingers up and down her channel, lightly, gently, spreading the liquid heat of her arousal, and dipping lower to explore very gently the entrance to her body. She moved under him, her hips rolling as she panted. "Robert?"

"Yes, sweeting, it's all right, just let me . . ." He swirled around the entrance and then gently pushed a finger inside her. She stiffened and gasped. He withdrew, swirled some more and pushed again. "Is that all right?" He nuzzled at her neck.

"Ah! Yes," she gasped.

"Good," he whispered. "Let me . . . more," his words getting lost in kisses on her neck. His thumb working around her clitoris. She arched up into his touch and he groaned. *Fuck, yes. Come, Sarah! Come please . . .*

"Spread your legs a little more, darling." He pushed his finger deeper, his thumb continuing to trace circles round her bud of pleasure.

"Oh!" She flung her head back, panting and arching her body, one hand clutched at the sheets, the other grabbed his shoulder, her nails digging into his flesh. "Robert!" she gasped again, her hips bucking under the determined onslaught of his fingers. He pushed another inside her, stretching her, trying to make her ready. She was wet, so wet, and his cock thrummed with the need to be where his fingers were.

He slid them in and out, swirling his thumb gently, increasing the speed as she arched and trembled, graduating from whimpers to outright moans that made him push his cock harder against her flank with a groan. *Fuck, I am going to lose all control in a moment and rut myself on her hip!*

He ignored it, panting to gain control of his body. He continued sliding his fingers and rubbing around her clitoris. She had come easily for him the other night.

"Come for me, Sarah," he whispered hoarsely, kissing and nuzzling her neck and across the top of her bosom, as his fingers moved faster in and out of her. He found a nipple and sucked, swirling his tongue around the hard bud.

She gasped, arching under him. Hooking his fingers inside her, he sought the spot that would send her over the edge. She moaned, tossing her head, panting, grabbing at him, her hips jerking, her legs trembling. *Close. So close . . .?*

"Come, Sarah! Come!" he begged her, panting with her. His

fingers sliding frantically now.

Her body stiffened and she groaned, her head flung back as she arched up into his touch and he felt her flesh tighten and flutter against his fingers. Her moans as she trembled and slowly collapsed back onto the bed, panting, made his cock tremble sympathetically, a bolt of desire making him leak further. He groaned, pressing himself into the bed to assuage the ache.

He stilled his fingers, cupping her gently as he withdrew slowly. He found her mouth and kissed her. "Sarah?" He leaned over her, scanning her face. She was flushed, her eyes heavy. "Will you take me into your body now?"

Her eyes widened. "Yes, Robert." Her voice was low and slumberous.

His heart was beating fast, his groin hard and heavy. He doubted he would last all that long this first time. He settled between her legs, his weight on his elbows. He bent and kissed her softly. "This may hurt, I'm sorry. It will be better next time, I promise." His voice strained, hoarse with a desire he was barely able to control.

She nodded, and he reached between them to position his cock at her entrance. Notching it in place, he took a breath and pushed. There was a little resistance and she gasped, he pushed again, and the resistance gave, and he slid inside her tight wet heat.

He groaned, closing his eyes. *So good!*

Resisting the overpowering urge to push deeper, to thrust hard, he held still and opened his eyes. He searched her face for signs of pain. Her expression was strangely blank.

"All right?"

She nodded, and reached up to stroke his hair, which had fallen forward over his face. "Yes, just a—a pinch."

He moved forward until he was fully seated. Her face registered a slight grimace, and he held still, his heart thudding. "I'm sorry," he said, dropping apologetic kisses on her face. She shifted under him, her arms coming round his shoulders.

"It's all right," she said softly.

He found her mouth and, holding still inside her with a supreme effort, he kissed her deeply. "Lift your legs up a bit. It might help."

He was going to explode in a moment if he couldn't move. It was an exquisite form of torture. She lifted her knees and the angle changed, pushing him deeper. She gasped and he groaned.

"Better or worse?" he asked anxiously, panting.

"Better," she said, moving under him in a way that made him moan and move his hips involuntarily.

"Sarah, I need to move, I—" His breathing was erratic, his heart thumping.

"Yes," she said, slightly breathless. "Yes, please . . ."

With a groan, he moved, withdrawing slowly and plunging back in, his desire rising even as he battled to contain it. Watching her as he did it, straining to hold a slow pace, she smiled, and with relief he kept moving, gradually gaining momentum until he had a steady rhythm. *It felt so damned good . . .*

Irresistibly, his speed increased, she moved under him, restless, panting with him. He kissed her, random kisses, hard, soft, deep, her hands stroked over his back, sending tingles down his spine, making his buttocks go taut.

*Fuck!* He broke the last kiss, his head flung back in a loud groan as he hit the point of no return and came shatteringly hard. His body convulsed with a wave of deep pleasure; his seed loosed in a hard rush of pulsing heat. The wave was exquisite, flooding his whole body and taking him from bowstring tight to limp in a wash of eddying pleasure. He collapsed on her, panting, little grunts of residual aftershocks trembling through his body.

*My God . . . devastating . . .*

He lay listening to his heavy heartbeat and recovering his breath.

# Chapter Twenty-Two

S ARAH LAY BENEATH him, stunned by what had just happened. The little she had known about marital congress had in no way prepared her for this. The throbbing pleasure she had experienced left her limp and dazed. The invasion of her body by his, had been at once both painful and fulfilling, a contradiction she could not reconcile. His weight on her ought to feel heavy and suffocating, instead it was comforting.

Her fragile heart swelled with warmth and longing and pride. *I have given him pleasure, yes? As a wife should?* She put her arms round him and stroked a hand down his sweaty back. His body was perfection. She breathed in his musky, masculine scent and pressed a kiss to his shoulder, the only bit of him her mouth could reach. His head was lying beside hers on the pillow. She could feel his heart thudding slow and heavy like her own. His breathing had returned to normal, a soft exhalation, warm against her ear, but his body was still limp and heavy on hers.

He stirred and lifted his head to gaze down at her, his expression as dazed as she felt. "Sarah," he breathed her name as if it were a reverence and kissed her mouth with a soft, tender kiss. A contrast to the barrage of passionate, devouring kisses he had lavished on her before.

He cupped her face tenderly. "Are you all right?"

"Yes," she said with a tender smile. She felt open and vulnerable, all her shields down.

"Did I hurt you?"

She was about to say no when he moved, and a sharp stab of pain made her wince.

"I did!" He moved again, making her gasp as he extracted himself from her body. He rolled onto his side and pulled her against him. "I'm so sorry. I'm a selfish brute." He kissed her hair and she subsided against him, her face buried in his chest, his tenderness a balm to her body and heart. *Can he care for me, truly? Is this how the bond is formed between husband and wife, through the physical connection of their bodies?*

"It's all right. I don't mind."

"I do!" he said, stroking a hand down her back. "I had hoped to avoid that."

"You're not pleased?" she asked, raising her head to look at him. "Did I do something wrong?"

"No. You did nothing wrong."

"I don't understand. How was it supposed to be then?" *If this was to be avoided, what was supposed to happen?*

"I should have held off longer until you reached your crisis again."

"Oh." She didn't really understand what he meant but was afraid to ask more questions in case he thought she was unhappy.

"Did you experience any pleasure at all while we were joined?" he asked.

"A great deal," she said softly, her cheeks flushing at the memory. "I can't explain it, but it was pain and pleasure all at once . . ." Words failed her.

He hugged her. "Sweet Sarah. Next time we are joined, I hope you will spend with me."

"Spend?"

"It's a word to describe that explosive feeling of release. The pleasure you felt before we were joined? You should feel that also when our bodies are joined."

"As you did?"

"Yes. Oh, yes. The most powerful, pleasurable experience of my life."

She raised her eyebrows, and that warm feeling stole into her chest again.

"I completely lost control of myself at the end there," he said ruefully. "The next time will be much better for you, I promise."

"And when will the next time be?"

"When you have healed sufficiently that I do not hurt you."

"Oh. How long will that be?"

"A few days—a week perhaps."

"Oh." She stroked a hand over his chest, enjoying the scratchy hairs that curled there in dark profusion, and rubbed her sticky thighs together. A pulse between them prompted her to say, "Do we really have to wait that long?"

He groaned. "Sarah, don't tempt me."

She leaned up daringly and kissed him. When he finally broke the kiss, he said, husky voiced, "I can pleasure you without us joining, as I did before." He ran a hand down her back and squeezed her bottom. "There are lots of ways to achieve orgasm, Sarah." She squeaked at this treatment, and he grinned. "Let me demonstrate, Your Grace."

She started at the term of address, but then as he rolled her onto her back and ran a hand down her belly, she hitched a breath. And when he touched her between her legs again, she sighed.

He then proceeded to stroke her between her legs while he made a meal of her breasts. She was getting hot and flustered, her hips behaving as if they had a mind of their own, when he moved farther down her body, tracing kisses as he went, until his head was level with the juncture of her thighs.

"What are you doing?" she asked, bewildered. He merely grinned and set his mouth on her, *down there!*

When his tongue speared her flesh and lapped at it, her hips jerked upward in shock. Holding her hips firmly and keeping her legs spread wide by his arms, then using only his mouth, he subjected her to some exquisite torture for the next several minutes.

Her flesh was quaking and aching by the time he raised his head and looked at her over the curve of her belly.

"I think," he said softly, "you need a little more persuasion to come."

"What does that mean?" she panted, her flesh twitching. "You kept telling me to come before. I didn't know what you meant."

"Another one of those words for spend," he said, wiping his face with the sheet.

"Oh. How will you persuade me?" she asked. "I feel quite ready," she added, flushing at her boldness.

"Oh, Sarah!" he groaned and returned to his assault on her flesh with his tongue. This time he moved lower and began lapping at the entrance to her body, wriggling his tongue and pushing it inside her. It was soft and gentle, yet teasing. At the same time, his fingers played with that most sensitive spot that she noted seemed to be the place of most intense pleasure.

Her breathing became completely erratic, and the sensations began to build alarmingly. This was more intense than the last two times. The sensation of his tongue invading her body, where his . . . member had been, combined with whatever he was doing with his fingers, was sharply pleasurable, and it was making her heart race and her breath come short. She grabbed at the sheets and strained her legs wider to take more of his tongue, quite longing for his member to stretch and fill her again. She really didn't want to wait another week for that.

"Robert!" She grabbed at his head. "Robert, I want you, please!"

He raised his head, "I don't want to hurt you."

"You won't!" she panted. "Please, I want you now! Inside me!"

He blinked and rose over her. She was pleased to see he was erect and hard again. He hesitated a moment. "Are you sure?"

"Yes, yes, I'm sure. Please, Robert."

"Oh God, Sarah, no man could say no to that!" He pressed forward, guiding himself into her, slowly. There was a slight pinch, but she ignored it because the deeper ache inside her was begging for his full length. He moved agonizingly slowly, and she pulled at him, wrapping her legs around him in an attempt to speed things up. But it seemed he wouldn't be hurried.

When he was finally fully seated, he looked down at her. "Are you sure this doesn't hurt?"

She nodded. "I want it. I want you," she said more boldly than she would have thought possible mere hours ago. The events of the past hour had changed her into a woman she didn't recognize. Her earlier anxiety seemed absurd now.

He began to move. Slowly at first, then gradually he built up speed, as he had done before. He was still being careful with her, and it wasn't enough. As if he sensed that, he shifted to take his weight on one arm and reached between them to stroke her rapidly at that place where the sensations were sharpest and most exquisite.

He was breathing quite quickly, but it was clear he wasn't in the same state of frenzy he had been before. She on the other hand, was fast approaching a condition in which she was becoming completely swamped by desire. Her body clenched on his frantically, and the sounds that she uttered she would have been embarrassed about if she were in her right mind, which she wasn't.

Her hips thrust up into his, and she twisted and moaned and trembled as the crisis barreled toward her like a runaway carriage. She arched and flung her head back and groaned loudly, her body contracting as he thrust deep and held still, while her world truly came apart.

The explosion of pleasure was so intense her breath stopped, and she hung in a state of suspended bliss for several seconds when everything went blank and nothing existed except the intense pleasure coruscating through her trembling, pulsing body.

She collapsed back onto the bed in a panting heap, her body going completely limp as a state of lassitude filled her, and she closed her eyes, floating on a warm tide of bliss.

She vaguely registered that he continued to stroke within her. A moan from him and a harsh gasp made her open her eyes to the sight of his face twisted in a grimace of desire. He groaned again and again as he closed his eyes, and she felt that rush of heat within her as his body jerked and he filled her with his seed in a series of violent spurts.

He collapsed forward onto her body.

It hit her then that the act which they had just performed (twice) meant that she could soon be with child. She was well enough acquainted with the mechanics to know that it only took once. *If she was as fertile as her mother . . .* She swallowed, her heart giving a flutter.

He lifted his head and looked up at her with a half-smile. "And that is what I should have done the first time." He withdrew from her slowly and flopped onto his back. Groping with his hand, he found hers and raised it to lips. "Thank you, that was so good! For me. I hope you enjoyed it?"

"Yes, it was wonderful," She rolled onto her side toward him, rubbing her thighs together. "I think I'm leaking," she said with an embarrassed smile.

He smiled and stroked her cheek. "I'll get a cloth." And before she could protest at his waiting on her, he was off the bed and back with a damp cloth. Which he used to clean her up, wiping gently between her legs before climbing back into the bed and pulling her into his arms for a cuddle.

His gentleness and consideration were pummeling her heart into a mush.

*I love him so much! But can he ever love me?*

She settled into his arms, curling in and hoping against hope that he could, for if he couldn't, she was destined to die of a broken heart.

# Chapter Twenty-Three

ROBERT WOKE TO a sensation of relaxed contentment. He opened his eyes slowly, and turning his head, spied his wife—*his wife*—asleep beside him. She was curled toward him, her hair loose on the pillow, one bare shoulder showing above the covers.

He stretched his body, feeling muscles and bones crack deliciously. He watched her sleeping for a bit. Sarah's responsiveness and her eagerness to join with him the second time filled his chest with warmth and his groin with heat.

He quietly left the bed to relieve himself and wash. A noise behind him made him turn to find her regarding him sleepily.

"Good morning," she said round a yawn.

He came back to the bedside, sitting down on the edge.

He took her hand and kissed it. "Thank you for last night."

Her cheeks stained a deeper pink. "Why are you thanking me for something that is expected between a husband and a wife?" She glanced up at him. *She was shy this morning, that was what it was. Understandable in the circumstances.*

"Because I experienced great pleasure. And I hurt you more than I intended to."

She shook her head, "I too experienced great pleasure, so I should thank you, too."

"I will pleasure you more, given the chance," he said softly. She blushed. The air crackled between them, and he fought the impulse to flatten her to the bed and have her again. *Where have these brutish impulses come from? I have never in my life wanted to behave so much like an animal as I do with Sarah. It is completely inappropriate; she is my wife!*

He found himself pressing kisses to her hand and then taking one finger into his mouth and sucking, all the while his eyes holding hers.

Her mouth fell open as he did it, her eyes widening, and her gasp was audible.

*Fuck!*

He did groan then, and releasing her finger, he leaned forward and kissed her, taking her mouth in another devouring kiss.

His hand loosened his robe, and he shrugged it off, easing her down into the pillows. He maneuvered himself under the covers with her and took her in his arms, renewing his fervid kisses. His hands all over her body, cupping, squeezing and stroking her lovely breasts, her belly, her hips and waist, her delicious thighs and buttocks. Her response was no less than it had been last night. Whatever constraints they felt in talking seemed to fall away when he touched her.

His hand slid between her legs and cupped her, a finger splitting her lips and sliding into slippery wet heaven. He groaned, "Sarah! My Sarah! So deliciously wet for me!"

He kissed her again, his fingers pressing inside her as she shifted her legs to accommodate him. He lifted one of her legs over his hip, pulling her to lie facing him as his hand continued to delve between her legs, making her ready for him.

She panted and mewled at this treatment, and he pulled his hand free to set his cock at her entrance.

"Ready?" he panted, hoping she was. *Fuck, I want you, Sarah!*

She nodded, panting. "Yes Robert, please!"

*Fuck yes!*

Holding her close against him, he pushed inside her, until

they were fully joined. His hand clamped onto her bottom, and he moved his hips against her, finding her mouth with his.

This position would slow him down, prevent him from ravaging her into the bed like a beast; he wanted this to be good for her, too. His breathing was ragged, and his heart raced. Wanting her was like a fire in his blood.

He rubbed against her, rather than thrusting, her body responding in like fashion, her inner flesh clenching on him in a way that made him delirious with lust. "Fuck, Sarah!" *Did I say that out loud?*

His hips began to thrust, he couldn't help it. His hand held her bottom, mashing her against him with every deep thrust. He was panting and groaning as the stabs of pleasure built. *It felt so fucking good to be inside her.*

"Sarah!" his voice cracked.

"Yes, Robert! Yes!" she responded brokenly, clinging to him. Then he felt it, the pulsing clench of her climax as she trembled in his arms and buried her face in his chest, her arms tight around his waist and neck.

Her muffled moans of release were too much, and his cock loosed its seed in a flood of hot pleasure, accompanied by a deep groan. He held her tight through the crisis, his face buried in her hair.

"Sarah, my sweet Sarah!" he whispered, kissing her hair repeatedly as the paroxysm ebbed, and his body slowly relaxed. His pulse dropped to a slow heavy beat and his breathing returned to normal. But he didn't let her go.

Not until his body was ready to withdraw from hers did he finally relax his tight hold on her. Rolling onto his back, he said, "I think we're getting better at this."

"Are we?"

"You don't agree?" He moved his head to look at her.

"I've no basis for comparison. It all seems incredible to me." She flopped an arm above her head on the pillow. "I had no idea it would be like this. No one warned me."

"Warned you? Of what?"

"That it would feel so good!" she said with disarming frankness. "Now I know what all the fuss is about! I shall have to warn my sisters. Mama is most remiss. I perfectly understand now why I have so many siblings!" He laughed, and she caught his eye and giggled. "I cannot for the life of me picture my parents doing this, and yet I know they must have, at *least* eight times!"

"Our children will think the same thing of us no doubt," he responded with a smile, a certain contentment at the notion of children taking up residence in his heart. He had always been so focused on the idea of finding the woman he would marry; he had not thought much about its natural sequel. But with the house now full of young ones, he was reminded that he might find himself a father in less than a twelve month.

"Yes, I suppose," she said slowly as if the idea was just settling in for her, too. "Naturally you will want an heir."

"And another boy and a couple of girls as well. My sisters will love to be aunts."

"Mine will, too." Her expression changed, and he reached for her hand and kissed it.

"Don't be too concerned. It may take a while." He fondled her fingers.

"Or it may take no time at all." The hollowness in her tone prickled at him.

"You are concerned." His tone was more accusing than he meant it to be.

"What makes you say that?" She looked startled.

"I would have thought that as the eldest of eight, you would be eager for children." His tone getting an edge in spite of himself, the disappointment in his stomach at her seeming reticence making him querulous.

"I didn't say I wasn't." He couldn't mistake the defensive note in hers.

"You're not. I can tell," he insisted, even as he wanted to drag the words back, return to the peace and congeniality of their previous conversation.

She sighed and he flinched internally. *She doesn't want my children.* He swallowed the lump forming in his throat. After what they had just shared, the knowledge cut him to the quick.

He flung the bedclothes back and got up. They were arguing again. *How could they go from that level of affinity to this in no time at all?* His chest ached.

He picked up his dressing gown and shrugged it on, tying the belt with a jerk. Disappointment, hurt, chewed at him. *He felt like crying, for fuck's sake! He hadn't cried since his father died.*

"Good morning," he said stiffly and headed for the door to his room. He didn't slam the door because he wasn't that petty, but the harmony he had felt with her earlier was in tatters and the pain of loss ached like the devil. *Why, oh why, did this happen every time they got close? Was it her? Was it him?*

It was while his valet was shaving him that it hit him. He had a fixed idea of what happiness looked like, and Sarah refused to fit into the picture. Every time she said or did something that didn't fit, it hurt. And when he was hurt, he lashed out in some fashion. Which made him feel even worse for being nasty toward *her*. He seemed determined to push her away, despite his avowed desire to bring her closer.

*If I keep this up, she will loathe me, and very rightly so.*

SARAH WATCHED THE door snap shut behind him and gasped for breath. She felt flattened. *What had happened?*

But she knew what had happened. Her face had betrayed her. When he said *an heir,* she had been reminded of the terms of their marriage of convenience and the shadowy Madeleine, a lurking darkness between them. It wasn't that she didn't want his children. God help her, she would adore having his children. But her reaction had told him otherwise.

What could she possibly say to explain her peculiar reaction without revealing the real cause? The prospect of motherhood on top of all her duchess duties *was* a little daunting. Perhaps she could make more of that, use that as an excuse for her hesitancy? It was weak, but what else could she say? She couldn't tax him about his relationship to Madeleine—Daphne had made that very clear. She wiped tears from her cheeks and flung back the bedclothes.

She would find a way to apologize, reassure him that she did indeed want his children. The idea that she had hurt him in that way made her heart ache.

But by the time she came downstairs, the duke had left the breakfast parlor, and she learned he had gone riding with his cronies. She sat and forced down some tea and toast and then went to consult with Mrs. Jardin, the housekeeper, on the orders for the day. She was the duchess now, and she needed to behave like one.

WHEN HE GOT back from his ride, Robert went in search of Sarah. He had spent the ride thinking about their conversation and realized that he hadn't asked why she'd reacted the way she had. He had jumped to conclusions, put the worst construction on her reaction, and taken immediate umbrage. Even worse, he had behaved rudely, walking out on her. He needed to apologize for his bad manners and find a way to restore harmony between them. If he let this fester, it would just grow worse, and the notion of being at outs with her was unbearable.

He found her supervising a game of croquet for the children with Miss Pringle on the south lawn. She wore a broad-brimmed hat to protect her face from the sun and a simple but tasteful white muslin gown. She was always well dressed, he reflected, watching her through the drawing room window.

The adult guests were taking tea on the front terrace, and he ought to be with them, but he needed to apologize to Sarah first for his appalling behavior this morning. Opening the drawing room French windows, he stepped out onto the lawn and made his way round the croquet field to her side.

"Which team is winning?" he asked, coming to a stop beside her.

She glanced at him and returned her gaze to the field. "Mary's team is leading by one point, but I believe Heather's team will steal a march on them soon."

The two eldest girls were heading each team of four made up of the younger ones, except little Ewen, who was curled up asleep on Miss Pringle's lap. At only three, he was too young to play and would have made the numbers uneven in any case.

"Shouldn't you be with our guests?" she said, crossing her arms. *Hostile or defensive?* His chest ached; he *had* to fix this.

"Yes, but I wanted to speak with you."

She made no response to that, and he said softly, "I wish to apologize for my rudeness this morning."

She stiffened. "It is of no matter, Your Grace. In fact, it is I who should apologize." She turned to face him. "I led you to believe that I did not want children," she said softly. "Nothing could be further from the truth. I do. I just—" she stopped and swallowed, blinking rapidly, and his heart contracted to see her distress. He stepped toward her, but she held up a hand to stop him. "I just need a little time to adjust to my circumstances," she finished.

"Really?" His heart lifted and softened. He seized her arm and pulled her through the gap in the hedge that ran around three sides of the field.

"What are you doing?" she protested, half laughing, half alarmed.

"I understand," he said, moving closer and slipping his arms around her. "And I am oversensitive, forgive me." It was a lesson not to jump to conclusions or make mountains out of mole hills.

"Perhaps a little?" she said, peeking at him from under the

brim of her hat. He wanted to toss it away and kiss her senseless. He did neither.

"Of course," he said, moving closer and slipping his arms around her, "I shall endeavor to be less *in*sensitive to your circumstances in future."

"And less sensitive to imagined slights?" she asked, smiling, teasing, a light of relief in her eyes. *She didn't like to be in disharmony, either.*

"That too," he acknowledged with a rueful smile. She returned the smile, and he bent his head and kissed her, his heart lifting at the restoration of peace between them. He kept the kiss gentle, and she responded in kind, her hands clutching at the lapels of his jacket. He pulled her closer against him and deepened the kiss. A shout from the other side of the hedge forced him to break the kiss which had elevated his pulse and breathing and stirred his flesh to hardness once more. He simply couldn't get enough of his wife. She was flushed and breathing quickly, too. At least in that respect they were equally affected.

"I had better return to the game," she said.

He nodded. "And I to our guests." But he didn't let her go, instead diving in for another kiss, which he eventually broke lingeringly. "Until tonight," he said softly, loosening his hold on her.

She nodded and stepped through the hedge. He gave himself a few moments to calm his pulse and restore order to his breeches before striding off for the front terrace, well pleased with the outcome of his apology.

# Chapter Twenty-Four

SARAH WAS DRESSING for dinner that evening when Robert came into her room with a cursory knock. He was all but dressed himself, lacking only a neck cloth, waistcoat and jacket. Esme had just finished doing her hair and was about to help her into her gown.

"Your Grace," said Esme, dipping him a curtsy.

"You may go Esme, I will help Her Grace finish her toilette," he said, his eyes fixed on Sarah. His hands were held behind his back, and she wondered what he was up to.

Esme dropped a curtsy again and left the room.

Sarah turned on her dressing table seat to face him, and he came to her, dropped to one knee and held out a long slender case toward her. "I should have given you this yesterday."

She looked at him questioningly and then opened the case. Within was a fine gold chain with a blood-red ruby heart suspended from it the size of a shilling.

"Robert!"

He smiled tentatively. "Do you like it?"

"It's magnificent!" She stroked the ruby with a gentle finger. "Is it part of the Layne jewels?" He had given her the Layne diamond and gold necklace that went with the coronet the other day.

"No. I bought this some years ago, for my bride." He flushed faintly. "I intended it for the mythical woman who would steal my heart. It belongs to you now."

Sarah reeled. *Was that a declaration? Do I have his heart? Was that what he'd said? Was it what he meant?* Her heart skipped and thudded. Tendrils of joy escaped and danced through her veins at the notion.

"Will you wear it?"

"O-of course," she stammered. He shifted to both knees. She turned back to the glass so that he could lay the blood-red jewel around her neck and fasten the clasp. It nestled in the cleavage of her bosom and his eyes met hers in the mirror as he wrapped his arms round her and drew her back against him. He nuzzled her neck. "It looks lovely on you; I knew it would."

She turned, wrapping her arms round him, her heart full to bursting.

"Thank you, it's beautiful. I—"

He cut her off with a kiss, pulling her tight against him, her dressing gown parting and her legs splaying either side of his hips. Her bare flesh pressed up against his hardened groin.

"Sarah." His voice was a soft groan as he kissed her cheek and her mouth, one hand pressing her harder against him, the other finding a breast to squeeze and fondle.

"We'll be late for dinner," she panted, kissing him back.

"I don't care." He fumbled with the buttons of his falls, his stiffened cock springing free. He rubbed the head along her channel, and she moaned, rolling her hips, pressing closer. "Sarah please . . ." he panted.

"Yes." She angled her hips, lifting her legs, and he pushed forward, sliding inside her easily. Holding her hips he thrust into her rapidly, deliciously big and hard. His thrusts rocked the stool she sat on, but she clung to him, lost in the pleasure of his member and his tongue plundering her body.

He reached between them to stimulate her with his fingers, and he groaned into her mouth. "Come, Sarah, please." His thrusts were so rapid now, the movement threatened to dislodge her from the stool altogether. She clung to him, whimpering with rising passion. It felt so good it was almost painful.

"Robert!" she gasped.

"Yes, Sarah, come! Come please!" His voice was ragged with desire, his fingers rubbing her furiously. This was not the gentle touch he used on her before. This was fierce and urgent, and her body responded with a burst of rising heat. She was so close, her flesh throbbed and pulsed, the peak just out of reach.

"Oh God!" he groaned, and she felt him burst within her and the hot rush of his release triggered her own, a cascade of pleasure flooded her body in a trembling rush, and she jerked and shuddered in his arms. Gasping, she clung to him, riding the aftershocks of her own and his pleasure.

ROBERT HELD HER tight against him as he thrust through the dying pulses of his orgasm, his face buried in her neck, fighting for breath and the return of his pulse to a slow, heavy beat. *So fucking intense.* He went over before she did. *Fuck!* He had been waiting for her to come, and then he couldn't hold the orgasm back.

He nuzzled her neck, "Sarah, did you come?" He thought she had at the end there, but he wanted to be sure.

"Yes," she said softly, languorously, rubbing her face against his chest. She dropped her feet to the carpet, and he pulled back, dislodging himself from her body.

"Good." He kissed her. Leaning his forehead against hers, he said, "I know I should have waited but . . . I can't resist you."

She flushed with pleasure, smiling into his deep blue eyes. He was so handsome, and his expression so softened, her heart turned over.

"You know it's like the sun has come out from behind the clouds when you smile, Sarah." He kissed her forehead.

"Oh, Robert, what a lovely thing to say!" she whispered.

"You are lovely," he said softly. "I cannot wait to see you swelling with my child. You will be so beautiful then, too."

"Robert!" she gasped. "I want that, too. Truly!"

He pulled her close and kissed her hair. "Thank you, Sarah. I begin to think you are a gift beyond price," he murmured.

"Robert, Robert, stop it. You will make me cry!" she gulped. "We have guests to attend to, have you forgotten?"

"I confess I had. I'm lost in my wife's beauty," he said, softly.

He got to his feet and pulled her up into his arms. "I'll get you a cloth and help you dress. Hopefully we haven't kept our guests waiting too long."

⟫⟫⟫⟪⟪⟪

THE NEXT MORNING Robert was seated at Sarah's little writing desk in her room, making some notes for his steward, Neville, while he waited for Sarah to finish dressing for breakfast. Esme had done her hair and been dismissed. He was enjoying dressing his wife, tightening her laces, buttoning up her dresses . . . kissing her neck, cupping her breasts. He was intoxicated with her, couldn't get enough.

He glanced over his shoulder at her as she bent to retrieve a slipper and push her foot into it. They had made love again last night and this morning, and it was fair to say he was obsessed with his wife. If this wasn't love, he didn't know what it was. All he knew was he couldn't bear to be apart from her for long, he couldn't keep his hands and mouth off her, and just watching her made his heart swell with emotion.

He hadn't uttered the words yet, because he wanted to be absolutely sure he hadn't fallen victim to some sort of infatuation. The emotions he was feeling were a jumble, and it worried him. It was so unlike him to be erratic like this, up one minute and down the next should she frown or look sad or vexed.

This was nothing like he had imagined love would feel like. He had thought it would be comfortable, not uncomfortable. Peaceful, not turbulent. Tender and affectionate, not blazing with lust and feudal impulses. Not that there weren't tender moments, but they were punctuated by fits of lustful madness when he wanted to behave like a beast.

He also wasn't sure if his feelings were returned. He knew she had harbored a great deal of anger and resentment toward him over the forced circumstances of their marriage, and although she had appeared to absolve him of deception over the incident, he wasn't really sure she had. There were times when he caught a warm light in her eyes that seemed to denote at least a level of affection for him, but then she would often retreat behind a wall of shyness or, if he ruffled her feathers, sharpness of tongue.

Then there was Lannister and her feelings for him. He hoped that was behind them. She never mentioned him. Neither did he, but the notion that she cared for the blackguard still teased him with occasional flashes of insecurity and, God help him, jealousy.

The ball that would mark the end of the wedding festivities was in two days, and their remaining guests would leave after that. He would tell her then how he felt . . .

He turned back to his notes and the pen broke. *Damn!* Pulling out the drawer he scrabbled around for a knife to mend it with, and among the debris of papers and pins and whatnot, his fingers encountered a calling card. It had an embossed coat of arms on the back. Flipping it over, he read the name on it: Reynard Fairbanks, Earl of Lannister.

His heart flipped and a sick feeling fell into his stomach. *What was Sarah doing with Lannister's card?* All his latent worries about the earl rose up and engulfed him. Recalling his last conversation with Lannister, a dread horror took hold of him.

Turning to look at Sarah, who was arranging a shawl round her shoulders and not looking at him, his heart contracted with pain. Did she truly care for Lannister? How could she? Yet she had his card, why would she have it if—?

He shook his head. That way lay madness. He slipped the card into his waistcoat pocket and with his heart thudding heavily, continued his search for a knife to mend the broken nib. He found it but his hands were shaking too much, and he abandoned the attempt. Shutting the drawer rather harder than he should, he rose and said abruptly, "I've just recalled something I need to talk to Neville about that can't wait. I'll see you downstairs later."

She looked round at him in surprise, but he was too agitated to respond rationally if she were to say anything to him. He left the room and bolted to the stables feeling as if he would choke or vomit if he didn't get some fresh air. He found Firefly chewing hay in his stall and saddled him himself rather than summon his groom, glad of something to occupy his hands while his mind raced round in circles.

Leading the stallion out into the yard, he mounted and kicked him into a gallop as if he could outrun the pain in his chest. An hour's hard riding brought him no closer to a resolution of his feelings. He was reluctant to tax Sarah with the possession of Lannister's card. If he had learned anything from their previous arguments it was to temper his propensity to jump to conclusions. Yet he had to find some way to address the issue, but how? Still unable to face Sarah, he sought out his steward and spent the rest of the day dealing with estate matters. There was enough to occupy him for days if he chose to bury himself there, but he was conscious that he couldn't hide from Sarah indefinitely. And the longer he avoided her, the more pointed the need to offer her some explanation for his precipitous exit this morning.

He allowed Bridges to help him dress for dinner and joined his family and their guests in the drawing room. As soon as he entered the room, Sarah came toward him. Her expression of concern pierced his armor and softened his heart with hope. Surely his fears were unfounded after the felicity they had enjoyed over the last few days.

"Robert, are you all right? Where have you been all day?"

With a jolt he realized he missed both breakfast and luncheon. "I'm sorry," he said. "A crisis with one of the tenants needed to be addressed." A slight exaggeration, but better than the truth in this instance. He knew himself to be a lousy liar and hoped that she wouldn't detect his evasion.

"Oh, what—" But fortunately, before she could probe further and uncover his deception, Jardin announced that dinner was served, and he was able to escort her into the dining room and deflect the conversation toward her day.

SARAH, TAKING HER seat to his left, shook out her napkin and snuck a covert look at him as he spoke to his mother, seated on his right and opposite Sarah. Was it an estate matter that had taken him away so abruptly this morning and kept him occupied all day? He seemed calm enough, but his manner was a little stiff and formal, reminiscent of his demeanor in London. She sighed inwardly. *Did I say or do something this morning to upset him?* She tried to remember their last conversation but could recall nothing that seemed a likely cause for his sudden exodus. *It must truly be something to do with the estate that has upset him. Yet—*

Ashford, seated to her left, interrupted her train of thought with a question, and she recalled her duties as hostess, pushing away the problem of Robert's unusual behavior for the moment. *Perhaps when we are alone I can get to the bottom of it.*

The evening seemed to drag interminably. The men had left the ladies to play billiards and not rejoined them for tea. At eleven she was able to retire to her room and hope that Robert would join her shortly. She dismissed Esme and climbed into bed with a book but found it hard to concentrate. A nagging worry had her senses alert for any sounds from Robert's adjoining room. When she heard the faint sounds of Robert and Bridges speaking, she abandoned her book altogether and waited tensely.

She heard the quiet snick of Robert's external door closing, behind Bridges she assumed, and bit her lip. *Surely Robert will open the door to my room any moment?* The minutes on the mantlepiece clock ticked loudly by with agonizing slowness and she had just flung back the coverlet to get out of bed and go to the door herself, unable to wait another second, when it opened, and Robert appeared in his dressing gown. His hair was damp, and her heart which had been racing with anxiety, settled a little. *He'd been having a bath!*

Relief made her smile at him and elicited a smile in return. "You're still awake," he said, coming toward the bed.

"I was waiting for you," she said, lifting the coverlet invitingly.

ROBERT UNDID THE sash of his dressing gown and slipped the robe off to join her in the bed. He had wrestled with whether to come to her or not and decided he couldn't bear not to. Her welcoming smile at the sight of him went some way toward easing his anxiety, and he wondered again if he was reading more significance into that damned calling card than he should.

She snuggled into him, and he wrapped his arms round her, deciding he was an idiot.

"I missed you today," she said.

"Likewise," he murmured against her hair.

"I suppose it is something I shall have to get used to," she said, tracing a pattern over his chest with a fingertip that sent tendrils of heat to his groin. "You have duties, and you've been neglecting them to dance attendance on me, haven't you?"

"Somewhat," he temporized. It was true, to a certain extent, he assuaged his conscience. He tightened his hold on her. *Really, I'm a fool to be threatened by Lannister. If there was ever anything between him and Sarah, it is long over.*

Just then she lifted her head and smiled, "Then we had best

make the most of the time we do have," she said.

"Oh, Sarah," he murmured, bending his head to kiss her and push her back into the pillows.

"Oh, Robert," moaned Sarah a little while later.

"Yes, sweetheart?" he said raising his head from between her legs.

"You're very good at that," she said, panting.

He grinned and returned to his labor.

In the wake of their mutual crisis, their bodies still joined and slowly cooling, he was glad he had said nothing to her of his discovery of Lannister's card. His fears were surely unfounded, and to raise them with her would drive a wedge between them when all he wanted was harmony.

He pushed thoughts of Lannister from his mind, steadfastly ignoring the faint niggle that persisted. Why did she have his damned card? *I neither know nor care!* he thought, tucking his wife into his embrace and preparing to sleep. *If I cannot trust her as I expect her to trust me, what do we have?*

# Chapter Twenty-Five

THE DUCHESS, NOW the dowager duchess, had left the planning for the ball mostly in Sarah's hands.

"It will be good practice for you, my dear," she said with a smile.

Sarah had nodded and tried to smile confidently back. "Of course. Thank you for the opportunity."

Her mother-in-law wasn't fooled. She patted her hand comfortingly. "Don't fret, Sarah. I am still here if you want my advice, but I have confidence in you."

"You are most patient with me. I am sorry to be so poor a pupil."

"You are not a poor pupil at all!"

"Am I not? I feel as if I can never remember all the things you tell me."

"You are doing extremely well," said the dowager.

"Thank you, Mama Duchess," said Sarah gratefully, and the two women embraced. Sarah reflected that she could not have been more fortunate in her mother-in-law.

Her parents and younger siblings did not remain for the ball, as the vicar needed to return home to attend to his flock, but Deb and Ruthy were permitted to remain to enjoy their first ball. Mary was most upset to be excluded from this treat, particularly as Heather, who was the same age, was going to attend. The two girls had formed a fast friendship during the Watsons' stay and Mary was devastated to be forced to go home early.

Sarah asked her mother if Mary could stay, but Mama shook her head. "Your father says she is too young for such frivolity, and I agree. Mary is impressionable. She hasn't the sophistication and experience of the Layne girls. She may be the same age as Lady Heather, but she is less worldly."

Sarah had to concede this was true, and so Mary was torn away from her new friend, protesting bitterly, weeping and red eyed.

"I shall write, Mary!" said Heather, weeping too, for she was a sweet-hearted girl and distressed by Mary's excess of emotion.

Thus, Sarah took a tearful farewell of the rest of her family, and the cavalcade lumbered down the drive with the boys hanging out the windows waving to them. Though Robert had assured her parents that he would bring her to visit with them shortly.

Sarah wiped her cheeks and had the comfort of Robert's arm around her, squeezing her against his side. Their attunement to each other had been quite wonderful these last days especially, and she knew herself hopelessly lost in terms of defenses against him. If the heat between them in the sheets was not enough to cement the relationship, he was also making every effort to please her. His absence all day yesterday she put down to the demands of his role. Last night he had shown her in no uncertain terms how much he had missed her during the day and the tender way he held her until she fell asleep had been very comforting.

Her only worry was over Madeleine. The woman cast a long shadow that Sarah could not dispel. Her vulnerable heart trembled at the notion that he would return to her when they went back to London. She didn't think she could bear it.

She could only hope that his evident desire for her since their wedding meant that he was developing stronger feelings toward her. Yet he never voiced them, except in the throes of passion, when his speech became hot, extravagant, and frequently crude, or in its aftermath when he uttered such lovely sentiments that her heart quaked with tenderness. Like the other day when he had said such lovely things to her in the wake of their passionately fast coupling on her dresser stool. She had been more than halfway convinced he must be developing deeper feelings for her then. He had followed them up with more passionate, hot compliments that night when he took her on her knees.

She blushed thinking of that. The position was so obscene, surely no lady should enjoy it, yet in the heat of passion it seemed one could do almost anything and love it. It was a mystery, but it underlined that fact that she couldn't trust what he said in that state. For if she was transformed by it into a wanton creature, he was also transformed into something other than himself.

Therefore, she dismissed anything he said in that state as an indication of lasting emotion, for when restored to his normal faculties he was quite proper in his manner toward her, treating her with respect and teasing affection. *Surely that should be enough?* But it wasn't. She wanted the words to underline the actions, to convince her that she held his heart. She longed to find the key to unlocking his reserve outside the bedroom and to unlock his voice in regard to his deepest feelings.

ADDITIONAL ATTENDEES FROM the surrounding neighborhood had been invited to swell the numbers for the ball, and Sarah knew a moment's pride when she could view the ballroom from the vantage point of the balcony above filled with their guests. The room was decked out in flowers and greenery, candles shimmering in the vast chandeliers hanging from the ceiling, and music gave a tuneful backdrop to the buzz of conversation.

She stood and watched as couples began forming for the next dance. Among them, she spotted so many faces that she now knew quite well. Her husband's friends, not only Ashford and his wife, but the dashingly handsome Marquess of Ravenshaw and the tall and awkward Earl of Pendrell.

She had only met him a couple of times. He was present at Ava's ball and now at the wedding. The man was so harsh featured that when his face was in repose it was positively quelling. But she had seen him blush and stumble awkwardly when trying to address any lady, even herself, and she felt sorry for him. He was like an overgrown schoolboy, who had no clue how to talk to a female. In marked contrast with the polished and charming Ravenshaw, who was still making Daphne blush and giggle.

Then there was Baron Greathouse, Ashford's friend. He was another dashingly handsome gentleman, a dark-haired Adonis with soft brown eyes and a gentle, calming manner. He quite put poor Ashford, with his disheveled appearance and unremarkable looks, in the shade. Yet the two men seemed to be friends, for the baron went everywhere with the Ashfords. She recalled having met him briefly in their company at the Castlereagh's ball where the four of them had formed a set for the quadrille.

She noted also in the line of dancers her sisters and Robert's eldest two. The girls who were not yet out would not be permitted to waltz, but they were allowed the country dances. Deb and Ruth had never before attended more than a provincial dance at Winchester's assembly rooms.

She frowned, noting that Deb's partner for the dance was Kenrick, recalling her conversation with him about Deborah at Ava's ball. She needed to keep an eye on that situation. She would speak to Robert about it. Deb was an innocent, and the last thing Sarah wanted was her sister falling for Kenrick's particular brand of charm.

She looked for her husband in the throng of guests and spotted him against the wall with his mother. He was looking around and his gaze swept up and found her. She smiled, and he smiled back. She indicated that she was coming down and headed for the stairs, a warm feeling of proprietary happiness in her heart. She was finding her feet, and this, her first ball was showing signs of being a success.

Several hours later she rather thought it *was* a success, moving among her guests, ensuring they had everything they needed, accepting the congratulations of neighbors and compliments upon her gown of rose-colored silk and ivory lace. She wore it with the Layne diamonds, an intricate necklace and diadem with delicate gold leaves between diamond flowers. The duchess had given her the diadem at her wedding, but Robert had produced the matching necklace the next day.

"Mama reminded me it should be worn with the diadem," he'd said with a smile at her expression.

"I shall be terrified to wear it. What if the clasp should fail or one of these delicate fronds breaks off?" she had said, touching one with a delicate finger.

But wear it she did. And paradoxically, she found it gave her confidence. She was beginning, she thought, to feel like a duchess at last.

A waltz was forming when Viscount Ashford approached her. Robert was leading his sister onto the floor, and she had been contemplating finding a quiet corner to sit down, as her feet were getting sore.

Ashford bowed and said, "Can I tempt you to a waltz, Your Grace?" His usually disheveled appearance was enhanced by a hectic color in his cheeks and a blazing fire in his eyes that made her wonder if he had been drinking. However, he seemed steady enough on his feet, and his speech wasn't slurred.

"Would you mind if we sat this one out? My feet are aching," she confessed.

His shoulders dropped which made her realize how tense his body had been, and he said, "Of course. Would you like to sit in the garden? It's devilish hot in here."

"That would be lovely," she said, resting her hand on his arm. She wondered what was amiss. His usual smile was absent, and he seemed to be laboring under the effects of some strong emotion, despite his obvious attempts to mask it.

He led her over to the double doors that gave onto the terraced gardens that dominated the rear courtyard. The air was appreciably cooler out here, the sky a velvet midnight blue scattered with stars, and a rising moon to plate everything silver. Jasmine filled the air with its scent, and Sarah reflected it was a romantic setting. If only Robert were here to share it with her. Instead, she had a troubled viscount for her companion. She glanced at him, but he was frowning directly ahead and appeared oblivious of her scrutiny.

Lanterns, set on poles at intervals, lit up the terrace and the paths that meandered among them, each terrace separated by a hedge. They wandered along one until they found a bench set back a bit from the main path, by a fishpond.

Seating herself, she folded her hands in her lap and watched the fish flitting about in the water, flashes of silver catching the light.

"What troubles you?" she asked, turning to look at her companion. He was seated with his elbows on his knees his hands clasped loosely, and his head slightly bowed as he contemplated the pavement before him. She suspected it wasn't the pavement he was seeing. He had been so kind to her when she was troubled, and she wanted to return the favor, for he was quite one of her favorite people.

He started as if pulled from his thoughts and said, "My apologies. I was woolgathering. What did you say?"

"I asked you what was wrong. You are not yourself tonight. Is one of the children ill?"

"No, they are all robustly healthy, thank the lord." He hesitated, as if not sure if he should say more.

She laid a hand on his arm. "You have something on your mind, however. A trouble shared is often a trouble halved, Emrys."

He swallowed, visibly moved, and said with a husk in his

voice, "I doubt that in this case, Sarah, but I thank you for your kindness."

She waited in silence as he appeared to gather himself. Finally, he spoke. "I discovered tonight a letter addressed to my wife." He stopped, swallowing again. "I wasn't trying to pry, you understand. I was looking for a tie pin that I had mislaid, and I opened a drawer. I found this letter stuffed at the back. It had my wife's name on it. Of course I shouldn't have opened it, but"—he took a breath and expelled it forcefully—"I thought I recognized the handwriting as belonging to a friend of mine. At least someone I thought was a friend."

She patted his arm comfortingly and waited, her heart wrung by his obvious distress and alarmed by what all this might mean.

"I shall not reveal the name of the individual, but the tenor of the letter made it clear that this person has strong feelings toward my wife. And from what I can gather from the missive, she has done nothing to dissuade him from sharing those feelings with her. She has, I can only conclude, in fact encouraged them."

"Oh dear! Have you confronted her about it? Or him?"

He shook his head. "I only discovered the letter just before we came down for dinner this evening. I have had no opportunity—I have been trying to decide what to do!" He rubbed his eyes as if they ached. "I do not want to cause a scene and ruin your ball, nor do I want to create a scandal. If there is the slightest chance that I have misread, misinterpreted what is meant . . . I—" He stopped and dropped his face in his hands, and his shoulders visibly shook, although he made no sound.

She put a hand on his shoulder awkwardly. She was accustomed to comforting little brothers when they scraped a knee or fell out of a tree, but she didn't quite know what to do with a grown man in tears. "Indeed, if you are mistaken—"

"Unfortunately, my instinct tells me that I am not." He lifted his head, and finding a handkerchief, he mopped his face and blew his nose. "Things have been strained between Caro and me for some time. I thought it was just a passing thing, that time would mend it, but—"

"Surely, if you speak with her? It sounds like nothing irrevocable has occurred, that this is perhaps just a warning and that if you take steps to rectify the situation, all may be well."

He smiled grimly. "Perhaps you are right. I hope so, but I fear . . ." He sighed heavily. "We have been married for almost ten years. We were very young. I was twenty-two and Caro only eighteen when we wed. But I was quite sure I had met the love of my life, and she seemed equally smitten with me. You are only newly married and will not know, but two people who live very closely can hurt each other immeasurably without even meaning to. In fact, it is often far worse where strong emotions are involved. If one cared less there would be less damage done.

"I love her to distraction and would not hurt her for the world, but I know that actions of mine have hurt her, though I never intended it so. I thought she had forgiven me, but I fear not. It is possible, you know, to live day to day and for everything to appear to be harmonious on the surface, yet for there to be deep undercurrents of resentment building in the shadows. I see now that she has been telling me for some time that she is not happy, but I was oblivious."

"Then it is not too late!"

"I hope not." He heaved a sigh and put his handkerchief away. "Thank you for your counsel. You were right, speaking of it has helped me find some perspective and perhaps some hope."

She smiled, and it seemed the most natural thing in the world to give him a hug, as she would a brother. His arms wrapped round her, and she hugged his solid frame, attempting to convey some comfort to this dear man, who didn't in her view deserve such pain.

"Ashford!" The duke's thunderous roar made them spring apart as Robert barreled toward them, his face red with rage. "You wolf in sheep's clothing! How dare you maul my wife?"

Ashford rose to his feet to protest but didn't have the chance.

"Robert!" shrieked Sarah as her husband pulled back a fist and punched Ashford square in the face. The viscount staggered under the blow, and Sarah caught his arm to steady him, rounding on Robert. *What has got into him? Is he drunk? How could he hit his best friend?*

"What are you doing? Stop this at once! There is no need—"

"There is every need!" snapped the duke, breathing heavily. He turned his attention back to the viscount. "You will answer for this—name your second!"

*Good God, did he mean to duel? He had taken leave of his senses!* Her heart thudded furiously. Surely, he could not think there was anything between herself and Emrys? It was absurd. All this for a simple hug? *How does he trust me so little?*

"I will not! For God's sake, Layne, see sense! It is not what you think!" Ashford said, nursing his eye which was swelling rapidly.

The altercation was already attracting attention, and Sarah gasped with horror. So much for her first ball being a success. It would be a scandal instead, and its hostess at the center of it. *Is this my fault? Had she behaved wrongly?* But no. It was *his* intemperate behavior that had made a scene, not hers. Even if she was somehow the motivation for it, he was the one who had lost control of himself. *Could he be so overtaken with unfounded jealousy that he was lost to all propriety?* The notion made her heart race.

Just then the dowager duchess appeared, and Sarah got another first-hand lesson in how to be a duchess.

"There you are, my dear," she said, looping her arm through Sarah's and drawing her away. She smiled at the assembling company and said, "The viscount has fallen and bruised his face. There is nothing to see here. Please return to the ballroom." She transferred her gaze to the duke and said, "You will see him attended to, Robert." She then sailed off down the path towing a hapless Sarah with her.

"Mama Duchess, I—"

"Never admit to anything, my dear," said the dowager duchess calmly.

ROBERT, BROUGHT TO earth abruptly by his mother's intervention, bottled his fury and escorted the viscount away from the scene to his library. Shutting the door, he rounded on his erstwhile best friend and said, "What the hell were you doing with your arms round my wife?"

Even as he said the words he knew he was being unreasonable. *So much for having buried my fears over Lannister!* It was only insecurity over Sarah's feelings for Lannister and his unresolved anger toward the absent earl that had boiled up and spilled over at the sight of Sarah in Ashford's arms, not any true misdeeds on their part—he knew that. It was Lannister he truly wished to hit, but he'd taken his anger out on Ashford instead and caused the kind of scene he abhorred. *I'm a bloody fool.*

The viscount cupped his swollen eye and sank into a chair wearily. "Take a damper, Robert. I've no designs on your wife as you'd bloody well know if you paid any attention to anything around you!"

"What is that supposed to mean?" asked Robert stiffly. He was aware he was being ridiculous, but he couldn't seem to stop. He stalked to the cabinet and poured out two glasses of whisky. He shoved one at Ashford and tossed off his own.

"You've had no eyes for anyone but Sarah for the past month." Ashford tossed back the whisky and sighed, closing his other eye as well as the one that was all but swollen shut.

"And who gave you leave to call her Sarah?"

"You did, you idiot!"

"Yes, well, I didn't give you leave to sneak off into the garden and hug her! What the hell were you doing?" That ache in his chest was back.

"Sarah," said the viscount somewhat belligerently, "was giving me counsel on a marital matter, if you must know!"

"I don't see how that gives you the right to put your arms

round her!"

Ashford sighed. "It was a sisterly hug. Nothing more. I was upset, and she was giving me comfort."

Robert rounded on him, the image of Sarah in the embrace of another man still far too vivid in his mind's eye. "Well, I'll thank you to find comfort in your own wife's arms!"

The viscount rose at this point and said wearily, "I'm going to bed. I suggest you calm down before you speak to Sarah, for if you rail at her like this, you'll do more damage than you can undo in a twelvemonth!" He opened the door and with uncharacteristic temper slammed it behind him.

Robert sank down at his desk and put his head in his hands with a groan. *What was he going to do?*

IT WAS WELL over half an hour later that Robert returned to the ball, where Sarah and the dowager duchess were trying to behave as if nothing had happened. The rest of the evening passed in some species of nightmare for Sarah. Robert may as well have been an automaton, he was so stiff and proper. She longed to shake him, but of course she couldn't, and did her best to behave with all decorum until the last of their guests departed or retired to bed.

The dowager had a few words to say to Robert, but Sarah didn't hear what they were. Instead, she bade them both goodnight and retired to her room, where she waited in vain for Robert to appear. It was the first night since their wedding he had not come to her.

She wept tears of hurt and frustration into her pillow. Should she go to him? They needed to speak about what had happened. She argued with herself for a few minutes then flung back the coverlet and, tying on her robe, went to the door between their rooms. She hesitated, then gathering her courage, she tried the door handle and found the door was locked.

Shocked, she dropped her hand as if stung.

Surely, he couldn't think there was anything between her and Emrys? But then why was he treating her this way, as if she were an adulteress? She had done nothing wrong except comfort a friend. *His* friend.

She stepped away from the door and walked on numb legs back to the bed. Crawling in, she clutched a pillow to herself for comfort. Was this simple jealousy run amok or something more troubling? Did he trust her so little that he meant not to allow her any friends of her own? She recalled his words about Lannister when they were in London and his insistence that he wasn't a man Robert would tolerate her calling a friend. But there was a world of difference between the earl and the viscount. Her heart contracted with apprehension. Even if Robert loved her, and she wasn't yet sure that he did, this was alarming behavior that she didn't understand.

It was almost dawn before she finally fell asleep.

# Chapter Twenty-Six

T HE PAPERS WERE full of the scandal. Madeleine read avidly.

*A certain duke who was recently married has suffered an unwelcome lesson for marrying beneath him. His new bride has been caught in a compromising position with a certain viscount. Anyone who doubts the veracity of this shocking tale need only see the dreadful bruised eye the viscount is sporting as a result of the duke's wrath.*

*We wait with bated breath on the sequel to this dramatic turn of events. A play upon the stage could not be more entertaining or shocking.*

Madeleine sat back staring at the opposite wall of her breakfast parlor done out in pretty white and pale green striped wallpaper. She played absently with the teaspoon in the sugar bowl. How might this unexpected turn of events play to her favor? Would Robert seek solace with her now, after this shocking betrayal by his duchess?

Her hand crept to the curve of her belly, the evidence of her mistake she could no longer deny. *Can I convince Robert that the babe is his?* He would not turn his back upon her if he thought the child was his. She was bigger than she ought to be for only three months along. But she'd had her courses after her last time with the duke, so it couldn't be his, could it? But perhaps it was? She hoped, she prayed it was.

She didn't know the identity of her mysterious blond lover from that night of the masked ball. They had only exchanged first names. It might be enough for her to track him down if she really tried, but she hadn't tried, because she kept clinging to the hope that it was Robert's child. She had even made up her mind last night that she ought to try to find him, then this . . .

*What should I do?*

DESPITE THE DOWAGER duchess's best attempts to quash the scandal, the tale of the duke's attack on the viscount spread like wildfire, getting more lurid in the telling.

The viscount and his family left The Castle early the following morning, and it was easy to see that marital discord was high between Lord and Lady Ashford.

The lady ignored Sarah altogether and stalked toward the carriage, also ignoring her husband's hand proffered to help her up the steps.

Ashford, his eye black and purplish blue this morning, swung up behind her, and the horses started forward, the lead carriage containing the lord and lady, followed by the second containing the couple's valet, personal maid, and their three offspring.

Sarah turned to walk back up the steps into the house but was stopped by a hand on her arm.

"Will you take a walk with me?" asked Robert stiffly. They were the first words he had addressed directly to her since the previous evening. After finding his door locked against her last night, she was still both hurt and angry. *I have done nothing wrong, so why is he treating me as if I have?*

She inclined her head, every bit as stiff as he was, and allowed him to lead her round the side of the house to the south lawn. It was deserted except for a few birds pecking in the grass.

"I must apologize for my—loss of control last night." he began.

"Did you apologize to Emrys?" she asked him.

"Not exactly."

"Why not?"

"I was too angry last night, and this morning there was no opportunity."

"He has done nothing wrong, and you *hurt* him!"

"You are mightily exercised over his welfare, madam!"

"And you are ridiculous! You call him your friend and you treat him thus?"

"Will you at least tell me what compelled you to hug him?"

"No! I will not!" said Sarah, furiously. "If Emrys did not confide in you, I will not break his confidence. If you have so little trust toward him and toward me, I see no value in satisfying your idle curiosity."

"It is not idle curiosity; I simply wish to understand—"

"The reason was sufficient. And for that you will have to trust *me!*" She turned away from him, but he reached out and pulled her back around.

"Must you make everything into a fight?"

"Must *I*—?" Sarah gasped and almost choked on her indignation. "It is not *I* who started this, Your Grace! *You* are at fault here. I will not be browbeaten by your arrogance!" She pulled her arm from his grip and stormed off, too furious with him to continue the conversation. Her heart was thudding and her eyes prickling with tears. His lack of trust and his readiness to jump to the worst possible construction of the circumstances broke her heart. *Does he have so little faith in me?*

ROBERT WATCHED HER walk away in despair. He knew he was being unreasonable about Ashford, that there was nothing in it.

He acquitted both of them of amorous intent, but the idea that Sarah might give Ashford comfort still provoked him. It seemed that instead of truly letting go of his feelings over Lannister, he had merely bottled them up and they had festered. It was an ugly side of himself he didn't like, didn't want. A sharp contrast, he realized, to both Sarah and Ashford's kindness of spirit. Ashford was the kindest man he knew, and Sarah was quite naturally drawn to a kindness that was an echo of her own. They also shared that trait of generosity, which he seemed to lack. Something he loved them both for.

It was the same spirit that inspired Lannister's admiration of her. The notion was bitter gall. It still rankled that Lannister understood his wife better than he did. Perhaps that was the true root of his insecurity.

Either way, it was really Lannister he wanted to hit on the eye. He could not rid his mind of the suspicion that she harbored feelings for him that she had not admitted to. Why else did she still have his card? He kept coming back to that, worrying at it like a dog with bone. They should have had a conversation about it after all.

His normal confidence was shattered by the thought of her returning Lannister's esteem, even in the smallest degree. He couldn't fathom it. The man was so unworthy of respect, let alone love—he was sure of it. If she harbored feelings for a man such as that, she couldn't be the woman he thought her to be. Not the woman he loved. And that thought was truly why he had shied away from asking her about the card. It wasn't some determination to be reasonable or to trust—no, he just couldn't bear to discover any painful truth.

Wretched, he flung off to the stables to take out Firefly for a good gallop, as he had the other day, anything to run off his sick despair. He learned later that his sisters-in-law had left while he was out, and he felt a twinge of regret to have missed them, but in the current circumstances he felt it might be for the best.

The conclusion he had drawn on his ride was that the less he saw of Sarah for the moment the better. It was clear that he couldn't deal with the thought of her possible feelings for Lannister or discuss it with her rationally in his current state, so until he could be civilized about it, he was best to avoid her and wait until he could. He had thought he had found a way to deal with this jealousy, but he was mistaken. All he'd done was bury it, and the mere sight of Ashford's arms round her had set off every nerve of insecurity he had.

The rest of their guests, including Lady Holbrook, left in dribs and drabs throughout the day. Ravenshaw and Pendrell were among the last to leave and both attempted to speak to him about Ashford, but he had no desire to discuss what he knew was his own folly and rebuffed them, suggesting they apply to the viscount for the story.

That night it was Sarah who locked her door.

Robert spent the next two days mostly with his steward, following up on the work he had begun two days ago and setting in motion much needed repairs to the estate that were now possible with access to Sarah's fortune. It gave him a good excuse to stay away from the house for the majority of the day and avoid any private speech with Sarah, not that she showed any inclination to talk to him. Which, perversely, just made him more upset.

After discovering her door locked against him, he was too hurt—or too stubborn—to try again, quite forgetting that he had locked his door to her the previous night. Thus, he spent another night alone, prey to fears that his behavior was destroying any burgeoning feelings she might have for him and instead fanning any flame of affection she had for Lannister. And if that truly were the case, everything was at an end and their marriage was a hollow shell. Such gloomy thoughts were uncharacteristic, and he tried mightily to head them off, but they kept intruding, showing him the bent of his mind.

He had learned early that he needed to stay in control of his emotions and remain the cool head when others lost theirs. And he had lived much of his life in that artificial condition, not really feeling and believing that was self-control, even being proud of himself for that. What he hadn't realized until now was that his control was a veneer. It merely masked much stronger emotions he had never known—or admitted—he had and when they exploded as they had the other night, he discovered he had no practice, no methods for preventing it.

And further, in the aftermath, he found himself mired in a mud of conflicting feelings, paralyzed by shame, hurt, and fear—emotions he was not accustomed to entertaining. He had made a wretched, self-serving attempt to apologize to Sarah, but when she pointed out that he had hurt Ashford, guilt had made him lash out at her! Which was unforgivable.

Every time he opened his mouth, he made things worse. He knew he was behaving like an arse and yet he couldn't seem to do otherwise. So he took refuge in being the Duke of Troubridge and continued to behave like an arse.

MADELEINE WAS INFORMED by the duke's servants that he wasn't in residence at Berkeley Square—he was at his country seat. She decided to make the journey into Leicestershire. It was not her preferred option, but perhaps she could contrive to send word to him and seek an interview in private?

ON THE THIRD day, Robert's mother bailed him up and demanded that he repair the situation.

"I have received several letters from my acquaintance in town, asking if it is true that your new bride was caught in flagrante with Viscount Ashford! I cannot return to town with Ava until you fix this! You must do something, Robert. You know as well as I there was nothing in it, yet you are punishing Sarah unmercifully! What is the matter with you? I thought you loved her!" He had seldom seen his mother so furious.

He paced to the fireplace, his back to her. "I do!" he admitted wretchedly. "But she doesn't love me!"

"Doesn't she?"

"How could she, after the way I have behaved?" he turned back toward her, his eyes stinging. "I've made a mess of it, Mama. I don't know what to do! She won't speak to me! I pressed her to offer me an explanation, and she turned me off, said I should apply to Ashford for an explanation." He couldn't admit that the real problem was Lannister and his own behavior, that he had made only one meager attempt to speak to his wife about it before giving up. He had never loathed himself so much as he had in the last few days.

"Perhaps you should. The rumors are that Caroline has left him."

"What?" He stared at her aghast. *My God have I destroyed Emrys's marriage with my intemperate behavior? Is there no end to the damage I have caused?* "Then Caro must believe there is something in it! Why would she—?" He stopped, reflecting on the little that Emrys had let fall when they'd spoken in his study. Guilt sent a spike through him. Emrys was his friend, and he had done this to him! He chewed his lip. "You're right. I do need to talk to Ashford." He bent to kiss her cheek and strode to the door, feeling a bit better now he had some sense of direction.

He turned back at the door. "Will you tell Sarah where I have gone and why?"

"You would be better to speak to her yourself," Mama looked at him with a frown.

"I know, but—Mama, I fear she won't talk to me, and I feel so horribly to blame for this. I feel I must set things to rights before I try to speak to her," he confessed, feeling like he was five years old again.

His mother's expression softened, and she rose from the couch and gave him a hug.

"I'm glad you've realized it's your fault. All the same, you should hurry back, or you may find *she* has left *you!*"

He swallowed. "Please don't let her leave before I get back! I shall return to beg her forgiveness, which is what I should have done days ago."

"I still think you should speak to her now, but I understand why you feel you need to settle things with Ashford first. You were always one for taking responsibility. I'll tell her that."

"Thank you, Mama." He kissed her cheek again, and she patted him with an awry smile.

"You're very like your Uncle Ingram by all accounts. I never knew him, but your father always said so. It's why he admired you so much."

He frowned. "What do you mean?"

"Your father loved you, Robert. He thought the world of you, he was so proud. He loved all of his children, but you were special. To both of us." She blinked and swallowed.

"Oh, Mama." He hugged her. "I must go, but thank you for telling me that, it—it means a great deal."

SARAH RECEIVED THE news of Robert's leaving for London with mixed feelings. She was glad that he was going to talk to Emrys, for only then would he surely understand that he had blown everything out of proportion. But she was sad that he hadn't come to see her before he left.

The afternoon dragged, and she put on her bonnet and cloak to walk in the grounds. Returning to the house an hour later, she found a dainty carriage with two horses drawn up to the front entrance.

Entering the front hall, Sarah put off her bonnet and cloak and asked, "Who is our guest, Jardin?"

He looked uncomfortable, flushing faintly. Since Jardin never looked discomposed, this alerted her that something wasn't right. Just then the dowager duchess's voice, raised in indignation, came to her through the door of the ground floor front parlor.

"How dare you come here with your lies, you strumpet! Leave at once or I'll have you tossed out!"

Alarmed, Sarah crossed the hall and flung the parlor door open. The duchess stood quivering with indignation before a vision of loveliness. Sarah was struck breathless by the other woman's beauty.

She was petite and garbed in an expensive green pelisse trimmed with fox fur over a matching green walking dress. She had dark, glossy ringlets beneath a fashionable poke bonnet and her heart-shaped face featured a perfect nose and rosebud mouth, creamy skin and the most unusual violet eyes, large and fringed with long dark lashes beneath beautifully arched brows.

"Sarah!" the duchess changed color from the red of indignation to pale alarm. "My dear, this is nothing you need to be concerned about. Miss Kinsella was just leaving!" The dripping scorn with which she uttered the name made Sarah blink, and she didn't miss the young lady's flinch, nor the faint tremor in her bearing under the lash of the dowager's tongue.

The young woman directed those large violet eyes at her and said in a sweet, winsome voice, "You must be Robert's duchess." She curtsied as she uttered these words, and Sarah's heart flipped and a sick feeling stole into her stomach.

"I am," she said slowly, swallowing the lump in her throat.

"My apologies, I would have much preferred to speak to Robert about this privately, but I'm informed he is not here. Is that the case?"

"It is." Sarah gripped her hands together tightly, willing herself not to fall apart. "How may I help you?"

"Sarah, my dear, this doesn't concern you. Please leave, now!" said the dowager, trying to shepherd Sarah to the door.

Sarah evaded her and said quietly but firmly, "I believe it does. Miss Kinsella, is your name Madeleine, by any chance?"

The other woman colored faintly. "You've heard of me?"

"I have."

Behind Sarah, the dowager groaned and tottered to a seat. Sarah ignored her, her heart thudding hard.

"What did you wish to speak to my husband about, Miss Kinsella?"

For the first time, Miss Kinsella—Madeleine!—seemed a little discomposed. "I am sorry to bring this to you, Your Grace, but I am with child."

Sarah had been braced for it, but the words still hit her like a lash. She stiffened her legs to prevent them buckling and breathed rapidly to stop the wave of faintness that threatened her senses.

"Sarah, don't believe her. It's all lies!" urged the dowager.

Madeleine stiffened, her face turning pink and sudden tears starting to her eyes. "I assure you, it is not!"

"Then why have you waited until now to come forward with this tale, you wicked girl?" snapped the dowager.

"To be truthful, I had hoped that Robert would come back to me. And then I learned of his betrothal and marriage and"—she stopped, her voice choked by a sob—"I was so cast down I didn't have the spirit. But when I learned of the scandal—!" Her large eyes flashed at Sarah and a look of derision flickered across her face. "I thought of his hurt, and I wanted to comfort him!" She uttered this with a kind of defiance that Sarah, through the miasma of her own pain, found strangely touching. *This girl loves him?*

Sarah swallowed, drawing on all her self-possession, and said calmly, "You were right to come."

"Sarah!"

"The duke would wish to be apprised of such a circumstance; I am confident he will do the right thing by you." Sarah clutched her hands tightly in front of her. She had to believe he would, or everything, absolutely everything she believed about him, was false. Her head was too thick at the moment to work out when this could have occurred.

Daphne had warned her he had a mistress. Sarah had hoped he had ended things with her, and Miss Kinsella's words indicated that he had. *I had hoped he would come back to me . . .* So, it must have occurred before they'd parted ways.

"The duke is in London. I am sure if you return there and ask to speak with him, he will hear you out and—and make all the suitable arrangements," said Sarah. "Should that not be the case, please apply directly to me. I give you my word you will not be abandoned."

"You are most gracious, Your Grace," Miss Kinsella bobbed her a curtsy. She glanced at the dowager, bobbed her a curtsy, too, and left the room.

"Sarah, have you run mad?" the dowager wiped her face with her handkerchief.

"Mama Duchess, do you know Robert so ill that you think he would abandon someone he was responsible for?" asked Sarah.

"No, of course not. But we have no way of knowing if what she says is true."

"No, but Robert will," said Sarah doggedly.

"Women like her make their living by lying."

"I don't believe she was lying; I think she truly cares for Robert." Sarah swallowed and blinked. "If you will excuse me, I— think I need to lie down."

"Oh, of course, you poor child!" said the dowager, rising and rushing to Sarah's side. She put her arms round her. "Such a shock! You took it very well. I'm extremely proud of you. And Robert would be, too."

Sarah smiled weakly and hugged her back. "Thank you, Mama."

"I'm just thankful Ava didn't appear. That would have been disastrous! Go and rest, you poor girl. I think I will need a little rest myself."

# Chapter Twenty-Seven

M ADELEINE, GREATLY FATIGUED, decided to stop at Swinford for the night. Stepping down from her carriage, she directed the footman she brought with her as escort to take her baggage into the inn, where she requested a room and private parlor to take her meal.

"We've only the coffee room, ma'am. There is a gentleman in the private parlor."

Stripping off her gloves, she smiled and said, "I shall ask the gentleman if he will mind sharing with me," and sailed off to the private parlor. Knocking lightly and entering on her knock, she paused in the doorway.

"La," she said lightly, "I am awfully fatigued, and I really do not wish to sit in the public room. Would you mind terribly, sir, sharing the parlor with me?"

The gentleman was seated in a chair before the fire, only his boots and part of his breeches-clad legs visible to her. He rose and turned to face her, and she clutched the door frame. *It was her blonde lover!*

He clearly recognized her, too, and came toward her immediately, his hands held out. "Madeleine, what a delightful surprise!"

She shut the door hastily on the gaping landlord and moved into the room.

"Rey! What a shock!" she said, letting him draw her nearer to the fire, where she took off her bonnet and pelisse before sitting. "What brings you here?"

"I'm on my way to visit—a friend. I stopped for a meal, only. What a chance meeting. Where are you bound?"

"Back to London."

The door opened and the landlord bustled in with a bottle of whisky and a glass. "Your meal will be coming shortly, my lord," he said with an unctuous bow. "Anything for the lady?" He raised an eyebrow toward the gentleman, ignoring her completely.

"Will you join me for dinner?" he asked with a smile that made his eyes sparkle with the light that had captivated her through the mask he had worn that night. Without the mask, he was exceedingly handsome.

"Yes, please," she said with a demure smile.

"Dinner for the lady as well, and a bottle of wine instead of the ale."

"As your lordship desires." The landlord gave him another low bow and left.

"You never did tell me your full name, sir," she said, smoothing the fabric of her gown over her knees. He was clearly a peer, which she had thought at the time. *Perhaps she needed to rethink her plan?*

He was busy pouring himself a whisky. Returning to the fire, he gave her a bow. "Reynard Fairbanks, Earl of Lannister, at your service, Madeleine . . .?"

"Kinsella," she supplied, her brain running at a hundred miles an hour. *Lannister! She should have guessed!* His charm and good looks were as legendary as his financial woes. But she'd never had occasion to meet him before, and she hadn't connected the diminutive of his name that he had given her, *Rey,* with his full name and title. Despite his apparent wealth, she knew his pockets were notoriously to let.

He would be unlikely to be able or willing to shoulder responsibility for a child conceived in a momentary flurry of lust.

He was charming but completely lacking in the moral fiber that made the duke a far better bet for financial stability and reliability. It was also well known that the two men were not friends. She didn't think he would, but if the duke proved recalcitrant, Lannister might be able to help her bring him up to scratch. A lady in her circumstances needed to cover all eventualities.

"Miss or is it Mrs. Kinsella? I am delighted to meet you again," he said, kissing her hand with gallantry.

She smiled. "Miss." She frowned prettily. "But I would be better to be a Mrs., for you find me in a fix, my lord. I can rely on your discretion?"

He raised an eyebrow, and she saw a flash of cynicism in his eyes. Yes, her instinct was right. Robert was the better bet here. "You can," he said.

*Can I though? That might be the fly in my ointment.* "Your word as a gentleman?"

He frowned slightly and said soberly, "Yes, my word as a gentleman. What is it?"

She took a breath and plunged in. "I am returning from a visit to the Duke of Troubridge's estate. I had hoped to have speech with him on a matter of some delicacy, you understand, but he wasn't there."

"No, he's in London. Why did you wish to have speech with him?" Then his eyebrows contracted as if he had just made a connection. "Good God, you're his mistress!"

She flushed faintly. "Yes, I am, or at least I was until recently. Before you and I—"

"Quite!" he said a little grimly. "I'm not in the habit of poaching on another man's preserves. If I'd known—"

"We had parted company before. It was for that reason I attended that party. I wanted something to cheer me up, as I was quite melancholy."

"Hm. It would be typical of Troubridge to break things off before he entered into a contract to wed. Why are you telling me this?"

"I have discovered that I am in a certain condition."

He jerked, spilling his whisky. "And you believe I am responsible—"

"No, you misunderstand me. I had not realized at the time—I was quite distraught, you see—but my courses were late, very late. I had missed them altogether the previous month, before we ah—engaged in our little liaison."

"The duke. You believe the duke is—the father of your child?" The words came out a trifle strangled. The man looked strangely distraught for one who had dodged a bullet.

"Yes," she said softly and dabbed at her eyes with her handkerchief.

"But you haven't told him?"

"I was endeavoring to do so, but he wasn't at home. I spoke to the duchess instead."

"You what?" Lannister rose, spilling more of the whisky. He put the glass down on the mantelpiece in a distracted manner and ran his hands through his hair. His agitation was so odd, she just gaped at him.

"You spoke to Sarah about this?"

"Yes, you know her well enough to use her name?"

"She is a fr—. Never mind!" he waved distractedly, pacing the room. "Good God, what she must be suffering. As if it weren't bad enough that clod hit Ashford and caused a scandal over nothing!"

He turned back to her as she sat gaping at him, not following half of what he said. "I apologize, but I must leave you. I shall pay for the meal and wine, so the landlord doesn't throw you out. You will find Troubridge in London. If you have any difficulty with him, apply to me in Ryder Street. I should be back in London in a couple of days, although perhaps not. I don't know. Good day to you, Miss Kinsella."

He bowed and left the room before she could say anything further.

ROBERT ARRIVED IN Berkeley Square after midnight. He was greeted by Em, who had missed him. Truth to tell, he had missed her, too. Her comforting weight on his feet, once he finally crawled into bed, helped him sleep.

The next morning at the ungodly hour of eight o'clock, he was banging on Ashford's front door demanding admittance. The butler, who knew him of old, was astonished but let him in anyway.

"His lordship's still abed, Your Grace."

"Don't disturb yourself. I'll wake him," he said, striding to the stairs and bolting up them to his lordship's bedchamber. Barging in, he found the room swathed in darkness and rather stuffy. Going to the window, he dragged back the curtains and shoved up the sash to let some fresh air in.

"What the devil?" came the muttered groan from the bed. He turned to eye his friend, who sat up on one elbow, the sheets at his waist showing an expanse of bare, hairy chest, above a slightly rounded stomach and his unfashionably long hair a tangled mess round his stubble-covered face. The bruise round his eye had become purplish-green and yellow. He looked a right mess.

Robert crossed his arms over his chest, planted his feet, and said, "Right. I want the truth! What is going on? Is it true Caro has left you?"

Ashford slumped back onto the pillows with an arm across his eyes. "Fuck off, Layne!"

"I'm not budging until you tell me."

"Yes! Are you happy now? Yes, she's fucking left me! For Greathouse!"

"What?"

"They've been having an affair for months! I didn't bloody know until the night of the ball. I found one of his letters to her. Seems she loved that letter so damned much she needed to carry it everywhere with her. It's the one where he declared his feelings for her." Ashford swallowed. "They have gone to France. She left the children. I can't believe she left the children!"

"Oh God, Emrys, I'm sorry." Robert came toward the bed and sat on the edge of it.

Ashford blinked hard at the ceiling. "She used the kerfuffle you caused by punching me in the face as an excuse to leave. She felt justified then, like it wasn't her fault. I—" He cleared his throat. "She could blame me instead. I was telling Sarah about the letter when you found us. That was what we were talking about. Neither of us realized the letter dated back several months. I thought there was some hope, that things hadn't gone too far."

"If I hadn't hit you and caused a massive scandal, perhaps—"

"No, it was too late. They've been carrying on for months. I just didn't know. I thought we were having a rough patch, is all. You know the night we were at the club and Greathouse and Lannister asked if we wanted to play cards?"

"The night before I went to Almack's and met Sarah?"

"Yes. Caro stayed at home that evening because she had a headache."

"I remember," said Robert slowly.

"Greathouse was with her before coming to the club himself. While I was at the club with you fellows, he was with her. Do you remember what he said when I mentioned she had a headache?"

"Something about being sorry to hear it?"

"And to give her his regards and his hope that she would feel better soon!" Ashford looked as if he'd tasted something bitter.

"The gall of the man!" Robert let out a breath. "You've more self-control than I do, Emrys. Once you found out, what stopped you calling him out?"

Ashford shook his head. "Apart from the fact that I'm a lousy shot," he said with a wry grimace, "he was my friend."

"Some friend!" snorted Robert.

"And Caro loves him," he added quietly.

Robert just stared at him in silence, letting that sink in. *That. That right there was real love.* He swallowed.

"And besides, even if I was capable of that kind of violence, which I'm not, I'm a father. My children need me. Now more than ever."

"How *are* the children?"

"They don't know. I've told them Mama has gone to stay with a friend and threatened the staff with dismissal if they breathe a word to any of them. I'll have to tell them eventually, but not yet."

Robert nodded. "I'm so sorry, old man."

Ashford sat up and looked at him frowning. "Just tell me you've made it up with Sarah?"

Robert shook his head.

Ashford groaned. "Why the hell not? And don't tell me you're not crazy in love with her because you fucking are!"

"I know, I'm an idiot!"

"Well, I told you that!"

"The trouble is, I don't think she loves me," said Robert in a hollow voice.

Ashford snorted. "You're a double idiot!" He poked Robert in the chest. "She's been in love with you from the first!"

"No." Robert shook his head mournfully. "You're wrong. I behaved dreadfully. My cursed bad temper—"

"Blind, stupid idiot!" The viscount hauled himself out of bed and went to the washstand where he poured water into the bowl and plunged his head in it.

Dripping water, he groped for a towel, which Robert handed to him, and drying his face he said in a muffled voice, "Everyone can see she loves you—except you!"

Robert stared at him. "How do you know?"

Emerging from the towel, he scrubbed his hair, making it stand on end. "The way she looks at you, the way her eyes follow you round the room, the way she defends you. A million things."

Robert groped for a chair and sat down. "Oh, God!" he

groaned, putting his head in his hands. "I'm such a fool!"

Ashford rubbed behind his ears and said, "Well, you'd best get back to her then, hadn't you? And for fuck's sake, tell her how you feel!" he said to Robert's retreating back.

At the door, Robert turned. "If there is anything I can do about the situation with Caro—?"

"There is. Return to town with Sarah, your mother, and Ava, and carry on as if nothing happened at The Castle. Once the *ton* figures out we're friends again, I at least won't be a pariah. There isn't much anyone can do to save Caro from the scandal she is determined to make."

"Will you divorce her? You'll have grounds."

A spasm of pain crossed the viscount's face. "If I can't persuade her to come back for the children's sakes, probably. She wants to marry Greathouse." He swallowed hard.

"I'll support your petition in the House of Lords," he said, coming back to his friend's side. "Ravenshaw and Pendrell will, as well." He hugged the other man. "I'm sorry I hit you."

"So am I," said Ashford with feeling.

Robert grimaced and slapped him on the arm affectionately. "And bloody shave and get a haircut. You look like the devil!"

"Go and fix your marriage you grumpy-arsed marplot!" said the viscount with a half-smile and punch to the shoulder. "And give Sarah my regards."

"I will."

# Chapter Twenty-Eight

ROBERT RETURNED TO Berkeley Square intending to have some breakfast before he returned to The Castle, but he was met with the intelligence that a female was waiting in the front parlor to speak with him.

The expression of disapproval on Creighton's face as he said this was marked enough to raise the hairs on the back of Robert's neck.

"Thank you."

"You may rely on my discretion, Your Grace," said Creighton stiffly, but it was clear his sensibilities were offended.

Robert opened the parlor door, and taking one look at its occupant, shut the door hastily and crossed the room to her side.

"Madeleine, good God, what are you doing here? Are you well? What is it?"

She was sitting on the edge of one of the chairs with her bonnet beside her, and when he reached her, she sprang up and flung herself on his chest, sobbing. "Oh, Robert, I'm so sorry, but I had to come when I heard."

"Heard what?" he said with a sinking feeling. Her perfume, lavender, he used to find arousing, it now made him feel slightly ill, or perhaps that was just because of the sense of foreboding pervading his stomach. He patted her back gingerly and tried to extract her arms from round his neck.

"I was so cast down when I learned you were to be married, I was positively melancholy—it made me quite ill."

He frowned, taking her hands and guiding her to sit down again. Tossing her bonnet aside, he sat beside her and said calmly, "Madeleine, I explained that was what was going to happen. I haven't heard from you in months. I had assumed you were getting on with your life."

She sniffed and he gave her a handkerchief. "I was so sad, but then I heard about the duchess and Ashford and thought you might need me?"

*Oh God!* He groaned silently. *What a tangle!* "Well, thank you for the thought, but no, it—isn't what it looks like. I was at fault, not Ashford."

She wiped her face and sniffed again. "The duchess was very understanding."

"What?" He goggled at her dark glossy curls. Her dark beauty had ensnared him five years ago when they began their liaison. He had thought her the most beautiful woman he had ever met. Now he could only think black was no competition for chestnut.

"I was looking for you. When I came here, I was told you were in Leicestershire, so I went there, and the duchess told me you were here, so I came back again."

He took a breath and bit back a sharp imprecation. "What did you say to the duchess?"

"I told—I told her about the baby!" she sobbed.

"What?" Robert's world tipped on its axis, and he was grateful he was sitting down. His heart raced and that sick feeling increased.

"Are you telling me you are with child?"

She nodded, and standing up, she flattened her gown over her belly to show the gentle swell.

Robert closed his eyes for a moment and just breathed.

He opened his eyes and said through numb lips, "Why didn't you come to me with this earlier?"

She swallowed and sat back down, her hands plucking at her skirts nervously. "I—I wanted to be sure. I was so upset I didn't notice at first that I'd missed my courses, then I kept hoping they would start, and I was wrong. I felt so ill and tired and lethargic. I thought it was just grief at first."

He rubbed his face with a groan. "Madeleine, I had no idea you would take this so hard. You seemed fine when I last spoke with you, not happy about it exactly, but not distraught. I—I cannot believe you would wait this long to come to me with this. You must be five months at least—"

"Do you mean to cast me off?" she said tremulously.

"Of course not, I just need a moment to—adjust! This is not what I expected. I thought we were always careful, that you took precautions. How did this happen?" He rose and paced around the room. He felt sick to his stomach. He may not have loved Madeleine as he did Sarah, though it had caused him a pang to separate from her. But he had done it thinking it was best for her to have time to adjust and find a new protector before he was leg shackled.

He had looked forward eagerly to Sarah having his children. He had never expected—. He looked back at her sitting huddled on the couch looking woebegone and small. *God, I am a beast to treat her so. Why would she wait so long to tell me?* She was small for five months, he thought, but then what did he know of such things?

Getting a grip on himself, he returned to the couch, sat, and took her hands. "Do not worry, I will take care of everything. You will not want for anything, you or the child."

"The duchess said you would say that," she sniffed.

His heart contracted. *Sarah! She will never forgive me for this.* He felt the sting of tears under his lids and a deep ache in his heart.

"I do wish that you hadn't seen and spoken with the duchess. This will have caused her pain that I would prefer she didn't have to experience."

"Do you care for her?" she asked in a small voice.

"Yes. I'm sorry if it grieves you, but I do, very much."

And this would destroy his already fragile marriage. What a way for a marriage to begin! To his knowledge, even his father, despite his dissolute ways before he'd married Mama, had no bastards.

"I'm sorry!" she whispered, choking on another sob.

"What do you have to be sorry for? This is not your fault, or at least no more than mine." He rose and paced to the hearth, recalling his joy at the notion of Sarah being pregnant and the contrast with how he felt about this. *But that isn't the child's fault. I will love it, whatever it is, boy or girl, and do my best to ensure it has everything life could offer a baseborn child of mine.*

He recalled his father's joy at each birth of his siblings, in particular the girls. He had been a bit young to remember the boys' births, but he remembered Ava's especially. And Heather's. He had been away at school for Ingrid's.

"I can't do it!" Madeleine's anguished cry broke through his thoughts and jerked him back to the present. Returning to her side, he crouched down before her as she wept into her hands.

"Can't do what?" He felt helpless and empty inside. Madeleine needed comfort, and he had so little to give. She had carried this burden for months alone.

"I'm sorry! I'm sorry!" she sobbed.

Alarmed at the edge of hysteria on her voice, he tried to pull her hands away from her face. "Madeleine, what—?"

"I lied!" Her red eyed, tear streaked, and blotched face screwed up in anguish. "I'm sorry! It's not yours." She closed her eyes and dropped her head in shame.

He blinked at her, trying to fathom what she was saying.

He rose and paced away from her. "Who?"

"The Earl of Lannister!" she sobbed.

*Lannister? Lannister?* Incandescent fury erupted under his ribs. He clenched his fists and turned back to her.

"And that cur refused to help you? That is why you turned to me?" He was panting, he realized vaguely, his heart thudding violently.

She shook her head, a black curl shaking loose from her coiffure and falling down her neck. "I know he has no money. I didn't tell him."

"You thought you could get more from me?" His voice was raw.

"I wanted you back!" she cried. "But it was wrong, and I c-can't do it! I'm so sorry!"

"Tell me everything—when, where, how. Damn it, do you realize how much damage this has done to my marriage?"

She sobbed some more and then began to speak haltingly. "It was in February. I-I had been moping and miserable since you'd ended things. I decided I needed to—get on with my life. Needed something to help me get o-over you!" She gasped and wiped her face, sniffed and blew her nose.

"Did he approach you?" *Has Lannister always hated me, targeted those around me, without me realizing it?*

"No, not exactly. I don't think he knew who I was at the time. I certainly didn't know who he was. It was a masked ball, one of those public ones."

He nodded slowly. "So, you met by chance?"

She nodded.

"Was it only the once?"

"Yes, we exchanged first names but nothing more. He told me his name was Rey, I was pretty certain he was a peer, but I didn't work it out until—until I met him on the road back to London."

"What? What are you talking about?"

"On my way back from Leicestershire, from—from your estate, I met him at Swinford. It was only then we recognized each other."

"And you didn't tell him then? Why the hell not?" His voice rose a little.

She shook her head, pleating her skirts. "I made a split-second decision to continue the subterfuge. As I said, I wanted you, not him. I knew he didn't have your resources, or your"—she swallowed—"kindness."

"What did you say to him?"

"I told him I was with child, and it was yours."

"Why? Why tell him anything?"

"I am beginning to show. I can't hide it for much longer. He would learn of it anyway eventually, especially if it became known it was yours."

"And how did you convince him, in the circumstances, that I was the father and not him?" he asked grimly.

"I told him that I'd missed my courses after we—you—. But I was too upset to notice until later."

"And had you?"

"No, I had them as normal after we parted. It was only after I was with him that they stopped."

"I see. Well, that explains why you didn't come to me earlier. You're three months along, not five."

"Yes," she whispered, head still bowed.

"Where was Lannister bound, did he tell you?"

"No, but he left in a hurry when I told him that I had just come from speaking with the duchess."

"I'll bet he did!" Robert swore beneath his breath, pounding his fist on the mantelpiece. "My God, what a coil!"

She began to sob again, and he paced a bit trying to think. Finally, he came to a stop and said roughly, "Please stop crying, Madeleine. More properly, this is Lannister's problem, not mine, but I'll not see you destitute over this, for he's not likely to help you. Just wait here, I'll be back in a moment."

She raised her face and looked at him, blinking wetly. He left the room and went into the library, where his desk was located. He drew out paper, pen, and ink.

In a few minutes, he was back and handed her a folded sheet. "Take that to Coutts's Bank, it will ensure you have sufficient funds for your purposes. I will arrange for another house you can move into. If you continue at Clarges Street, everyone will assume the child is mine, and frankly I'd rather they didn't. You can take everything with you, including the servants. I don't expect we will see each other again." He walked to the doorway. "Good day, Creighton will see you out." He bowed and held the door for her.

She gathered up her bonnet and, still clutching his handkerchief and the folded paper, she left with one last wistful look over her shoulder at him. He watched as Creighton held the front door open for her, and she stepped over the threshold.

When Creighton closed the door on her, Robert's shoulders slumped. He felt gutted by the events of the past hour, but there was no time to delay. If he was right, and Lannister was headed to Leicestershire to see Sarah, it might already be too late. He felt sick all over again.

"Have my horse brought round, Creighton. I'll be leaving in fifteen minutes," he said, heading up the stairs to fetch his baggage.

# Chapter Twenty-Nine

SARAH RETIRED TO her room after Madeleine left and indulged in a hearty bout of tears, after which she felt so exhausted she fell asleep and did not wake until it was dark. Not feeling up to facing company, she rang for a bath, changed into a robe and ordered a tray for her room, not that she was very hungry. The pain in her heart made it hard to breathe, let alone eat. She spent the evening desultorily reading and staring into the fire, trying to fathom what to do.

Her instinct was to go home, back to the comfort of her family where she knew she was loved and cared for. Where she could be herself. She had assumed the mantle of a duchess, but she didn't feel her title in her bones the way the dowager did and the way Robert did. He was the duke as much as he was the man, Robert Layne. She didn't feel like a duchess or a Layne, yet she was no longer just a Watson either.

She wiped a tear off her cheek. *Neither fish nor fowl.* Where *did* she belong?

And now this baby. It must have been conceived before Robert approached her at Almack's, she thought, but how much before? *Did he still love Madeleine?* She was a beautiful woman, older than Sarah, she thought, and still stunning. It was obvious that Madeleine loved him. How long had they been together?

Daphne had implied it was quite a while.

Her head ached almost as much as her heart.

She nodded over her book and dragged herself off to bed, tossing and turning until the small hours, finally falling into an exhausted sleep and not waking fully until close to midday.

After a wash and another tray in her room, she realized she couldn't stay penned up all day and decided to go for a walk to clear her head. It wouldn't help the state of her heart, but at least it might make her feel a little more like engaging with the world.

She feared Papa would be disappointed with her, giving in to such melancholy. She knew the antidote was hard work, but as the duchess she had none. The hardest things she had to do were order the meals and see that the household ran smoothly, and she had no doubt that while she was malingering in her room like this, the dowager had resumed those duties. So, there was no real need for her to do anything if she didn't choose to. Which was so depressing she almost crawled back into bed.

Straightening her shoulders, she bade Esme a good afternoon and went downstairs where she collected her bonnet and cloak, and with a nod to Jardin, who held the door for her, she set off in the direction of the ruins she had heard so much about.

The scatter of stones and remnants of an old tower and staircase were all that remained. She tromped about miserably, staring at the ground. She was so lost in her thoughts that she didn't realize she wasn't alone until a voice hailed her.

"Your Grace."

She started and looked up and around, her eyes widening in shock. *Lannister.*

The Earl of Lannister stood several feet away, removing his hat and bowing to her. He was dressed for riding, and in fact she now saw his horse tethered a little way off beneath a tree.

*Oh, gosh, if Robert got wind of him being here . . .* "My lord, what are you doing here?"

"I confess, looking for you," he said with a smile, stepping closer to her.

"You must leave at once!" she said stepping back. "If the duke knew you were here—"

"He won't if you don't tell him," he said, stepping closer.

The tower was behind her and the ground uneven beneath her feet.

"My lord, you must leave now!" she insisted, looking around. There was no one in sight, but that didn't mean there wouldn't be at any moment.

"Please, Sarah, I just wanted to speak with you, nothing more. I've ridden all the way from London. Will you turn me away without a word?"

She swallowed her heart thumping in panic. *He has come from London where Robert is. Did they speak, fight?*

"Is Robert hurt?" she blurted her terror.

"No, I don't believe so. Why?"

"You haven't seen him?"

"No, I haven't." He looked down at his booted foot set on a rock, and then back up at her. "I had not expected to be so fortunate in running across you out here. I had thought I would be forced to some form of subterfuge to attempt to speak with you. I know I am not welcome in the house. The duke made that clear in our last conversation."

"Indeed, it is not safe for you to be here. You should leave."

"I will, but not because I am afraid. I came to speak with you on this matter of a falling out between the duke and Ashford."

"You know about that?" she said, aghast.

"My dear woman, it's all over London. And that you are the cause of it. It was that circumstance that prompted me to come."

"Why?" she clutched her hands together in distress. *This is dreadful!*

"I wanted to know if you needed rescuing."

"What?" she said faintly.

"I promised you I would come if you needed me, remember? It occurred to me that in the circumstances you might not be able to send me word."

She blinked at him, bereft of speech.

"At the risk of appearing a lurker, I watched you for some time, Sarah, tromping about. It would be obvious to the meanest intelligence that you are unhappy. I need to tell you also that I met Madeleine on the way here. She told me she'd had speech with you."

Sarah reeled. She put out a hand to steady herself as the earth seemed to move under her feet. He stepped forward hurriedly to clasp her arm. "My dear, are you all right? You've gone horribly pale!"

She clutched at his arm. She shook her head to clear it. "Yes, yes I am. Thank you."

"Please come and sit down on this rock," he said coaxingly. "I don't want you to fall and hurt yourself." His words of concern, the warmth in his eyes, threatened to undo her. She felt raw and wretched inside, beaten down by shock after shock. His care was a balm that she must not accept. For his sake as well as her own.

She shook her head, "None of this is your concern, my lord. Please leave."

"How can I, when I know you must be in so much pain?" He caught her hand and held it tightly.

She looked away, sympathy at this point would make her cry, and she had to get him to leave for his own sake. But he was still speaking.

"Your husband, my dear, is an ass."

She stiffened, her hackles rising instinctively in Robert's defense, and tried to pull her hand away, but he held it fast. "I will not stand here and listen to you denigrate him. I am aware that the two of you do not see eye to eye."

"That, my dear, is putting it mildly." He raised his other hand to her face. "How your dolt of a husband could fail to appreciate what a warm, vital, loving creature you are, with such a soft heart and caring nature, I cannot fathom. He doesn't deserve you, and so I told him."

*Warm, vital, loving creature . . .* She recalled Robert repeating those words. He didn't claim them himself, but that someone else had said them.

"It was you!" she whispered. "Those are your words?"

His stormy blue eyes connected with hers. "Yes, why?"

"I cannot tell you that, my lord." Her heart raced. This man loved her, she could see it in his eyes. She closed her own. "I am a married woman. For the last time, please leave."

"Lannister! Unhand my wife!" Robert's bellow caused them to spring apart guiltily. The earl moved in front of her as if to protect her from Robert's obvious wrath. *God in heaven, if he hit Emrys just for hugging me, what will do to the earl?*

Robert covered the ground between them at a rapid pace. He must have only just arrived home and come in search of her immediately. Her heart thudded painfully. *What did he know? Had Jardin told him of Madeleine's visit?*

ROBERT REACHED THEM, his heart fairly jumping out of his chest, his breathing so accelerated he was almost panting. He made a grab for Lannister's lapel, his vision red and narrowing.

"You cur!"

"Robert, don't!" Sarah's obvious alarm only fueled his anger.

"Sarah, you should go back to the house! This doesn't concern you!"

"I won't, and it does!" she said defiantly. "Let him go! He's done nothing wrong!"

"That is where you are mistaken, Sarah." He transferred his attention back to Lannister, who had made no attempt to remove himself from Robert's grip. In fact, he was standing remarkably passively, his hand at his sides, though they were clenching into fists. "He has done a great deal that is wrong!" With an effort, Robert let go of Lannister's lapel and stepped back. "But he may not be aware of it."

Robert scanned Lannister's face. The man's expression was

closed, but there was fury in his eyes. He would like to hit Robert as much as Robert wanted to hit him. He could see it was Sarah's presence that restrained Lannister, and Robert had no intention of letting fly in front of her ever again. Already he was regaining control over his initial fury at the sight of the man.

"I saw Madeleine in London," he said steadily, aware of Sarah's shocked, indrawn breath. "I'm aware that she was here, Sarah, and what she told you. It was all lies."

"What?" Sarah's voice came out a hoarse whisper.

"She is not with child?" asked Lannister quickly.

"She is, but the child is not mine," Robert watched Lannister's face as his eyes widened and his color leached away.

Robert nodded. "Yes, it's yours. I absolve you of trying to foist your child off onto me. I believed her when she said she'd deceived you, too. You needn't concern yourself with her welfare. I'll make sure she doesn't suffer." The dripping contempt in Robert's voice made Lannister's eyes flash.

"Damn you to hell, Layne! What kind of a worm do you think I am? Don't answer that, it's obvious." Lannister seemed to gather himself. "If the child is mine, of course I'll take responsibility for it!"

The duke raised an eyebrow. "See that you do. I'll be checking. Sarah, please stay here a moment." He grabbed Lannister's arm and tugged him a distance off out of Sarah's direct hearing, although she could still see them. Fortunately, she didn't follow them.

"Do you recall what I said I would do to you if you went near my wife again?" he said, keeping his voice low.

"Attempt to put a bullet through me, I believe? To which I responded that you were welcome to try." Lannister had the audacity to grin, seeming to recover his sangfroid with remarkable rapidity. He eyed Robert's fist and said, "Are you proposing to give me a blackened eye like you gave Ashford? You'll be getting a reputation."

"If Sarah weren't here, I would." Robert swallowed, trying to rein in his emotions. "What are you *doing* here?"

"Seeing if your wife was all right," said Lannister roughly.

"What damned business is it of yours?"

"None, yet I was concerned when I heard that you'd knocked Ashford's daylights out over Sarah. And then when I met Madeleine on the road, I was doubly concerned."

"You thought to capitalize on the situation?"

Lannister turned away from him in disgust. "To what end?"

"Why did you give Sarah your card if you didn't mean to make mischief between us? Admit it, you still have designs on her. Was her fortune too tempting to give up?"

"For fuck's sake, no! I was motivated, believe it or not, by pure concern for her. Nothing else!"

"By God, you love her," whispered Robert, staring at him dumbfounded.

"I said as much the last time we spoke, but I don't think you were listening." Lannister looked away, pointedly not at Sarah, although Robert was sure the other man was as aware of her presence as he was himself.

"She knows how you feel?"

"She does. And she told me to leave."

"My God." Robert squeezed his eyes shut and swallowed hard. The pain in his chest was making it hard to breathe.

Lannister seemed to get himself under control again and went on. "There really is no need for any of this, you know. Your wife loves you. You're just too thick headed to see it."

Robert scrubbed his face, staring at the tumbled-down rocks around them. "I've castigated myself for being all kinds of an idiot from here to kingdom come, but I think you've just crowned it."

"Having an epiphany, are you?" Lannister smiled at him derisively. "Good." Lannister shoved his hands in his pockets. "The field is yours, Your Grace. Don't fuck it up. Or I'll put a fucking bullet in *you*!"

"Noble of you."

"Yes, it's very unlike me, but then Sarah"—at a glare from

Robert, he amended—"the Duchess of Troubridge is a unique woman."

Robert nodded and said softly, "Yes, she is."

"Will you allow me to take my leave of her?"

Robert nodded and watched Lannister tread over to her and bow.

"I KNOW YOU'RE determined to have none of my help," said Lannister ruefully. "And I hope that leaving you with your husband is not a mistake."

She clasped her hands and said quietly, "I thank you for your concern. It—it is unfounded, however. Whatever you may think of my husband, I do not share your view."

He watched her for a moment or two, then he inclined his head and bowed. "Your sentiments do you great credit, Your Grace. You are a lady to your fingertips. I will of course respect your wishes, but please do know that I am always yours to command, should you ever have need of me."

She nodded, wholly unable to respond to that. He then turned and walked over to his horse. She watched as he mounted, waved his hat to them, and set off across the fields toward the road.

Robert had returned to her side, and they stood watching him leave. There was so much unsaid between them, she didn't know where to start.

# Chapter Thirty

WHEN THEY REACHED the house, Robert drew her into the library, and as soon as the door was shut, he seized her hands, words tripping over themselves. "I am an idiot. I am so sorry, Sarah. I behaved abominably toward you. I need to tell you that I found Lannister's card in your desk drawer that morning I left you abruptly. I—"

"Is that why you disappeared all day?"

"Yes. I was beside myself over Lannister. I tried to forget about it, but clearly I couldn't."

"Why didn't you tell me?"

"I was afraid of what you might say, that you might confirm my fears. I confess I am a coward. I told myself that it was absurd to be jealous of Lannister and I pretended to believe it, but when I saw Ashford's hands on you, it all just boiled over. It was actually Lannister I wanted to hit. Instead, I hit Emrys. My behavior is appalling."

"Did you apologize to Emrys?"

"I did."

"Good." She paused, as if gathering herself. Raising her eyes to his, she asked, "Is the child truly the earl's?"

"Yes. I broke with Madeleine before Christmas, and Lannister was with her in February, well after she knew she could not be with child by me. She confessed the whole of it was a fabrication when I saw her in London. She wanted me to return to her and thought this was the best way to achieve it. But then she realized the damage she had done and recanted. Even so, I said I would take care of her; I didn't expect Lannister to step up."

"I think you paint him blacker than he is," Sarah said with a sigh. "I think you are prejudiced against him. He has the instincts of a gentleman in spite of all."

"Time will tell," Robert said, reluctant to allow Lannister any virtues.

"He only ever treated me with respect, Robert," she said quietly.

"And so he should." He was tempted to say more, but he wanted to leave the subject of Lannister behind them, to instead focus on each other. He hoped she did, too, and his eyes scanned her face for some indication of her feelings, but she stared back at him impassively. It seemed he would have to go first and risk her rejection. *Very well. Nothing ventured, nothing gained.*

"I love you, Sarah." Her hands jerked in his hold at those words, but he tightened his grip and barreled on. Having begun, he didn't intend to stop until he had made a clean breast of all of it.

"I have long had some very strange notions about love. Our relationship didn't seem to fit into that framework, so it has taken me some time to recognize my own feelings. But I can assure you they are solid. I love you to the point of madness, as you see. I am wretched when we are at outs with each other." He dropped to his knees, kissing her hands.

"Can you forgive me for being a complete fool and for making you bear the brunt of my ill temper? Can you love me even a little in return?" He swallowed, conscious of the tears on his cheeks as he spoke, and waited, his heart beating heavily, aching, his throat tight.

She squeezed his hands as tears started to her eyes. "Robert, I feel I am somewhat at fault. I allowed you to think I had a partiality for the earl when I did not, and that led to this trap of jealousy you have been in. I am sorry. Will you forgive me?"

He rose to his feet. "There is nothing to forgive. You are blameless."

She loosed her hands from his and flung her arms round his neck, burying her face in his chest. "I'm not blameless. I felt jealousy myself—of Madeleine."

"There was no need to. I never felt for her what I feel for you, and as you now know I broke with her several months before we even met."

She gave him a rueful smile. "Actually, we had met before. But you never recalled the occasions."

"No, I didn't. What were they? I confess my brain is still a blank."

She traced a pattern on his lapel with a finger. "The first time was in Hatchards, in my first season. You reached a book down off a shelf for me." She looked up, and he frowned in an effort of memory but shook his head. "The second time my umbrella got away from me in a sudden squall and slapped you in the back—"

"That was you?" He had been sodden. His memory of the bedraggled young lady was vague at best. The rain had been coming down so hard it had been difficult to see through it.

She nodded. "The third time—"

"There was a third? My God, no wonder you were annoyed with me."

"The third time was at Almack's two years ago. The Countess Lieven introduced us, and you *didn't* ask me to dance."

"I was a blind, stupid fool. I'm so sorry. I could have been married to you two years ago if I hadn't been such an idiot!" he said, tightening his arms round her.

Her face softened.

"Robert, I love you so much, I thought you would never love me! I confess I was infatuated with you on sight. I thought you were so handsome, just like a fairytale hero. Of course, you never noticed me, for why should you? I was a mere vicar's daughter and nothing out of the common way."

"That is untrue, for you are quite extraordinary."

"I was furious with you for only noticing me when I had money," she admitted.

"And rightly so." He winced. "Idiot!" When she looked at him, he said hastily, "Me! I'm the idiot!"

"I thought my infatuation with you was dead, then I got to know you better and I began to fall in love with you all over again." She swallowed. "When Daphne conspired to trap us, I blamed you because I was afraid you would break my heart. I used everything I could to try to resist you, to put a barrier between us to shield my heart. I refused you because my affections *were* already engaged—by *you!*"

He pulled her tight against him, his heart swelling with joy and dismay in equal parts at her words.

"Oh, Sarah, I was such a bloody fool! I was blind to your love *and* my own. I am so, so sorry to have hurt you. Can you forgive me, love?"

She squeezed him close. "I have missed you so. I was sure you would want nothing more to do with me after the scandal. I had failed you as a duchess to be the cause of such a scene, but indeed I never meant to cause it. People are so judgmental and see things that are not there. Emrys was in pain, all I did was give him a hug as I might one of my brothers."

"I know, I know. He explained it all to me and told me I was a blind, stupid idiot! He told me you loved me and that everyone but I could see it." He held her tight and kissed her hair. "Lannister said the same thing." He paused and asked the question that was burning through his chest. "In spite of everything, do you care for him?"

She scanned his face and smiled. "Only as a friend. I know that he cares for me, though. Even so, I told him repeatedly to leave before you arrived. I was afraid if you knew he'd been here you'd find him and hit him—or worse, after what you did to Emrys."

Robert swallowed the pain he felt listening to that.

She went on, "Can I make you understand? I had no friends in London, Robert. This is your world, not mine. When Daphne betrayed me, I lost my only confidant. Emrys was kind to me, and in his way, so was the earl. I realize I don't know the proprieties of having friends in society, but—"

"No, I was wrong. Emrys is a good friend to us both, and I promise I will not object to him. Lannister—" He stopped. "Lannister is a man of so different a stamp to me he makes my blood boil. I can't even pretend to like him."

"You're not so different, you know."

"What?" Robert was thunderstruck.

"The earl is at bottom a gentleman of honor, as you are."

"He is not! That is precisely my objection to him. He has no honor."

Sarah just looked at him in silence. Then she said, "When has he broken his word, that you know of?"

Robert blinked. Opened his mouth and shut it. "All right, perhaps he does keep his word, but in every other respect he is nothing like me."

"No, I suspect he is like your father, and *that* is why he makes you so angry," she said softly.

The image of his sire rose up in his mind's eye. A big handsome, charming man, who constantly failed to shoulder the responsibilities of his title. His eyes stung as a lump rose in his throat. "Oh God, Sarah, you're right!"

She wrapped her arms round him, and he clung to her as things fell into place. "I loved my father, but he let us all down, time and again. I had to step up and fill his shoes, look after the rest of them."

"I know," she said softly, stroking his hair. She smiled up at him her eyes misty with tears to match his own. "And you did, but it wasn't fair. You shouldn't have had to."

"God, I love you, Sarah." He hugged her close, overcome with love for her. "I wanted you from the moment I took you in my arms at Almack's that first night. It has just taken me all this time to realize that you were the woman I've been waiting ten years to find."

Her tremulous smile pierced his chest, and he raised a hand to cup her face and kiss her. A gentle, loving, tender kiss with all his heart in it.

"Sarah, are you sure you can love me, truly?"

"Yes," she said huskily. "For I have loved you for three years. I am not going to stop now."

# Postscript

"THE EARL OF Lannister."

Madeleine looked up from the lady's magazine she was flipping through, startled. Flustered, she rose, "My lord." His expression lacked its usual humor. Her heart quailed.

He waited until the door had closed upon her butler before he said, "I understand we have some unfinished business?" His tone was silky but not in a pleasant way. She shivered. For the first time in her adult life, she was afraid of what a man might do. Being under the duke's protection had made her forget what that felt like.

"I—"

"Was your opinion of me so low that you thought I would shirk responsibility for my own child? Or was it sheer avarice, the duke being a bigger golden goose?"

"No!" she said, wriggling with distress and guilt. "I wanted him back. I thought—" She shook her head. "I was a fool. It was a stupid thing to do."

"Yes, it was. And extremely selfish. You hurt two innocent people in the process."

Her mouth fell open in surprise.

"No, not me. The duke and duchess."

She swallowed, digesting that. *Why did he care?* As far as she was aware, there was no love lost between him and Robert.

"The duke did everything right by you. Why would you serve him such a trick?"

"I told you I wanted him back." She spoke a little sullenly, sinking back onto the sofa. She felt a bit dizzy.

"Very well then, why not stick to your plan? Why confess?"

"I realized I'd hurt him—and the duchess. I wanted to hate her for stealing him, but I couldn't. She was too nice, too kind. The dowager would have thrown me out on my ear. The duchess wouldn't let her."

She looked up and caught a softened expression on his face. He murmured, "Yes, that is Sarah all over."

Tears welled in her eyes, and she reached for a handkerchief hastily. "I love him. I know it's foolish, but I do, and I couldn't deceive him in the end. I just c-couldn't."

She bowed her head, covering her face with her hands, and sobbed.

She felt the sofa dip beside her as he sat.

"There is a delicious irony in this that, if I weren't so damned affected, would be highly amusing. As is it, I'm as trapped as you are."

She sniffed and looked up. "I don't understand."

"No, you probably don't." He was sitting sideways toward her with his arm along the back of the couch. "I love the duchess; you love the duke." He smiled bitterly. "You see, irony."

"Oh." She wiped her eyes.

He took her hand. "I can't pretend to have any real feelings for you, Madeleine, but I'm not a monster. You're carrying my child. I'll care for you and it to the best of my ability. I give you my word as a gentleman."

Oh," she said again. "Thank you." It was then she felt it, a flutter in her abdomen. She put her hand to it, unthinking.

"What is it? Are you well?" He leaned forward, concern in his expression.

"The baby," she said softly. "I think I felt something. It—it hasn't done that before."

She glanced up at him and caught an expression on his face she couldn't read.

"May I?" he asked, holding out his hand.

She took it and, leaning back, placed his hand on her lower abdomen where the swell of the child was most prominent.

They both sat in silence for a moment or two, and then she felt a distinct kick. The look of wonder on his face made her smile.

"Well, little fellow, you've got some power in those legs," he murmured, clearly pleased.

*Will I bear him a son? Will that make up for what I have done?*

She placed her hand over his, and he wrapped the other arm round her shoulders.

"Don't worry, Madeleine, everything will be all right," he murmured against her hair.

# Epilogue

*The Castle, two months later*

SARAH OPENED THE letter on the top of her pile of correspond-ence and spread out the single sheet. Reaching for her cup of tea, she sipped as her eyes scanned the letter.

"Good heavens!"

"What is it, my love?" asked the duke, peering round his newspaper.

"Daphne writes that the Earl of Tavistock has won the battle for Cecelia Woodrow's hand."

"Who?" asked the duke blankly.

"Did she make so little impression upon you that you don't recall her name? Cecelia was one of your heiresses—the pretty blonde." Sarah raised her eyebrows at him.

"Oh, the spoiled one?" he grimaced. "I wish him well of her. And she was not my heiress. None of them were, save you." He bestowed a smile upon her.

Sarah smiled back and returned to her pile of letters. Putting the one from Daphne aside, she reached for a piece of toast and cut it in two. "Have you heard how Emrys is faring after the funeral? That whole affair was so terribly sad. I so felt for him at the ceremony. He looked devastated."

"A horrible conclusion to a shattering situation," agreed the duke. "Emrys did not deserve any of that. If it were not bad enough Caro should leave him for Greathouse, for her to perish in a carriage accident with Greathouse at the ribbons was tragic."

"I cannot help but feel a little sorry for Greathouse, too. By all accounts, he loved her to distraction."

"You are more compassionate than I, my love," said the duke grimly.

Sarah considered this in silence for a moment, finishing half her toast. "Is Emrys still in London?"

"No. He has taken the children to visit his grandmother in Bath." The duke sipped his tea. "Do I gather that you have finally forgiven Lady Holbrook, since you are receiving correspondence from her?"

"I have. Her motives were perhaps self-serving in many ways, yet I think she genuinely thought she was doing the right thing by me. She was inadvertently correct, as it turned out—my happiness did lie with you." She paused to refill her teacup and his. "Do you mean to write to Emrys again soon?"

"I will. In fact, I would like to extend an invitation for him to bring the children here when Mama and Ava return at the end of July. See what we can do to cheer the poor fellow up."

"What a lovely idea! I should be delighted to see him. I wonder if he has found a nanny for them yet."

"As of his last writing, no. He was full of complaints about it."

"If you mean to invite Emrys and the children, should I invite Zibby and the boys to stay as well?"

"An excellent notion," replied the duke warmly. "Although Miss Pringle may abandon us if Emrys can't find a nanny. I don't think she relishes assuming responsibility for so many little ones."

"No indeed. I shall make enquiries, see if I can locate some-one suitable for him, shall I?"

The duke nodded. "Who is your last letter from?"

"Mama Duchess." Sarah broke the seal and reviewed the crossed sheet. "She says that she expects more of Ava's suitors to apply to you forthwith."

The duke made a harrumphing noise, and she looked up at that. "What does that mean?"

"She has refused three of them already. I doubt she means to accept anyone at this juncture."

"How many have applied to you, so far?"

"Six. I knocked three of them back as unsuitable and Ava refused the other three herself."

"Well, she is a very pretty girl, and with such vivacious spirit, it is no wonder she is popular." Sarah spread jam on the last of her toast and took a bite. "I have got Papa's permission to bring Deb out in the little season. You will be happy to return to London in September?"

"As you wish, my love. Parliament resumes in October in any case, so I shall have to be present then."

"With any luck, I can then bring Ruthy out next year. It will be at least a couple of years before Mary is ready."

"Has anyone told Mary that?" he asked with a smile.

"No. Making her wait so long is going to break her heart, poor love. When will your mother bring Heather out, do you think?"

"As soon as she has Ava off her hands, I am guessing. Why?"

"Mary will be so miffed if Heather is presented before her."

"Well, perhaps you can speak to Mama about that. Thornbury won't be ready for her and the girls to move into until at least August." He paused to finish off his tea and settled the empty cup in its saucer. "Would you care to take a ride with me this morning, love? I would like to show you the repairs being made to the tenants' houses. See your money at work."

"I would," she smiled and leaned across the table to take his hand.

He tugged on it and said, "Come over here. I want to kiss my wife." She rose and came round the table, whereupon he pulled her down into his lap and kissed her.

After a bit she said, flushed and breathless, "The servants or even Miss Pringle or the girls could walk in at any moment, Your Grace."

"Let them," said the duke and resumed kissing his wife senseless.

# About the Author

Wren St Claire lives in Brisbane with one confused Mini Schnauzer and six mad Bengal cats. She writes Steamy Historical Romance, where the heroes spoil the heroine and readers get to tag along for the ride, enjoying a roller coaster of emotions. Wren has a Masters Degree in Egyptology and used to lead tours to Egypt up until the Revolution of the Arab Spring in 2011.